ABOUT THE AUTHOR

Penny Freedman is a teacher, academic, actor and director. She lives in Stratford-upon-Avon, where she indulges her passion for Shakespeare and theatre. She has two grown-up daughters.

*Little Honour* is the sixth book in a series. Previous books are *This is a Dreadful Sentence, All the Daughters, One May Smile, Weep a While Longer* and *Drown My Books*.

# LITTLE HONOUR

## PENNY FREEDMAN

Matador
9 Priory Business Park,
Wistow Road, Kibworth Beauchamp,
Leicestershire. LE8 0RX
Tel: 0116 279 2299
Email: books@troubador.co.uk
Web: www.troubador.co.uk/matador
Twitter: @matadorbooks

ISBN 978 1789015 294

British Library Cataloguing in Publication Data.
A catalogue record for this book is available from the British Library.

Printed and bound in the UK by TJ International, Padstow, Cornwall
Typeset in 11pt Minion Pro by Troubador Publishing Ltd, Leicester, UK

Matador is an imprint of Troubador Publishing Ltd

*For Robert*

*The odds is gone*
*And there is nothing left remarkable*
*Beneath the visiting moon.*

*Ha! Little honour to be much believed*
*And most pernicious purpose!*

*(Measure for Measure* Act 2 Scene 4)

# Acknowledgements

My thanks to Naomi Perry for putting me right on the organisation of barristers' chambers, to Madeleine O'Beirne of Wise Owl for insightful and constructive comments beyond the remit of simple proof-reading, and to Elsa Lake for convincing me that a bright and competent ten-year-old could do all that Freda is required to do here.

My thanks, too, to my family and my friends who ushered me gently through the dark months when I was completing this book.

## Great Ormond Street Hospital

In the course of this book, four-year-old Nico Biaggi is treated in hospital. It was necessary, for the working of the plot, that the hospital should be near Gina's home in Bloomsbury, so Great Ormond Street was the only choice. I could have given the hospital a fictional name, but that seemed pointlessly coy, given its location. This is a work of fiction, however, and I have only the most superficial knowledge of the hospital, so the Great Ormond Street of this book is a fictional place and I would not want my imagining of the staff, the organisation or the medical procedures there to be taken as an informed representation of the real hospital.

## SOAS

My version of SOAS as Gina's workplace is also entirely an invention, and Maria does not work there and does not represent anyone who does.

*vii*

# Chapter One

## AB INITIO

*Monday 18th July 2016*

It starts, I suppose, with the phone call from Freda. 'Granny,' she says, 'what's wrong with Mum?'

Now, this is the kind of question that sends the room spinning around you. One minute you are engaged in some safely mundane task – in my case, sorting books – feet securely on the dull ground, not so much as a warning tremor to disquiet you, and the next everything is in free fall – no safe purchase at all. I sit down, hard, on the floor, since there is nowhere else to sit, and ask, 'What do you mean by wrong, Freda?'

'Hasn't she even told you?' Freda asks.

Well, obviously she has not. I haven't, in fact, spoken to my daughter for ten days, and that's my fault, although I have been busy telling myself that it is hers. Ten days ago, I told her that I could not drop everything, yet again, and take the train down to Marlbury to look after my four-year-old grandson, Nico, who seems to go from one minor ailment to another – coughs, colds, earache, general malaise – just bad enough for the nursery not to want to take him. Ellie has a full-time job as a teacher, so Nico's being ill so often has made life difficult for her, I know, and I have done my best to help, but I have a full-time job too. I teach English Language at SOAS, the School of Oriental and African Studies, and – yes –

1

as Ellie has pointed out, the university term has finished, but I have much to do, including finishing a paper to present at a conference next week and negotiating a complicated house move, more of which later. Ellie got tearful, I got stubborn and neither of us has picked up the phone since.

'What makes you think something's wrong?' I ask, striving for a sympathetic-cum-reassuring tone but somehow managing to sound only irritated. 'It's the end of term and things always get stressful, and Nico hasn't been well...' I trail off.

'She keeps crying,' Freda says. 'She and Ben keep whispering together and today Ben was crying too.'

*Divorce*, I think. *Divorce or death. Ellie is seriously ill.*

'Haven't you asked what's wrong?' I ask, and there's that irritated tone again.

'Of course, I have.' Freda can be snappy too.

'And?'

'And she said she couldn't tell me yet, but she would when things were sorted out.'

'Right.'

'And she said not to worry, it would all be all right.'

'Well. There you are then.'

'Except...'

'Except?'

'Except she doesn't tell me things. She keeps saying she'll tell me about my dad, but she doesn't.'

'No. Well, that's a difficult one, Freda. And you've got Ben now, and he's a lovely dad, so...'

'Can't you tell me?'

'I can't, my love. She hasn't told me, either.'

This was always going to be an issue one day. Ellie got pregnant at the beginning of her first year at university, possibly in freshers' week. She has never talked about the boy concerned, but I suspect a drunken, thoughtless encounter with disproportionate consequences. Anyone else might

2

have gone for a quick abortion but Ellie was too stubborn for that. She saw it through. Now she is married to Ben, a nice musician who teaches at the same school as her, and who is being a lovely father to Freda, and they have Nico as well, and it's all happy families, except that Freda is wondering who she is.

'I can't help you there, Freda,' I say, 'but I will ring Mum when she gets back from work and try and find out what's wrong.'

I look at my watch. 'Why aren't you at school, anyway?' I ask.

'It's lunch time. We're allowed to have our phones at lunch time.'

'OK.'

'Bye.' She rings off.

Ellie said she would let Freda know when things were sorted out. That sounds more like divorce than illness. I get up off the floor.

I should probably explain why there is nothing to sit on here. I am not at home. I am sorting out books which I abandoned two and a half years ago, when I left the seaside hovel in which I had been living and swapped it for a studio flat in Bloomsbury, where I now work. The hovel went unsold for two years and the books stayed here, as there was no room for them in the flat, which is so small that I have felt like a battery chicken in it. Now, however, the hovel and the chicken cage are both sold, and I am about to move upmarket to a flat which I shall describe later, as it is my pride and delight and deserves your full attention.

The hovel has sold for more than I had any right to expect. It is one of a terrace of six, overlooking the sea on a depressed and unattractive bit of the Kent coast. In the fall-out from a murder on the beach, virtually on our doorsteps, all the inhabitants, for various reasons, tried to sell up, but the place felt jinxed and no-one was buying. Now a property developer is purchasing the whole lot, ready to knock all the houses down and put up a block of luxury seaside apartments. *And good luck with that*, I think, as I look out at the sea, which, even in July, manages to look greyly uninviting.

I turn back to my books, which are, in fact, wrecked. Two years of damp and neglect have ruined everything, actually. I took nothing with me to my new London life: the furniture, such as it was, went to a charity and everything else in the place – clothes, bedding, rugs, kitchen equipment – was left to moulder, and has now been consigned to the giant skip outside the front door. The books, I decide, will have to join the rest. I was already moving to that conclusion before Freda rang – the pages have all gone crinkly and have stuck together – so now I can vent my anxiety and self-blame by hurling the lot of them into the skip. My favourites and my work books are safe in London; these are for pulping.

It is good exercise heaving the bags out to the front and swinging them over into oblivion, and by the time I have finished it is four-thirty and Ellie might be home from work. I take my phone and go and sit on the sea wall. I need to be in the open air for this.

'Oh, it's you, Ma,' she says. Her voice sounds flat.

'You sound tired,' I say, fatuously. 'How many days to go?'

'What? Oh – three. Three till the end of term.'

'How's Nico?'

'He's ...'

She stops.

'The summer holiday will do him good, won't it?' I rush on, feeling blame coming my way. 'When do you go to Italy?'

'We're not.'

'What? Why not?'

*Divorce.*

'Nico's got to have an operation.'

4

'Why? Is this his ears? Are they putting grommets in or something?'

Suddenly, she is shouting. 'No, they're not putting bloody grommets in his ears. He's having heart surgery. That's what they're doing.'

I have to lean forward because I feel dizzy and I could easily topple backwards off the wall and become another fatality on the beach.

'Why?' I ask, stupidly. 'What's wrong with his heart?'

'He has an atrial septal defect – it's a hole – ' her voice wobbles '– a hole in his heart.'

I gather rapidly anything I think I know about this.

'It's an operation they do quite a lot, isn't it? I mean, it's serious, of course, but... '

'Don't!' she says. 'Don't tell me it's just a routine operation. They're mending his heart. How can that be routine? He's four years old and they're having to mend his heart. And I didn't even see. I didn't see. I just saw it as a problem – him being ill all the time and me having to take days off work and you not being here – and all the time his little heart was struggling, and I didn't even know!'

She is crying now, and I am forty miles away, without a car and with no possibility of wrapping my arms round her, so all I can say is, 'It's not your fault, Ellie. It's not your fault.' And then I stay sitting on the wall and I cry too, because actually it is my fault, isn't it?

Eventually I ask, 'Have you got a date?'

'Next Monday. A week today.'

'At Marlbury Royal?'

'No. Great Ormond Street.'

I feel dizzy again and decide it will be better to stand up.

'Ellie,' I say. 'My new flat is about two hundred yards from Great Ormond Street. You and Ben must come and stay there. How long will Nico be in for?'

'They say five days to a week. We'll get the train to and fro, and maybe one of us will sleep on the ward – they do let you – '

'You'd be exhausted. Stay with me. I can feed you and look after you.'

'Ma, you haven't even moved into the new place yet, have you?'

'Friday. We complete on Friday and I move in.'

'But you won't be sorted out. You won't be able to manage with us around.'

I have no idea how I'm going to manage, but I say, 'Course I will. Give me the weekend and it'll be all ready for you. You can sleep in my room and I'll sleep in my study. I'm putting a single bed in there so Freda will be able to come and stay.'

'That's the other thing,' she says. 'What are we going to do with Freda?'

Freda. I think about her taut little voice on the phone: *Granny, what's wrong with Mum?*

'What were you thinking of doing?' I ask.

'I was going to ask you to have her as first option.'

*Of course you were.*

'She's welcome, of course,' I say. 'I can sleep on the sofa.'

'Are you free to look after her during the day, though? She won't be allowed to hang around in the hospital and she won't want to.'

Am I free? No. In fact, I'm not. I'm due to be giving a paper at the three-day conference at UCL next week – my usual shtick on cross-cultural pragmatic competence – and it's quite important that I give those three days my full attention. I'm on a discussion panel, as well, and I was quite flattered to be asked. I'm up for a senior lectureship so I really need to put myself about next week and appear to be an asset to the university. I can probably manage to do that after nights spent sleeping on the sofa, but I can't look after Freda as well.

'I've got this conference...' I say.

'Of course you have. Why didn't I guess?'

This is not fair, but for once I bite my tongue.

'Monday to Wednesday,' I say. 'After that – '

'I'll see if Charlotte's mother will have her. Otherwise I'll have to ask Lavender.'

'What about Annie? Couldn't she help? Then, at least Freda would be in London and she could visit Nico.'

'Annie's working, Ma. She's got a job to do.'

'So have I.'

'She's a lawyer.'

Law, it appears, trumps education. I say nothing.

'Freda won't be happy,' Ellie says. 'She likes Lavender but she's not comfortable with Dad and she doesn't like the boys.'

'They do seem to be little monsters.'

'They're not like Nico.'

'No.' I wait, helplessly, for something better to say. 'Nico will be fine, Ellie. It will all be all right.'

'Yes,' she says.

I stay on the wall for a long time. My legs are so stiff when I stand up that I can barely totter as far as the steps down to the beach. It had always been my intention to have a walk on the beach, for old times' sake, regardless of its homicidal associations. I walked my dog here every morning for two years, in the odd sabbatical from my life that I had decided to take. At the time, I didn't think of it as a sabbatical – I thought I had given up the world for good – but it turned out that the world – Forster's world of telegrams and anger, I suppose – came and found me, and I couldn't resist its lure. Only a light breeze plays on the beach today, but I turn into it, remembering how driving into a gale could knock all thoughts out of my head, and that was peace, of a kind.

I have thought about going to see Caliban, my dog, who was my companion and my excuse for those battering walks.

A friend – Lesley - who lives here took him on when I defected to a London life, so he still has his sandy playground. I don't think I loved him, but I would quite like to see him again. What holds me back? I suppose it is that I shall find out what he felt about me. Either he loved me and will greet me ecstatically – in which case, I shall feel terrible about leaving him again – or he didn't really like me much at all and will greet me with indifference. I suspect that this is the more likely scenario, and I shall mind, because I have a sneaking feeling that dogs are rather good judges of character. I tell myself that it would be an imposition to turn up unexpectedly on Lesley's doorstep, and call a taxi to take me to the station.

# Chapter Two

## ALTERNATIVE VERDICT

*Saturday 23rd July 2016*

When I told Ellie that I could easily get the flat ready over the weekend, I was, of course, lying. It's not that it takes long to arrange a few pieces of furniture, or to unload kitchen tools into drawers, clothes into cupboards and books onto shelves. It's the technical stuff that's the problem, and there are, it pains me to admit, some jobs for which I need to get a man in. I am not helpless. I did manage to work out the complexities of the hot water system and the state of the art shower last night, because I was determined not to go to bed dirty, and today I will work out the cooker controls, which look as though they belong on a flight deck, but I am too small and – yes, all right – too female for other jobs, and I would be in despair today if yesterday evening had not brought an overdue piece of good luck.

I had a phone call.

The call was from David Scott – Detective Superintendent David Scott, of the Metropolitan Police. The eight-year journey of my relationship with David has been one of ups and downs, blind corners, hairpin bends, accident black spots and more than one emergency stop. Our relationship is partly bedevilled by the fact that I was once his teacher. This is not as bad as it sounds: I was a very young teacher and he was in my A level class. Our relationship then was perfectly proper, but years later he investigated the death of one of my students, and I could tell you that romance blossomed, but it has never really been like that. Although we can't seem to leave each other alone, we are, in my view, fundamentally unsuited: he is stubborn, I am obsessive; he thinks he is clever, I think I am brilliant; he needs always to be right, I need to be righter. A marriage made in hell is signified, and that is what I told him four years ago, when he took it into his head to propose to me. This brought us jolting to our second emergency stop and we didn't see each other at all for two years, during which time I went into a deep sulk in my seaside hovel and he forged ahead with the Met. Then I got this job in London at SOAS and I thought we might resume our journey – just a little gentle pottering about together, no commitment on either side, no destination in view. I found, however, that David had another passenger. (If you are finding this over-extended metaphor irritating, I apologise; I wanted to see how far I could take it, and I think this is it).

David presented Anthea for my inspection. *Anthea, I ask you* – a name that is at least one generation out of date and hasn't been modified to something with cooler vibes (how about *Thea*, for instance?) signals elderly parents and a daughter who hasn't noticed. But I don't really know her, of course. We had an awkward conversation in a pub, with David refereeing, and we bumped into each other once at King's Cross Station. Anthea works for the Met, but not as a police officer; she is in admin of some sort, and she didn't seem to want to talk about it when I made polite enquiries. She is youngish, feminine – all pastel sweaters and on-the-knee skirts – and no doubt wants to settle down and have a family. She is my fault. She is exactly what I told David he needed when he proposed to me and I refused him for his own good, pointing out that forty-three was too young to be settling down to step-grandfatherhood, which was all that marriage to me offered him.

Well, their relationship has been hopeless, of course, but it has limped on in a stop-start way for the best part of two years. The stops, I assume, are when Anthea can't stand the sense of stasis, or when David decides that the boredom is life-threatening. I know when things are in stop mode because that is when David rings me with an oh-so-casual suggestion of a drink somewhere, and I go because, to be fair, he doesn't use me as a listening ear for a moan about Anthea, seems genuinely pleased to see me, sometimes entertains me with (heavily anonymised) titbits of cases he has been working on, and isn't crass enough to suggest going to bed. It's crumbs from the table but I haven't found another man who interests me as much, so I stick with it.

Last night's call started in the usual way, but I managed to turn it to my purposes. As I recall, it went as follows:

He: Gina.

Me: David.

He: How are you?

Me: I'm very well.

He: It's been a while.

Me: Yes.

*Pause*

He: Are you busy?

Me: Pretty much. New flat. Moved in today, so –

He: So how does a drink somewhere by the river sound?

Me: When?

He: Now?

Me: Hardly. I'm filthy and there's loads to do. Come round and help, if you like.'

He: I –

Me: How's Anthea?

He: Um –

Me: That good!

He: It's over, in fact.

Me: Over as in irretrievable breakdown or over until one of you apologises?

He: I think I said some irretrievable things.

Me: Really? Your usual tact and diplomacy deserted you?

He: Let's meet for a drink and I won't talk about it.

Me: Why don't you come round here? See the place. I'm very proud of it. Come for coffee tomorrow morning. Better, come for breakfast.

He: Well, I –

Me: Bacon and eggs in the garden. I have a garden. How can you resist?

He: If you're sure it won't be too much trouble.

Me: I'll text you the address.

So now, here I am, waiting for him. I have been out for bacon, eggs, orange juice, croissants and coffee, the French doors to my garden are open, and I am waiting for the doorbell to ring and admit David into my sticky web. Once he has been fed, after all, how can he refuse to do a few manly tasks for me? Blinds and curtain rails, a couple of wall-mounted mirrors – anything that requires an electric drill, really.

When the bell rings, I usher him in and show him briskly through the flat. It is what the estate agent's blurb called a *lower ground* flat, which means basement, and my front door is the old servants' entrance to a four-storey house in an elegant nineteenth-century terrace. I imagine cheery boys with flat caps and bicycles delivering to the kitchen via the steps down to my door. Inside, the flat has *nice levels of natural light*, also agent-speak about which I was sceptical until I saw the place and found it was true. The windows at the front may be at the level of feet in the street, but doors at the back open onto my secret garden, which is quite up to Hodgson Burnett standards, with climbing plants rampaging over its walls and a random assortment of things growing in pots, left behind by the previous owner. In the garden of the seaside hovel, I grew salty, hardy vegetables and wrestled them into edible form; here, the garden is tastefully paved, with no soil available for vegetables, so I shall buy my vegetables from M & S, and won't even have to wash them.

Walking David through my subterranean domain, I show him the bedroom, mentioning, lightly, that the previous owners have taken their antique-brass-effect curtain poles away with them and that it was quite annoying to be woken by the light pouring in at five o'clock this morning. We proceed through to the living room, which has no natural light of its own, but mirrors on the walls will, I point out, make all the difference, reflecting the light that flows through from the kitchen, and here I wave an airy hand at two mammoth mirrors which stand propped against the blank walls waiting to receive them. In the kitchen, I allow him to appreciate the glory of my little garden, and then fill him in on the Nico, Ellie and Ben situation. I point out that I (and Nico tomorrow night, in preparation for an early appointment at the hospital on Monday morning) will be sleeping in my 'study', which is just a sort of bulge, really, without a door, accessed by an archway from the kitchen and open to the light from the lovely French doors leading to the charming garden.

'So, you can see,' I conclude, 'that blinds in here are a bit of a priority.' For good measure, I indicate the blinds, rolled in their cellophane wrappers, leaning by the doors.

He is properly empathetic about the prospect of Nico's operation, because he is a good man, but he doesn't make the move to offer help because he is not, to be honest, a terribly practical man. His own flat, I swear, is exactly as it was when he moved into it; he could be living in a hotel. However, he is all I've got, and I can be patient. Once I've fed him, the credit will be on my side. So, I can wait. We move the kitchen table out into the garden and I settle him there with a glass of orange juice and the newspaper while I fry bacon, eggs and bread. While he eats these, I make coffee and warm up croissants in my top oven, the controls of which I have now mastered.

I join him for the coffee and croissants and we chat idly about the possible names of the plants that burgeon around us – David is no better at horticulture than I am – about the books we have been reading and, briefly, about work. I tell him about my forthcoming gig at the conference, and he tells me how fed up he is with government interference in the workings of the Met.

'Which reminds me,' he says, reaching into an inside pocket of his jacket and bringing out a plastic bag with a piece of paper inside it, 'there was something I was wanting to ask you about. A language thing.'

So, he wants something from me, too, and this is my moment.

'Ulterior motive!' I say, pointing an accusing finger. 'Not my delightful company you wanted – nor even my delightful breakfast. J'accuse! You're here under false colours.'

I watch the blood come up into his face. His tendency to blush is one of the things I've always liked most about him.

'No, really –' he starts to say.

I give it a moment and then I relent. 'Why do you think I cooked you breakfast, David? Didn't you think I might have an ulterior motive too? So, a deal. If you'll show me yours, I'll show you mine. I suspect that what I want from you is a good bit more than what you want from me, if it's just taking a look at that piece of paper you have in mind. So I'm a breakfast in credit at the moment, but if we think I'm in debt by the end of the morning, I'll buy you lunch at my favourite Italian. How's that?'

He eyes me with deep suspicion. 'It depends what you want me to do.'

'Can't you guess?'

'Obviously not.'

'Curtain poles, David. Blinds. Wall mirrors. I need manly assistance.'

He looks, briefly, quite panic-stricken.

'That really isn't my line,' he says. 'I never – '

'It's easy. I've looked. There are instructions on the blinds and on the pole – actual words, not just diagrams, in real English, not translated from Japanese.'

He opens his mouth to protest.

'And,' I add, 'I've got this.'

I retrieve from the kitchen a metal box with a neat Black and Decker drill inside it. It belonged to my former husband, Andrew, bought for him by his father when we got married. It has hardly been used, as DIY wasn't really Andrew's bag, either. He regarded our house as a place to rest and refuel when not doing the more important stuff, and whatever happened there was my responsibility. I didn't embrace DIY myself, but I have held onto the drill, taking it with me on all my house moves, and now its moment has come. I was afraid it might have seized up through disuse, but I plugged it in this morning and it whirred around all right, so I think it will do. David eyes it warily.

'How hard can it be?' I ask.

He rallies. 'I think you ought to reconsider your gender assumptions,' he says. 'Why should I be any better at this than you are?'

'You're taller and stronger – and younger – for a start. And how about *your* gender assumptions? You could quite well have cooked your own bacon and eggs, but you assumed I would be better at it.'

He glowers.

'And anyway,' I say, 'I don't like machines. I once had a very nasty encounter with a sewing machine.'

That gets him. He laughs. 'Lead me to it,' he says, 'but you're going to have to help.'

And so we get started. We move through the flat from front to back, dealing with curtain rails, mirrors and blinds, and the scene that unfolds seems to me a perfect paradigm of domestic DIY: he drops things, swears, gets things the wrong way round and shouts at me; I pick things up, make soothing noises, hold the other end of things, and occasionally shout back. Really, we could have been married for years.

It is almost two o'clock by the time we finish, and I nearly push my luck too far when I suddenly remember that there is a little window in the study in need of a blind as well, but there was a television drama recently in which someone was murdered with an electric drill, so I say nothing. I shall improvise something temporary and see if Ben might see to it later in the week.

'Lunch,' I say. 'Old-fashioned Italian. Things should be quietening down by the time we get there, and I'll look at your piece of paper.'

We walk round to Great Russell Street. It is a still, close, day – no great help to us in our exertions this morning. I do sometimes miss the sea breezes of my coastal sojourn, but I remind myself that they were more often gales than breezes, and frequently laden with icy rain. There, I used to have to brace myself for the outside world as I opened my front door; here, it is like stepping into a bowl of tepid soup.

Cucina Nonna, where we are heading, is a stone's throw from the flat, and the throw of another stone from SOAS. I have been patronising it a lot in the past two years and I am greeted as an old friend by Alessandro, the proprietor, who shakes David's hand while casting an appraising glance over him. I like to think he is checking on whether David is good enough for me. Settled at a corner table, I order us each a glass of prosecco and we both refuel with bread and olives before I say, 'So, what's the story with your piece of paper?'

He does not produce the paper immediately, but takes a swig of his prosecco and says, 'Does the name Isha Anand mean anything to you?'

'Should it?'

'She was murdered. Near here, in fact – very near your flat.'

'Really? When?'

'A month ago. 26th June.'

'Well, if it was in the papers, I wouldn't have noticed. Three days after the Brexit vote, I was in such a rage. And I was obsessed with what the pundits had to say, and the psychodrama of Gove and Johnson and the other turds, so … no, I don't remember.'

'It got pretty much buried, and the powers above were happy with that.'

'Why?'

'Isha Anand was a student lawyer, doing her pupillage in chambers in Gray's Inn. Her uncle is a senior minister in the Indian government. With the spike in racist attacks after the vote, the last thing anyone wanted was for it to turn out that this was one of them. Bad for potential trade deals with India, disastrous for universities' recruitment of overseas students.'

'Was there anything to suggest there was a racist motive?'

He shifts a bit and empties his glass. 'It's not my case,' he says. 'This,' and he again draws the paper out of the pocket of his jacket, which is hanging over the back of his chair, 'was sent to me, so I can share it with you – in the strictest confidence, obviously – but I can't tell you anything else. Or nothing that wasn't reported in the papers.'

'Because you don't trust me?'

'Because it would be unprofessional.'

'And you don't trust me?'

'You haven't always been as discreet as you might have been.'

'But you still want my help?' I feel inclined to sulk at this point and refuse to cooperate, but we did have a deal and, besides, I am interested.

'Just with this,' David says. He takes the paper out of its plastic bag and hands it to me.

'Shouldn't we be wearing gloves,' I ask, 'if it's evidence?'

'It's a copy,' he says. 'Do you think I carry evidence around with me in my pocket?'

'It was in an evidence bag.'

'Habit,' he says.

I open up the paper and study it. It is a word-processed letter, printed on quite ordinary A4 printer paper, and it reads as follows:

20.06.16

*Dear Detective Superintendent David Scott,*

*Please can you help to protect a young woman who is in danger? The young woman's name is Isha Anand and I have reason to believe that she will be attacked if nobody prevents it. Her address is Flat 6B, Woburn Court, Russell Place, WC 1B.*

*I know you can not protect her all the time, but please put some sort of guard on her flat. I would protect her if I could, but I am not able to.*

*This is serious. Please help.*

As I am reading it through for the second time, Alessandro arrives with our bowls of spaghetti alle vongole and a carafe of house white. Manipulating the spaghetti and the clams demands our full attention for a while, but eventually I say, 'So, written five days before she died. Why was it sent personally to you?'

'I'll tell you in a minute. How about the writer? What do you think?'

'Well, it's a young person, obviously. Using your first name – it's someone who's not used to writing a formal letter. The directness of the appeal, too, and naïvety about what sort of action the police could take. Did you do anything?'

'A community support officer went to see Isha Anand. She told the officer it was nonsense – a hoax – but the officer thought she was upset by the letter.'

'Well, I'd certainly rule out the letter's having been written by her – unless she was playing a very subtle game. It's too naïve for a young lawyer, isn't it? But the writer is well educated. He or she understands about a formal register – doesn't use contractions like *who's* or *I'm*. In fact, he hypercorrects when he writes *can not*. *Cannot* is the standard form now.'

'You said, *he writes*. More likely to be male than female, do you think? '

'I'm not sure. Marginally, maybe. I suppose, *I would protect her* seems like a boy who feels he has a responsibility.'

'Mm.'

We concentrate on eating for a bit, enjoying our fishy broth.

'So, why did the letter come to you?' I ask, when I have wiped the juice off my chin.

'I was involved in a case in the chambers where Isha Anand was doing her pupillage. A harassment case. A woman barrister, who had lost a defence case, was being threatened by her client's friends. He was a nasty piece of work – Steel, Jake Steel – and was sent down for twenty years. His cronies didn't like that and started a very ugly campaign – death threats on social media, stuff through her door, even a packet of shit delivered to her chambers. She's an experienced lawyer, but she was close to cracking.'

'Did you get them?'

'Oh yes. They were nasty but not very clever. The social media stuff made them easy to track down, and we had a fair idea of who they would be, anyway.'

'What did they expect to gain? The guy had been convicted, hadn't he? They couldn't change anything. Was it just random viciousness?'

'It seems they had some benighted idea that if they could get her to crack up, then there would be grounds for appeal for a retrial on the basis that she was mentally unstable and hadn't given him proper representation.'

'My God.'

'Yes.'

'So, you think the writer of the letter knew your name from that case? Was it reported in the papers?'

'No. These cases are more commonplace than you might think. And it's generally women who come under attack.'

'So, our writer has to be associated with the chambers to have heard of you. But it really doesn't look like a letter written by a lawyer – unless the style is a deliberate disguise.' I stop, with a sudden thought. 'Was Isha Anand involved in the case where the guy was convicted?'

'She was. She was a pupil of the woman who led the case.'

'So, the people who threatened the barrister could have killed Isha?'

'In theory, yes. If we didn't get them all. But we think we did and they were all in custody by 26th June.'

'But you could have missed someone.'

'The thing is,' he says, 'and I can tell you this because it was in the papers, Isha Anand had a seventeen-year-old brother, Bimal, who is – was – at boarding school here in the UK, in Surrey. The day after his sister died he flew to Delhi, and his family are refusing to send him back.'

'So…' I am thinking hard and can't make much sense of this. 'So, he might have written the letter – he could have known about you from Isha. And when she was killed, he thought he was in danger too?'

'That is what you might think. It's not what our political masters want us to think.'

'Why?'

'Bad publicity, as I said. The daughter of a prominent Indian politician murdered by gangsters, the son having to flee for his life. How does that make us look?'

'So, what's their scenario?'

'An honour killing.'

'What?'

'The official line – and we deviate from it at our peril – is that Bimal Anand killed his sister because he believed she had dishonoured the family, and then fled, with the connivance of his family. Bimal won't be extradited – his uncle will see to that – so he remains a convenient prime suspect, and the case is quietly buried.'

'Well, that doesn't do much for international relations, does it? Is there any evidence of her having dishonoured them?'

'There is, but I can't tell you about it. That's not in the public domain and, as I say, it's not my case.'

'So, you've involved me in this and got me interested, and now you're going to clam up and leave me dangling. And when I'm buying you lunch. You are a bastard, David.'

'I'm not involving you,' he says. 'I just wanted to get your view on the letter.'

'Oh, come on. I know you. I know when something's nagging away at you. You don't believe for a moment that the boy murdered his sister. You feel guilty because you think her death might be connected with your harassment case, and because the letter came to you and you think you didn't do enough to protect her, but you can't do anything about it because the inquiry has been closed down and it was never your case anyway, so you've thought around it and come up with a cunning plan. There's someone you know who can't leave a mystery alone, who gets steamed up about violence to women and who will just need a bit of a push to send her off, bumbling about in her amateur way, to try to find out the truth – never mind that you're not prepared to give her any of the information that might help her – or keep her safe.'

I lean back, out of breath. 'Pour me some more wine,' I say.

He pours for both of us, taking his time.

'OK,' he says. 'I did think – when I realised how near you were going to be living – that you might – '

'When you realised? You didn't have my address till you rang me yesterday evening. So, you didn't ring just to get me involved in this?'

'I – ' He stops. 'I did know you were moving to near here. Annie told me.'

'Annie? How the hell have you been talking to Annie? When you haven't talked to me?'

'I bumped into her.'

'What?'

'In Gray's Inn. Her chambers are in the same building as Isha Anand's were. I just bumped into her when I was working on the harassment case. She told me you were moving.'

I need a moment to digest this – my difficult daughter and my tricky ex-lover having casual chats about my life.

'Do you want pudding?' I ask.

'Oh, no…'

'Yes, you do. They do a very good frangipani tart. The portions are vast, so we'll have one, and two spoons.'

Alessandro comes to clear the plates, and I have a feeling that he has been waiting for our body language to relax a bit before he dares come near us. I order the tart and two espressos.

22

While we wait for our pudding, I say, 'I can't believe you're actually asking me to get involved in an investigation. I've always had to fight you to get a look-in.'

'I'm not!' he protests. 'The last thing I want is for you to go probing, asking questions. This was a murder. There's someone very dangerous out there. I don't want you in danger – nor Annie.'

'Annie! How is Annie involved in this?'

My voice has risen almost to a shout, I realise, and I look around to find that the restaurant is empty. It is three-thirty and everyone else has gone home. Still, I lower my voice.

'What do you mean about Annie?'

'Just – I think she probably knew Isha Anand.'

'Probably? Have you asked her?'

'No, I don't have – that is I'm not in regular contact with her. I just bumped into her once on the stairs, going into her chambers.'

'How did she look?'

'She looked – you know how she looks.'

'I don't know how she looks at work.'

'She looked every inch the bright young female lawyer. You could have cast her in the role for TV.'

'Good.'

Our tart arrives. It has been cut into two and served on separate plates. Maybe Alessandro didn't trust us not to fight over it. We eat.

'So why do you think Isha and Annie knew each other? Any reason other than that they were in neighbouring chambers?'

'I think they were supposed to be in a play together. *Measure for Measure*. Some sort of lawyers' theatre group, performing it somewhere in Gray's Inn. Annie told me she was going to be in it, and Isha told the officer I sent to see her that she was going to be out in the evenings, rehearsing for

23

something she was doing with people from work. It might not have been the same thing, of course, but – '

'But I could ask Annie?'

'Yes.'

'Well, *Measure for Measure* is certainly the play for lawyers to be doing. It's all about the law, really. Do you know what Annie's doing in it?'

'I don't know the play, so I don't remember the name of the character, but she's the lead, she said.'

'Isabella?'

'Yes, I think so.'

'Good Lord! She hasn't told me.' Of course, she hasn't told me because she knew my reaction would be *Good Lord!* I persistently underestimate Annie and she knows it, so she's always wanting to make me believe that everything in her life is a great success, and when things aren't going well, and she could do with some support, she won't talk to me because she can't admit to failure. It makes our relationship toxic, and it's my fault. She was a stroppy underachiever at school and I have never properly got used to the change in her, despite her Oxford degree and a blossoming career. I have to do better, but it may be too late.

I put down my fork; I haven't enjoyed my tart as much as I should have done. I drink some coffee.

'So, what exactly is it you want me to do, David?' I ask.

He puts down his napkin and pushes himself back in his chair as if to make more distance between us. 'I just wanted you to think about it,' he says. 'Not investigate, not talk to people, not go to her chambers, nothing like that. Just mull it over. Look up the news reports online and see what Annie can tell you, and think about it. Then tell me whether I'm crazy to think that a murderer, a possible danger to other young women, is walking free.'

'And what are you going to do meanwhile?'

24

He shrugs, 'It's not my case.'

'Well, it's not mine, either,' I say. 'And I don't know what you think you're doing trying to offload it onto me. Talk about unprofessional! And you may have noticed that I'm a bit busy at the moment – not just a house move, but a sick grandson, a flat full of his distressed parents and a career make-or-break conference next week – so really the last thing I need is to be doing your job for you as well.'

We pay the bill. There is an unseemly tussle over it as David insists that he is paying. Alessandro deals with it gracefully, as we both thrust our credit cards at him. He puts out a gentle hand to push away my card and tweaks David's deftly from his fingers. He shakes both our hands and sees us out onto the pavement, where we part without so much as brushing cheeks. David, I assume, heads for the Tube, and I walk home.

As I approach my flat, I get out my phone and I call Annie.

# Chapter Three

## FAMILY COURT

*Sunday 24th July 2016*

I invited Annie for supper last night. She turned me down but then instead volunteered herself for supper with Ellie and Ben tonight. She's on her own at the moment; her boyfriend, Jon, who is a junior doctor, is working in Uganda for six months. I think she's feeling quite lonely and is glad to be with us, even if we're not the most exciting company. So here we are, sitting round my new kitchen table, eating roast chicken, which was Nico's choice. He has been allowed to stay up because he will be sleeping in my doorless study, and when he goes to bed the rest of us will either have to go to bed too or be very quiet – something my family finds difficult.

I haven't mentioned the play to Annie. I was peeved at the thought of David and Annie talking about me, so I expect Annie will feel the same if she learns that we have been talking about her. If I want to ask her about Isha Anand, though – and I'm not sure yet that I do – I shall have to come clean. As it turns out, it's Annie who mentions the play. She leans across to Ellie and says, 'Guess what, I'm playing Isabella in *Measure for Measure*.' This is perfect, because Ellie reacts with unfeigned delight. Ellie is making such heroic efforts to be cheerful this evening that it is breaking my heart.

'That's brilliant,' she beams. 'You'll be fab.' She turns to me. 'Won't she, Ma?'

So I find myself able to say, 'Absolutely. You're perfect casting, Annie,' and mean it.

Annie relaxes. She has obviously been bursting to talk about it and now she has her opening. 'It's just an ad hoc group,' she says. 'Most barristers are frustrated actors, so it wasn't hard to find people. It's going to be open air. Later on, there's a company doing *Comedy of Errors* in Gray's Inn Hall – it's where the play was first performed, apparently, and they're doing it for Shakespeare's quatercentenary – but that was too expensive for us, so we're doing it in one of the courtyards. Fingers crossed for the weather.'

'Have you got a good Duke and a good Angelo?' I ask.

'Yes. Roderick's playing the Duke.'

'Roderick?'

'Roderick Gillard – he was my pupil master. I've talked to you about him.'

'Yes, of course. It's just I pictured your group as all young, somehow, and I got the impression that your pupil master was quite old.'

'Well, we are young, and he is old. About your age.'

'Thanks.'

'It's really good of him to do it. That's one of the good things about him; he doesn't stand on his dignity.'

A tremor of unease insinuates itself into the small part of my brain that isn't occupied with worrying about Nico and my conference paper. I have been here before. Annie has a tendency to hero worship and then to get hurt. An older man – probably married – with an air of experience and authority worn lightly, could be lethal. And Jon is in Uganda.

'And how about your Angelo?'

'He's fine. It's easy to find an Angelo in a group of lawyers.'

'Smug, self-righteous and given to specious self-justification and dodgy personal ethics?' I say.

27

'Oooh,' she says, 'steady on, Ma. This is me and my colleagues you're talking about.'

I have drunk too much wine, I realise, and am pushing my luck, but Annie sounds surprisingly good-natured about my attack on her chosen profession. 'Sorry,' I say. 'I was just thinking of one in particular.'

I catch a glance between Annie and Ellie.

'You're not fair to Dad, you know, Ma,' Annie says. 'He's terribly well respected by people in chambers.'

I feel suddenly very tired. It has been a physically trying couple of days, I'm worried about coping with the coming week and I'm terrified about Nico. I have no fight in me. 'I'm sure he is,' I say. 'Well respected.' I know quite well that it was Andrew's contacts that got Annie first her pupillage and then her place in chambers. Gray's Inn. Our surname is Gray, you see. Well, mine isn't any more – I have reverted to my maiden name, my real name, as I like to think of it – and Ellie is mostly Mrs Biaggi, but Andrew and Annie are Grays and Andrew started his career in chambers' at Gray's Inn, and was dying for Annie to follow in his footsteps. He likes to claim some sort of descent from Baron Gray of Wilton, who founded Gray's Inn, but I think it's spurious.

I look at Ellie. 'I wonder how Freda is doing with Andrew and Lavender,' I say.

'I had a text exchange,' she says. 'She sounded a bit stiff-upper-lip.'

I look round the table at our little gathering. *She ought to be here*, I think. *If I were any sort of proper grandmother, she would be here.*

Nico seems to have picked up my thought. He is half asleep, drooping over the remains of melting ice cream, but he sits up. 'Why isn't Freda here?' he asks.

'She's having a little holiday with Grandpa and Auntie Lavender,' Ellie says.

'While I'm in the hospital?' I can see him considering the unfairness of this arrangement.

'I don't expect it will be a very nice holiday,' I say. 'Grandpa's a bit scary, isn't he? And Freda doesn't like the boys much – she'll miss you.'

This is possibly a mistake. His face grows dark. 'I want Freda to –' he begins, but Ellie sweeps him up and says, 'Bed time, in Granny's nice little room. And we'll read *The Gruffalo*.'

We anoint him with kisses all round and Ellie carries him off. I don't know what Ellie has told him about what's going to happen to him tomorrow. Can a four-year-old really take in the idea that a doctor is going to be inserting a catheter into to his pulsing heart? Ben volunteers for the washing up, so I take Annie outside to show her my courtyard's secret garden potential, and – possibly – to ask her about Isha Anand. It turns out, though, that she has something she wants to ask me.

'I was wondering,' she says casually, while fingering a deep red climbing rose, 'whether you might have time to drop into a rehearsal some time. It's quite intimidating playing Isabella. It's the biggest part I've ever done. I wouldn't mind some advice.'

I never thought to see the day when Annie would ask my advice about anything. I am dumbstruck, but I must offer something.

'She starts off so well, doesn't she?' I say. 'The two scenes with Angelo are a doddle really. They're so well-written, you can just ride along on the lines, but then it gets tricky.'

'The scene with Claudio,' she says.

'*O you beast!*' I say. 'How the hell do you say that?'

'Exactly! And *More than our brother is our chastity*. It was easier, I suppose, when chastity was more of a thing, but now…'

I should probably explain, at this point, the plot of *Measure for Measure*, since it is not among Shakespeare's most often performed plays and you may not know it. The crux of it is that Isabella, a young novice in a convent, goes to see Angelo, the Duke's Deputy who is temporarily governing Vienna, to plead with him to pardon her brother, Claudio, who has been sentenced to death for getting his girlfriend pregnant. Angelo has a moral crusade going on, but the irony is that he falls in lust with Isabella and offers to pardon her brother if she will have sex with him. She refuses, of course, and after that the plot becomes both improbable and morally suspect, with the real Duke of Vienna returning in disguise and putting things right in a quite unnecessarily convoluted way. The final straw is that, at the end of the play, the Duke announces that he is going to marry Isabella, having forgotten, apparently, that she is planning to be a nun. What she thinks about the proposal we don't learn, as Shakespeare gives her nothing to say. My guess is that, since it is a comedy – though a pretty miserable one – Shakespeare needed to tie up the ends with a flurry of marriages, but could not imagine what a woman could possibly say to such a proposal under such circumstances. As you may have gathered, it is not a favourite play of mine. It has two great scenes in the first half, in which Angelo and Isabella debate passionately the conflicting claims of justice and mercy but, for the rest, the low-life comedy scenes are tedious and the plot dribbles away into absurdity in the second half. It has the longest and most implausible final scene I know of, except, possibly, the last scene of *Cymbeline*.

So, Annie is playing Isabella, and she has to find a convincing way of refusing to give in to Angelo, and still save Claudio's life.

'So,' I ask, 'would you – effectively – let yourself be raped to save Ellie's life?'

'Of course I would – or Freda's or Nico's. It would just be sex, wouldn't it? No big deal – not compared with the life of someone you loved.'

'Except it's not just sex, is it?' I say. 'You might not think chastity is important, but you mind about the way men take power over women for granted. Angelo isn't just exercising his power as the Duke's Deputy – he's exercising what he thinks is his right, as a man, to have any woman he chooses. It's Donald Trump stuff. If you had sex with someone on those terms, I think it might destroy you – eat away at you. In a way, that's what Isabella is saying. I think she means it when she says she would happily die to save Claudio. That would be easy because she wouldn't lose herself. For her, it's a religious self – her soul – but we all have that sense of our core self, and if we compromise that too far, we're lost.'

'That's not bad,' she says. 'I might be able to use that.'

'And, of course, Isabella is planning to be a nun. That does make a difference.'

We are sitting, now, on a rather grimy wrought iron bench, which came with the garden. Annie picks some of the peeling paint off it and says, 'I did talk to an Indian friend of mine – well not really a friend, but someone I knew – another lawyer. She told me she was still a virgin – at twenty-four or twenty-five – and she expected her family to arrange a marriage for her. It felt so odd, because she was really anglicised – she'd been at school here and everything – but she still had completely different expectations. And she had a younger brother she was really close to, but she said she didn't think she could have done that for him. So, I was trying to think about her as well.'

I take the plunge. 'Was that Isha Anand?' I ask.

Annie hasn't been looking directly at me, but her head whips round. 'How do you know about Isha?'

'It was in the papers – her murder – and you talked about her in the past tense.'

She gives me a narrow-eyed look.

'And David said you might know her,' I say.

'David?'

'My David – or once my David. He said he bumped into you.'

She is still looking hard at me. 'He did,' she says, 'when he was working on Cressida Long's case.'

'The harassment case?'

'Yes. But why was he talking to you about Isha?'

*Why, indeed?*

I shrug. 'He's a police officer and she was killed just around the corner from here.'

'So that's what you two do, is it, when you meet up? Have a nice cosy chat about dead people?'

Her voice wobbles a bit, with anger or distress, or a bit of both.

'It wasn't like that. I think the case bothers him.'

'Why? I thought they were trying to arrest her brother?'

'They are. But – '

I should tell you, before I go on, that I am now in possession of all the information given out by the news media after Isha Anand's death. Since yesterday afternoon, in between making up beds, cleaning the flat, shopping for food for the week, getting a haircut, collecting my conference jacket from the cleaners and cooking supper, I have trawled the internet, and now know that Isha Anand was found early on the morning of 26th June by a young lad delivering papers. Her body was lying in what used to be called *the area* of houses with basements – at the bottom of the steps – outside Woburn Court, where she lived. There is no indication in the reports of how she was killed. There is some background information about the Anand family, and it turns out that her father, like her uncle, was a politician, but he and his wife were gunned down by an assassin when the children were quite young and their uncle became their guardian. No wonder they were close, in spite of the age gap. Later reports

32

say that her brother, Bimal, is now believed to be in India, and that the police would like to interview him. Two reports raise the possibility of an honour killing. What none of the reports says is that Isha Anand was an impeccably behaved young woman with no sexual history.

'If her brother was involved, then the assumption would be that it was a so-called honour killing,' I say. 'But from what you say, no-one could have been further from dishonour than Isha.'

'I guess the police found out about the sexting,' she says.

'Sexting?'

'Yes, it's when someone sends – '

'I know what sexting is – sending sexually explicit texts or pictures. But who – '

'We got them the day before she died. I guess they went to everyone whose mobile number was on her phone – and that included the whole *Measure* cast. We all swapped numbers at the first read-though, so we could keep in touch.'

'What did the messages say?'

'They weren't messages. They were pictures.'

'What sort of pictures?'

'What do you think?'

'Well –'

'There was no-one else in them. It was just Isha – nude and doing – you know – stuff…'

'But didn't you think that was wildly out of character?'

'We didn't believe she had sent them – and we didn't believe the pictures were really her.'

'How do you mean?'

'It's easy to doctor photos if you know how. You can stick someone's face on someone else's body.'

'So, you think someone doctored the photos, and then put them on her phone and sent them out. Why?'

'It's usually revenge when people do that sort of thing. When people break up, one of them will use it as a way of getting back at the other. Sometimes it's blackmail. People get the photos and then threaten to send them.'

'What do you think the motive was with Isha?'

'I don't know. As you can imagine, we had a great flurry of debate about it – our phones were red hot – and most of us thought it was a cruel joke, but some of us thought it was a racist thing – especially coming after the Brexit vote – and others thought it was because she gave out those *noli me tangere* messages, and that had got up someone's nose. It was mainly the men who thought that. She was very beautiful and lots of people fancied her, but she had a kind of protective wall around her.'

'That might have made a woman jealous, as well. A woman who attracts men but doesn't want them could become a bugbear for a not very attractive woman.'

'I suppose.'

'What did Isha herself say about them?'

'No-one got to talk to her. We all texted her, of course, and tried phoning, but we went to voicemail. It was a Saturday, so she wasn't at work, and no-one knew her address. In the end we agreed that we would all delete the pictures from our phones and just try to downplay it. And then we heard she was dead, and we didn't know what to think.'

'If the pictures went out to all the numbers on her phone, then presumably her brother got them, too.'

'Well, that's the thing. I'm pretty sure Isha said Bimal was spending the week with her before he flew back to India on the Sunday, for the summer. So he would have been around.'

'So, there was nothing sinister about his flying off to India on the day her body was found? He was scheduled to go.'

'Yes.'

'I wonder if the police realise that.'

'But the other thing is, Bimal could have been the one who sent the pictures. He would have had photos of Isha he could use and, if he was staying with her, he would have had access to her phone. If he was tech-savvy, he could have used porn images off the internet, inserted Isha's face and sent them.'

'And then killed her for dishonouring the family? It doesn't make sense. Why would he do that?'

'Suppose he didn't kill her? Suppose he did it to put off some man who was after her, and it went horribly wrong because the man was so enraged that he killed her?'

'Was there a man after her?'

She hesitates. 'As I say, lots of men fancied her.'

We say nothing for a bit, while I think furiously. Eventually, I have to say what I am thinking, even though I am not sure how it will sound when I say it.

'The other possibility,' I say, 'is that the photos weren't doctored. Suppose Isha wasn't what she seemed. Suppose she actually had a secret life. Suppose those photos were for real – taken by her secret lover – and Bimal found them on her computer. Teenagers do odd things. He might have felt so angry, so let down by the sister he admired – she was eight years older than him, so she must have been almost a mother to him when their parents were killed and they were sent off to school in England. So, he decided he had to kill her, but he wanted to justify himself first – wanted the world to know why he'd done it – so he sent out the pictures.'

'It's hard to believe,' she says. 'I thought she was the real thing.'

'You liked her?'

'I did. I thought at one stage that she might get a place in our chambers and I'd have liked that.'

She stands up. 'So you'll come to rehearsal and tell me what I'm doing wrong?' she says.

'Not that, but I will come. Let me know when you're rehearsing the Claudio scene. And think about whether he's older or younger than Isabella. It should make a difference

35

to how you play it. Have you talked about that sort of thing with your director?'

'He doesn't go in for psychology much. He's more a moving people around sort of director. That's why I need some help. You may remember him, actually. He was in the Elsinore *Hamlet*. Tom Yeoman? He played Horatio. He's not a professional or anything – just another lawyer. He's what you'd call a safe pair of hands.'

'I do remember him. He suited Horatio. He didn't seem to have a big ego, unlike several of the other men in that production.'

'I'm not sure about that. He has his moments – entitlement, you know. And then there's Lyle, and Piers. They're both quite full of themselves.'

'Lyle is your Angelo, isn't he? What's Piers playing?'

'Claudio. He's coming over as a spoilt brat at the moment.'

When Nico is asleep, Ellie and Ben say they will walk Annie to the Tube and take a stroll around. I collect my conference outfit from my bedroom and decide to iron my shirt and polish my shoes. I'm not giving my paper till Tuesday, so this is my second-best outfit, but I aim to make a good impression. That done, I locate a spare duvet and pillow for my night on the sofa. When Ellie and Ben return, we all declare ourselves ready for an early night, though none of us, I think, expects to sleep.

I churn around on my sofa for a long time, but eventually doze off, to be woken by the sound of Nico crying. Ellie comes through the living room to go to him and I lie and listen to her soothing and then singing. When she comes back, I get up and make us a cup of tea. We sit in the kitchen to drink it, not saying much, knowing that it is useless to go back to bed and watching the sky lighten into a summer dawn. Eventually, Ellie says that they have to be at the hospital by seven-thirty and that she will go and get a shower.

I stay sitting at the table, and I can hear Ellie struggling with the controls of the state of the art shower. Above our heads is a very beautiful nineteenth-century house, and my basement has been imaginatively carved up into rooms, but the builders stinted on materials, and the interior walls feel no more substantial than hardboard in places. There is certainly little privacy in the bathroom; this is a one-person domain.

I shout out instructions to Ellie and then I pour myself more tea and reflect upon how casually I embarked on motherhood. I don't mean that it was unplanned. I wasn't like Ellie was with Freda – we did the prudent thing and waited until we had a house and a mortgage. What I mean is that I had no idea at all what motherhood would entail. I had some notion of the practicalities, and I expected to love my children, but I had no idea that my children would exert a lifelong pull on my heart, that my life would never be just mine again, and that I was opening myself up to vicarious pain on an epic scale. Joy too, of course; if you feel the pain, you are entitled to a bit of joy as well. *Joy and woe are woven fine*, Blake says, and he is uncharacteristically upbeat about it. *And when this we rightly know / Thro' the world we safely go*, he concludes, but it's a matter of percentages, isn't it? In the long run, doesn't woe always win out?

# Chapter Four

## FREDA

*Sunday 24th July 2016*

*It won't be as bad as you think.* Wasn't that what grown-ups always said when you were worried about something – maths tests, injections, the dentist? And then, afterwards, they would say, *There you are, it wasn't so bad, was it?* Well, this was going to be every bit as bad as she had thought, this week at Aren't-We-Grand Hall, as Granny and Mum called it. The house was actually called Nettlebourne Farm (although there were no animals there – except for the dog – and no nettles either, as far as she could see), but they liked having their own names for things, like always calling Auntie Lavender *TFL*, which stood for *The Fragrant Lavender*. Auntie Lavender wasn't really an aunt. She was married to Grandpa, but you couldn't call her *Granny* or *Grandma* because she wasn't old – only about the same age as Mum. Freda generally thought of her as just *Lavender*, because that was her name, but Mum said it would be rude to call her that, so they had agreed on Auntie. She was actually very nice. Mum and Granny always laughed about her, but Freda was glad to have her because she was beginning to see that she was quite short of relations, compared with other people. Most people had two sets of grandparents, but if you didn't know who your father was, then you missed out on one set. Nico had two lots, of course: Granny and Grandpa and Ben's parents, Maddalena and

Enrico. They were always nice to her when they all went to Italy to visit, but they had never told her to call them *Nonna* and *Nonno*, like Nico did, and she always felt a bit awkward when she was there because she didn't really fit in. Nico did. He looked Italian, like the rest of them, and Ben had started teaching him some Italian, which really pleased Nonna and Nonno. To be fair, Ben had offered to teach her too, but she had turned him down, which had been stupid of her, she realised, because Mum had been to classes and could speak quite a lot of Italian now, so she was the odd one out there, as well. It was the same with surnames: the others were all Biaggis but she was Freda Gray. Mum had said she could change her name to Biaggi, and Ben had said he would really like her to call him *Dad*, but it didn't feel right. She liked Ben a lot, but he wasn't her dad, and she would have felt stupid with an Italian surname, when she wasn't at all Italian. And somewhere in the world there was her real father, who maybe looked like her, who also had greeny-brown eyes like no-one else in the family had, and double-jointed thumbs. Only Mum said there was nothing much to say about him and Freda wasn't old enough yet to hear what there was to say.

Sometimes she was jealous of Nico, which she was ashamed of because she really loved him, and the thought of them doing things to his heart made her so scared that she felt sick nearly all the time. And what made everything worse was that they wouldn't let her be in London with them. Even Granny hadn't been on her side about this. Freda had pleaded with her, promised that she could stay in her flat and just watch TV and stuff while Mum and Ben were at the hospital and Granny was at her conference. She had promised she could be sensible and look after herself – she was ten now, after all – and then she would be there in the evening, when they got back, and know what they knew about Nico and not be worrying all on her own. But Granny, who you could usually rely on to understand, just said, 'It's against the law, Freda. Ten is too young We could all be sent to jail if we left you alone,' which Freda felt sure was just the usual sort of exaggerating that Granny did and was probably not true at all.

Anyway, when she watched Ben and Mum and Nico disappearing away down the drive, after they had dropped her off this afternoon, she had been really afraid that she was going to be stupid and cry, but Lavender had given her a big hug and said how glad she was to have a big girl staying with her, when she had only babies herself, and that had, surprisingly, made her feel better.

Then Lavender said she would show her round the house. She had been there a few times before, but they had mainly been in the garden and she hadn't really seen inside. Nico came here sometimes to play with the boys, but Freda was too old to play with babies, so she wasn't invited. The house was huge. You came in through a big front door with pillars outside, like those on a Greek temple, and then there was a big, square hallway, with a wide staircase going up from it – not straight, but in a curve. There were lots of doors from the hall, and Lavender took her to each in turn and showed her four rooms, which were all rooms Freda didn't have at home. In her house, there was the living room and the kitchen downstairs, and the three bedrooms and the bathroom upstairs – that was what most people had, wasn't it? But Lavender took her first to a door she didn't open, and said this was Grandpa's study, where he did his work, and no children were allowed into it.

'Even I'm not really allowed in there,' she said, 'and I don't expect you're allowed to disturb your parents when they're working, are you?'

Freda had said, 'No,' because that seemed to be the polite thing to say, but it wasn't true. Mum and Ben did their marking and stuff at the kitchen table, and only got cross if you kept on going and interrupting them.

The next room was the dining room. It had an enormous table in it, polished and shiny, and Freda counted ten chairs round it. Why did they need all those chairs when there were only four of them? Or five, maybe, because there was Monika too, who dropped the boys off to play with Nico sometimes. Freda looked at the table and tried to imagine Hubert eating here. He was the same age as Nico, but last time he was at their house he had spilt a pool of juice on the table and then floated pieces of bread in it. Maybe Lavender read her thoughts. 'This is just for dinner parties,' she said. 'Grown-ups only.' And Freda hoped she wasn't going to say it was probably the same in their house because, when Mum and Ben had parties, everyone ate standing up, in the kitchen or the living room or the hall, or sat down if they could find a chair. Sometimes people sat on the stairs.

She went over to look at some shiny silver things – a tray with bottles on it, a big bowl, two tall vases and some small things she didn't know the names of. Lavender said, 'Oh, the heirlooms. The family silver. From my family. I would pack them all away in a cupboard – they're extra work for Maggie to keep polished – but your grandpa likes to have them out.'

They went across the hall to a room from which a depressingly familiar noise was coming – the sound of Arthur and Hubert fighting. She didn't like Arthur and Hubert much, if she was honest. For a start, it made her feel weird to think that they were sort of her uncles, because Grandpa was their dad and Mum's dad, too. Granny thought this was a big joke and liked to ask, 'How are Uncle Arthur and Uncle Hubert these days?' but it wasn't funny, and then there was all the fighting. Today, they seemed to be fighting over some Lego, bashing each other and yelling. It was hard to tell whether there was a real disagreement or whether they just liked fighting, but it was always like that with them. When they came to her house to play with Nico, they shoved and pushed at each other all the time, and called each other stupid, rude names. She wondered if they really hated one another. Nico didn't join in, but he got sillier when they were around, and stayed silly after they'd gone. Lavender didn't seem to notice today's row, though, and just said, 'And this is the nursery.' Freda would have called it a playroom. Nursery was where Nico went, with a lot of other children, and where she had gone herself before she started school. You couldn't call a room for two children a nursery, could you?

Monika, the boys' nanny, was a tall, pale girl with sad eyes. She was standing by the window, looking out at the garden, and she turned round a bit as they came in, but she didn't smile.

'And you've met our lovely Monika, haven't you?' Lavender said, 'who looks after my naughty boys. Monika, you know Freda. She's a big girl and doesn't need looking after, but she will have nursery tea with the boys.'

Nursery tea? What was that? Freda had a picture of a dolls' tea set and the kind of games she used to play with her friend Charlie when they were younger.

'I thought you would rather eat with the boys, Freda,' Lavender said. 'They eat at about six, and Grandpa and I don't eat till eight or so, which is a bit late for you, and you won't want to listen to boring grown-ups' conversation.'

Conversation, however boring, would be better than watching the boys throwing food at each other, Freda thought, but there was no point in arguing. She looked at Monika, but she had turned back to the window. Freda didn't think she had ever seen a person look so miserable.

The next room was the most puzzling. Lavender said it was the drawing room, and Freda expected something like an artist's studio, but inside it was just a living room, with

42

sofas and a coffee table and a piano. There was no sign of anyone doing any drawing in here. There was a small table at one end of the room, with two chairs. 'Grandpa and I have our dinner here,' Lavender said, 'except on special occasions. It's cosier in here than in the dining room.'

It didn't feel cosy to Freda, not compared to supper at home, in the kitchen, with everyone talking about what had happened during the day and Ben being funny, because he was a music teacher and he could imitate the bad singers and make beginner violin player noises. *Stop thinking about that.* She gave herself a shake. 'Do you have a kitchen?' she asked.

Lavender laughed. 'Of course we do,' she said, and Freda felt stupid because it was a silly question, of course. It was just that she wondered about all these tables: the one in the dining room, the one in the nursery, where she supposed nursery tea would happen, and now this one, for being cosy. If you wanted to be cosy, why not eat in the kitchen? So that had made her wonder if they didn't have a kitchen table, and then she'd asked a dumb question.

Well, it turned out that they did have a kitchen table, a big one – about twice as big as the one at home – in a big kitchen with lots of wooden cupboards, and a door off it, behind which she could hear a dog whining and scratching. The dog. She had almost forgotten they had a dog now, a puppy, though Mum had warned her that didn't mean it would be small; it was a Labrador Retriever, and they were big dogs, even when they were puppies, Mum had said.

'Oh, that's Jasper,' Lavender said. 'He's in disgrace. He chews everything, and Grandpa says he has to stay in the kitchen till he's properly trained. I expect Maggie shut him in the scullery when she was cleaning in here.'

Lavender opened the door and a dog hurtled out, straight at Freda's legs, nearly knocking her down. The only other dog she had really known was Caliban. Granny had had him when she lived by the seaside. He was all right, and fun to chase around with on the beach. Freda was sorry Granny had given him away, but she had said he would be happier staying at the seaside than being cooped up in a flat in London, and her friend, who had him now, had lost lots of weight because of having to take him for walks so everyone was happy. Caliban was quite old, and quiet, except when something put him in a rage and then he barked his head off. Jasper was a different matter; she thought he would probably turn out to be a lot like Arthur and Hubert.

Nursery tea was horrible. The food was all right; Monika had made pasta and a tomato sauce with pieces of red and yellow pepper in it. The sight of the boys deliberately smearing the sauce on their faces was disgusting, though, and she couldn't manage to eat much although she tried hard, so as not to upset Monika, who looked all the time as if she was going to burst into tears. She felt sick again, and wondered what they were all doing at Granny's flat, and then had to jump up and run upstairs to her room before the boys could see that she was upset.

Upstairs, she saw that she had a message on her phone, which she had left on the bedside table. She was embarrassed by her phone, because it was so horribly basic, and she kept it hidden as much as she could. Everyone – *everyone* – else had smartphones, and she had so hoped Mum might change her mind and buy her one for her birthday, but Mum said no-one needed a smartphone when they had a computer at home, and people got so attached to the virtual world on their phones that they forgot to look around them and experience the real world. Which was all very well, except that just at that moment the real world was looking like something she didn't want to experience, and if she'd had a decent phone, she could have spent the next few days up here, playing games, listening to music and looking up stuff on the internet, and she would hardly have needed to see the boys at all.

And she would be happy to stay in her room because she really liked it. When Lavender had finished her tour of the downstairs rooms, they had gone up the big staircase and just glanced in at Grandpa's and Lavender's room, which had another door in it, leading to Grandpa's 'dressing room'. Why did anyone need a separate room for dressing? She had added it to the list of rooms they didn't have in her house. Then there were the boys' rooms, and Lavender had shown her the guest bedroom, which had a huge bed in it, and velvet curtains, and a bathroom of its own, and she had said she thought Freda might feel a bit lost in there, so she had taken her up another flight of stairs – a straight one this time, and quite narrow – and shown her this one. 'Monika sleeps next door,' she had said, 'and you can share her little bathroom. I hope you don't mind being up in the attic.'

Freda didn't mind at all. The further away from everyone else, the better. She thought that up here was a bit like the attic room Sarah Crewe had in *A Little Princess*, except that Sarah's room was cold and bare and miserable, whereas this room was pretty. It was a bit flowery, and Charlie would have laughed at it, but it felt summery and smelt nice and had a little window from which you could see not just the garden but places miles away.

She sat on the bed and picked up her phone. The message was from Mum, as she thought it would be. She took a deep breath before she opened it, because Mum meant home, and she might not be able to keep the homesickness, which she had tried to shut away in a box, from pushing its way out.

*Hi Freedie. We are safely at Granny's and about to have supper. I hope you're settled in and the boys aren't too annoying. Nico is being very brave. Everyone sends love. Granny says you can come and stay with her soon, and do shopping and museums and a play.*

45

*Fun! Her flat is lovely, with a garden. Love you lots xxxxxxxxxxxxx*
*Mum*

Push it away. Push it away. She quickly started typing. Later she would send a message to Charlie and tell her how she really felt, but, for now, she wrote:

*All OK here. My room is nice. We have just had supper. Tell Nico I am keeping my fingers and toes and eyes crossed for him. xx*

There.

She looked at the time. Nearly seven o'clock. Lavender hadn't said anything about bedtimes. After supper at home, Mum or Ben put Nico to bed and she was allowed to watch TV, but not after nine o'clock. There was something called a *watershed* that parents talked about – like children would be washed away if they watched things after that. She thought that Monika was probably putting the boys to bed now, and maybe she could go down and watch the TV she had seen in the nursery. If everyone forgot about her, maybe she could go on watching after nine o'clock and see just how scary the programmes really were, or whether there was just lots of swearing, which she and her friends all knew about anyway, though parents thought they didn't.

She read her book for a while. It was *The Ghost of Thomas Kempe*, which Granny had given to her as part of her birthday present. It was a bit old-fashioned, like all the books Granny liked, but still quite a good story about a family living in an old house with a poltergeist. Grandpa and Lavender's house was quite old, and she had wondered whether it would feel like it might be haunted, but it didn't. There was lots of light in it, and no dark corners. Nothing mysterious here.

When she thought the boys would be safely in bed, she went downstairs. She went to the kitchen first, to get a glass of water, and found Monika there, sitting at the big table all alone, eating her supper, which seemed to be the same as she had made for Freda and the boys earlier. Lavender and

Grandpa, she supposed, must be having their *cosy* supper in the so-called drawing room. Were they eating the same pasta and sauce as the rest of them, or had Lavender made something different for them? There were a lot of dirty pans by the sink, so she thought she must have done. It was all very odd, and she wanted to tell Charlie about it. It was too complicated to put in a text, though, and Charlie was on holiday with her family in Croatia, so she couldn't spend long talking to her or her phone would run out of credit.

'I'm just getting myself some water,' she said to Monika, who had hardly looked up from her supper when she went in.

'Glasses there,' Monika told her, pointing to a cupboard. She really did look sad, sitting there all on her own. Freda could see that she wouldn't want to eat with the boys, but maybe in future Freda could eat with her after the boys were in bed. It might be doing them both a favour. Tomorrow, she might suggest it.

She watched *Call the Midwife* and then flicked channels for a bit, looking for after-watershed thrills, but she found nothing interesting and decided that she quite wanted to go to bed. It was clear that no-one here was going to make her go to bed – they had all forgotten about her – so maybe one night she would stay up all night, just to see what it was like, but tonight she wanted to be in her little room and asleep.

Sleep came easily, but later, when the window behind her curtains was quite black, she was woken by a sound she couldn't at first identify. She had been having a dream, and in her dream Nico was crying, but now that she was awake, she realised that the sound wasn't from a person. It was a dog howling, and the howling seemed to be coming from right below her window. She got out of bed and stood on a chair to get a better look down from her window. She could see nothing, but the howling went on. She supposed it must be Jasper, but what was he doing out there? Granny, she remembered, used to let Caliban out into the garden for a pee before she went to bed. Maybe Lavender had let him out and forgotten to let him in again. And if she, Freda, was the only person who could hear him, because he was under her window, then hadn't she better be the person to let him in?

She turned the light on for the first flight of stairs, but then couldn't find a light switch, and had to grope her way down the main stairs and into the kitchen, where she found a switch and flooded the room with light. From the lit room, she could see nothing in the darkness outside, but she could still hear the dog. She had to wrestle with the back-door key, which was large and old-looking, but she turned it finally, and stepped out onto paving stones, which were gritty and damply cold under her bare feet. Jasper jumped up and down and started barking. She thought the barking was friendly, but it was difficult to tell with dogs. She braced herself for him to charge at her legs again, but he didn't, and then she saw why. In the light that spilled out from the kitchen, she saw that he had a chain attached to his collar, and the other end of the chain disappeared into a big kennel a few metres away from the house.

She moved towards Jasper and put out a cautious hand to pat his head, which seemed to be all right with him, and then she knelt down and looked into the kennel. It was, she had to admit, a luxury sort of kennel. She couldn't see much inside, but she could feel that there was a sort of dog's duvet in there, and there was a bowl of water and another of dog biscuits outside it. Well, obviously he hadn't been shut out by accident; he was meant to be here. But why? Caliban had slept in Granny's bedroom, which maybe was taking things a bit far, but why would you put your dog outside to sleep? She wondered if he was supposed to be a guard dog, but you wouldn't put a guard dog on a chain, would you? Because then it couldn't chase anybody, could it?

She felt sorry now that she had come down, because she had only got Jasper's hopes up, and now she was going to have to leave him. She patted his head again and took one of his biscuits out of the bowl and offered it to him, but he just bounced up and down and wagged his tail. She was turning to go back inside when she saw someone else coming out of the kitchen. She felt her heart actually jump up into her throat, just like people's did in books and you didn't quite believe it. It would be Grandpa or Lavender, and she would be in trouble for disturbing everyone. It wasn't, though. It was Monika, who came across to her and hissed, 'What you doing?'

'Why is he out here?' Freda asked. 'He was howling.'

'Mr Andrew says he must stay out. He pees on floor in night. Come.'

They went back inside and climbed up to their rooms. Outside Freda's door, Monika stood on one leg and examined her other foot. 'Dirty feet,' she said. 'Come, we wash.'

And so they sat on the edge of the bath in Monika's bathroom, side by side, and dangled their feet in a few centimetres of water, soaping them with Lavender's rose-scented soap, and once, when their arms bumped into each other, Monika smiled, and it was like she was a different person. *She's not really a miserable person*, Freda thought, *she's just miserable here.*

As she lay in bed, trying to get back to sleep, she realised what Jasper and the kennel reminded her of. Jasper was like Nana, the dog in *Peter Pan*, who gets shut out by Mr Darling, so she can't guard the children and they get taken away by Peter Pan. As she drifted off to sleep, she pictured Arthur and Hubert, in their pyjamas, cruising out of their bedroom window and over the garden, heading for Neverland.

# Chapter Five

## ADJOURNMENT

### Monday 25th July 2016

The ominous day does not turn out as any of us have expected. It starts predictably enough: Ellie gets Nico up, we all try, and fail, to eat pains au chocolat for breakfast, and then Ellie, Nico and Ben depart, after muted hugging, for the hospital. I attempt a transformation exercise – turning a grey-faced, sleep-deprived female, the wrong side of fifty, into a professional woman of pin-sharp intellect in the prime of her life. I have little to work with but a tube of concealer and a lipstick, but I slap one onto the bags under my eyes, paint on a bright smile with the other and don a blue linen jacket that is mercifully kind to a bloodless complexion. In this disguise I stride, insofar as my smart shoes will allow striding, to University College, and join the fray.

My performance holds up well, I think. I greet colleagues and acquaintances with well-calibrated levels of delight, and I sit in a plenary session on *Applied Linguistics and Communication Technology*, which is not as innovative as it thinks it is, and ask what I think is a pertinent question on the student sampling for research subjects. I then have coffee with a group from Edinburgh, some of whom I met at a previous conference, and listen to a paper on *Subjectivity and Identity in Additional Language Acquisition* before going for lunch with colleagues from King's College. I remember to turn my phone off during sessions and turn it on again as soon as they are over. By the time I go into the afternoon session, there has been no message from Ellie, but just as I'm about to turn off again, a text beeps in from Annie: *Nothing from Ellie. What's going on? Going nuts here, A*

*Join the club, Annie,* I think, and then see that I am getting an odd look from a young man who is sitting in front of me, and realise that I must have spoken my thought out loud. I smile placatingly, trying not to look dotty, and type quickly, *No news, good news. Breathe xx,* before switching off. Is that true? *No news is good news? Bad news travels fast?* Why not comfort ourselves with clichés when there seems to be nothing else available? *All shall be well, and all shall be well, and all manner of things shall be well.* It is possible that I say this out loud, too.

There follows a workshop session on the language of political protest, which ought to be fascinating but fails even to take the edge off my sharpening anxiety. When there is still no message at the tea break, I cut my losses, make a loose arrangement to meet some people for dinner later, and head for home, sweating into my newly cleaned jacket as I power my way, as fast as my elegant heels will take me, through the drifting tourists and the homeward-trudging workers in the airless afternoon. There was a time, during my life in the tourist hotspot of Marlbury, when you could distinguish tourists from locals, not just by the amount of paraphernalia they carried about with them, but also by their water bottles – as though, in this barbarous environment, you couldn't trust the water supply; here, everyone carries them. This gives the streets an apocalyptic air – a suggestion of disaster aftermath which is disquieting in my jumpy state.

I am not reassured when I get home. I find Ben sitting in the garden with the remains of the second bottle of wine from yesterday's supper, and looking such a picture of misery that my legs go helpless under me and it is all I can do to make myself walk out into the garden and ask, 'What's happened?'

He looks up and makes a vague gesture of apology at the bottle and his empty glass. 'They didn't do it,' he says. 'They got him prepped and everything and then said they couldn't do it. No explanation except *problems with the theatre*. One of the other parents said they'd found traces of a superbug in one of the theatres. I don't know if that's true, but I don't even know now if we want them to do it – if there's that danger.'

I pick up the bottle and pour some more wine into his glass. 'They won't operate if there's any possibility of infection, Ben. They didn't operate today, and they won't operate until they're absolutely sure it's safe.'

'Well ... meantime, he's in there and the waiting's driving us spare.'

'How's he doing?'

'Better than us.'

Perspective is all. I see how he and Ellie feel, but this is so much better than my worst fears as I walked home that I feel almost cheerful as well as almost cross at having been left in suspense all day. I go into the kitchen and fetch a glass for myself, and while I'm there I put some bread and cheese and tomatoes on a plate, take this out and put it on the bench beside Ben. 'Is there a drop of wine for me?' I ask. And then, when I've taken a swig, I say, 'There wasn't a moment when Ellie could have texted Annie and me?'

He looks slightly blank. 'Didn't she?' he asks.

'She didn't.'

'I told Freda. She rang here a few minutes ago.'

'Well, that's something. How about your parents?'

He fishes his phone out of his pocket. 'I should um ...' he says.

'You should. And you should eat something. Have you eaten at all since we didn't eat breakfast? Low blood sugar isn't going to make you feel any better.'

I sound unsympathetic, I know, but he needs to brace up. He gets up and goes as far away as he can, into a corner of the garden, to have a muted conversation in Italian with his mother. Meanwhile, I text Annie:

*Op adjourned. Hospital glitch and family communication failure. Breathe again xx*

When Ben returns, he says, 'I need to get back and relieve Ellie. I'm doing this evening so she can have a break.'

'Eat your bread and cheese,' I say, 'and don't tell Ellie I was cross that she didn't text. I know how it is. It's a separate world once you get into a hospital. It's easy to lose sight of the rest of us on the outside.'

I go back to the kitchen and fetch a bag of gingerbread men that I bought from the bakery with the pains au chocolat this morning. 'Take these for Nico,' I say.

Why do I think that feeding people is the antidote to misery? My mother wasn't like that. Ascetic is what she was, and food was never offered to me as consolation when I was a child, but I have always trusted comfort food, from bars of chocolate at exam time, to slices of Black Forest gateau from the deli for homesickness at university, to a smoked salmon sandwich for lunch after a testing morning's teaching in a collapsing comp (one term, things got so bad that I took a small pot of caviar to school with me). I don't need to excuse my feeding compulsion to Ben, though; his mother is Italian, so I imagine he is used to it.

After he has gone back to the hospital, I take off my conference uniform, have a shower and sag into baggy trousers and a loose shirt. Then, I read through my paper for the next day, so that I can devote the evening to Ellie. When she gets back, however, she is too exhausted to talk much, and she certainly doesn't want to hear about my day, so I make us a Spanish omelette and open a fresh bottle of wine, and we eat and drink more or less in silence, which is just about unheard of in our family. Then she says she thinks she will go to bed and try to catch up on some sleep. I wash up and wonder what to do with my evening.

Flicking through the TV Guide, I can see nothing in the way of distraction television that has any chance of actually distracting me, and I'm too jumpy to read, so I do some fussing over my clothes for the next day and then go and sit out in the garden as the dusk thickens, and I let my mind go into free fall.

This is not a brilliant idea, I know, because this is when worries I have forgotten to worry about come bobbing up to the surface. I am putting worry about Nico on hold until we know what is going to happen next, but there are plenty more lurking about in the depths, and what emerges, surprisingly, is not fear of my paper falling flat tomorrow, nor my iffy relationship with Annie (always a good standby), nor her iffy relationship with Jon, nor whether David and I are speaking to each other, but what, if anything, I am going to do about finding out who killed Isha Anand.

If I had pen and paper with me, I would start writing things down, but I am too tired to go and get them, so my list of questions has to be written in my head.

a.  *Random race attack?*

b.  *'Honour' killing?*

c.  *Attack for other reason by someone who knew her?*

Against a), to my mind, is this location. I may be wrong, but if you were a violent race-hater, out for blood, Bloomsbury wouldn't be the obvious place to strike would it? Unless, of course, someone was particularly infuriated by the idea of a young Indian woman being able to afford to live in an area like this.

If b), then Bimal becomes the obvious suspect, except that his flying off to India the day after the killing looks less suspicious now it seems this was his scheduled flight back for the summer holidays. And the idea that he fled because he thought he too was in danger from the killer is less convincing, as well. On the other hand, I think he is a very likely candidate as the writer of the letter to David. He could have heard David's name from Isha, when David was investigating the harassment case, and the letter's mixture of naïveté and formal correctness fits the style of an educated but sheltered seventeen-year-old. You might expect that, when he heard that his sister had been killed, he would have felt he ought to stay, but he is just a boy, and if his initial questioning by the police was aggressive, why wouldn't he want to get away?

So, c) seems to me most likely, but that doesn't narrow things down much. The photos may not be connected with the killing, but they are bizarrely coincidental if not. Assuming they are connected, then:

a)   they may be genuine and so have driven a potential lover to fury because Isha was not what she seemed

b)   they were doctored, as Annie and Isha's other friends believe, by somebody wanting revenge on her – a rejected lover/suitor/ colleague – and the same person killed her, using the photos to suggest an honour killing, or someone else did, for reason a) above. The photos suggest a sexual motive, but could it have been professional jealousy? Getting a place in good chambers is a cut-throat business. Could Isha have got a place someone else believed was theirs by right? In my mind, I have ruled out a female killer, but it's not impossible, if that was the motive. (It would help, of course, if I knew how Isha was killed. I didn't find that in any of the reports.) I try to remember what

Annie said about Isha. Didn't she say that she had thought Isha might get a place in the same chambers as her, but it hadn't happened? Did Isha get a better offer and displace someone else?

*Information.* I can't do this without information. What did David think he was doing, landing this on me and then refusing me the basic facts? Isha's phone is the key. Where is it? Have the police got it and what, if anything, have police forensics found on it? If this were *Silent Witness*, Clarissa would have found out everything about Isha's life and death from that phone. How am I supposed to work this out simply by the power of thought?

David and I parted badly on Saturday, you remember, and it may be that we are now not speaking, but I am phoning him anyway. I decide that the garden is the best place for the conversation, as there may be some shouting and I don't want to disturb Ellie. Shouting in the garden will disturb my new neighbours, but they might as well get used to it.

'David?'

'Gina.'

'Further to our conversation at the weekend, if you want me to be any use, I need more information than I can find in old news reports and casual conversation with my daughter. So, how did Isha die? Was she sexually assaulted? Where is her phone? Do the police have it? If so, what information have they got from it? Are the sexting photos on it? Were they taken on that phone? Are they genuine or were they doctored? Did they come from a computer? If so, whose?'

I have been expecting him to interrupt, but when I pause for breath, he is silent.

'And don't you dare tell me,' I hiss, 'that this isn't your case. You've made it mine, so you can bloody well make it yours.'

He speaks very quietly – *low and slow* – the formula for

dealing with difficult children. 'I can tell you how she died. That was in one of the tabloids, though how they got it I don't know. She was strangled. I can't tell you anything about a sexual assault.'

'Because there wasn't one?'

'Because it's not my case.'

'But strangling often goes with rape, doesn't it?'

'I can't – '

'Oh, shut up, David. Strangling means not a female killer, doesn't it? Women don't strangle people. And not a simple random race attack – those are knives and boots, aren't they?'

'You can't generalise altogether b – '

'But I have to, because I've got nothing else. What about the phone?'

'It's no good asking, Gina. I don't have access to that information.'

'But you could have.'

'No, I couldn't.'

'You could, if you'd just use a bit of initiative.'

'Break the rules, you mean. This isn't TV, Gina. I'm not a maverick detective, breaking all the rules but so brilliant that I get results in the end.'

'You're certainly not. You're the other one. If you ever watched TV crime, you'd know there's always the boring time-server who tries to thwart the brilliant and charismatic detective, because he's got no imagination or gumption himself.'

'Thanks.'

'The people at the top don't stick to the rules, David. They've deliberately shut down this investigation, and there's a family who will never know what happened to a clever and beautiful young woman. Why aren't they kicking up a fuss?'

'Because any further investigation would involve bringing Bimal back here for questioning, and they don't want to lose him, too.'

'So he's lost his sister and has to live with unjust suspicion hanging over him for the rest of his life.'

'If he's innocent.'

'Which you think he is.'

'Probably.'

'Then do something! Get off your backside and do something – other than telling me about it.'

'And what exactly do you think I can do?'

'Get me – us – the information we need. It's easy for you to do it. This case is connected to your harassment case. You think you got all the villains on that one, but you're worried that you might not have done, and maybe one of that gang was Isha's killer, because she was a junior on the case that got their criminal buddy sent down for twenty years. You breeze up to whatever DCI is nominally conducting Isha's case, while actually doing nothing, you pull rank and you ask, *'All right if I just review the evidence you've got on the Anand case? I've got a possible lead on another conspirator in the Long harassment case, and I just want to see if there could be a tie-in.'* Then he, or she, says, *'Of course, David. Feel free'* and off you go.'

I pause. He is silent. 'Not forgetting to report back to me when you've got what we need,' I add.

'You should be writing for TV,' he says, and cuts me off.

# Chapter Six

## FREDA

### Tuesday 26th July 2016

It was all very well telling herself she had to be brave, but a person only had so much bravery in her, and after yesterday she felt she had used up all her store for the entire week. Mum had promised her that she would ring as soon as Nico's operation was over, but hours and hours had gone by before she had finally got to talk to Ben and had found out that the operation had been put off. And it was worse because nobody else in this house seemed to be thinking about Nico at all, let alone worrying about him. Nobody even mentioned him. Monika said maybe they were thinking about him but didn't talk about him because they thought it might upset Freda, in which case they were quite stupid, because of course she was upset anyway. Monika hadn't even known what was happening to Nico until Freda told her. They were sitting together in the garden, watching the boys play. The boys had a separate part of the garden that was just for them, so that they didn't mess up Lavender's flower garden, which was what you saw from the windows at the back of the house. The flower garden had a wall all the way round it, like in *The Secret Garden*, except that it wasn't wild and secret at all, but very neat and tidy. The boys' garden was like a playground just for two children. There was a sandpit, and a climbing frame, and a swing, and a little trampoline with a net round it so you couldn't fall off. It was hard to believe how spoilt those boys were.

Sitting watching them play, Freda felt she would burst if she didn't talk to someone about Nico, so she talked to Monika, who was really kind, actually. When she talked about Nico's operation, she could see that Monika was getting all teary, and that set her off too. She hadn't wanted to cry, but Monika gave her a good hug, and she did feel better afterwards. And the boys were too busy trying to knock each other over on the trampoline to notice her crying, so that was all right.

She wasn't sure if, maybe, Monika had said something to Lavender about her being upset, because Lavender started being really nice, and asked if she would like to come and collect eggs from the hens. Freda hadn't even realised that there were hens here, and it was nice to find that this was a bit of a farm, after all. They found six eggs and brought them back to add to the bowl in the kitchen, and Monika made a huge omelette for lunch, with mushrooms in it, and chips for the children, and they all (except Grandpa, who had gone to work) ate together this time, in the kitchen, and the boys didn't throw their food about, for once.

Then, after lunch, Lavender said that she was going to take Jasper for a walk and that she didn't want the boys with her because they dawdled too much, but Freda could come, if she would like to. They went out through the garden, where a man was mowing the grass, and Lavender waved, and called out, 'The lawn's looking lovely, Ted,' before they went through the door in the garden wall, and then through the play garden to a big gate, which Lavender unlocked, and locked behind them, and then out into a field, where Jasper started rushing about among the long grass. He was enjoying himself so much that Freda quite wanted to rush about with him, as she used to with Caliban on the beach at Granny's, but she was ten now, and she felt that Lavender expected her to be grown-up, so they walked along together, and Lavender knew the names of all the wild flowers, and spotted rabbit burrows and a foxhole, so it was interesting.

They went right across the field, and then through a bit of woodland, and then came to a whole lot of caravans, with young people sitting on the ground, eating a sort of picnic. They looked very brown, and some of the men had bare chests. It looked quite fun.

'Strawberry pickers,' Lavender said. 'They're working at the farm down the road.'

Then Jasper decided to go mad, and rushed at them, barking, and it all got a bit out of hand, and so some of the men jumped up and shouted at him, and Lavender caught hold of him and put him on his lead, and said, 'I'm so sorry to disturb your lunch,' in that very polite way she had, and the men sort of mumbled 'OK', but they didn't look very happy, and Lavender turned quickly back for home. Freda asked what language the strawberry pickers were speaking, but Lavender didn't know. 'Something Eastern European,' she said, which was a bit vague, but Monika would probably know, Freda thought, and she decided she would ask her about them.

The first thing she did, though, when they got back to the house, was to ring her mum, because she still hadn't had a message. But Mum didn't answer her phone: *The person you are calling is unable to take your call*, the message said, and this gave Freda such a cold, hollow feeling in her stomach that she thought she might be sick. With shaky fingers, she called Ben's phone, and it was such a relief to hear his voice that she could hardly get her words out. He told her that Nico's operation had been put off, and after what she had been afraid of she didn't know whether she wanted to laugh or cry, so she did a bit of both, and then got angry because she had done all that worrying, and Mum could have told her, and now there would be worrying all over again when the operation did happen. Did no-one realise how much she was worrying? Did they think she didn't understand? Did they think she didn't love Nico?

She went to find Monika, because being with her made her feel better, and Monika agreed that she could have supper with her after the boys were in bed. That was the best bit of the day, really. Monika was a good cook and she had made a spicy chicken stew with little potatoes from the garden (not the flower garden, but yet another bit of garden, near the hens). Freda felt grown-up to be sitting eating with Monika – as though she was already a teenager. Monika was a quiet person, so Freda did most of the talking while they were eating – about school, and her friend Charlie, who she envied because she was having a cool holiday in Croatia. Then she made a mistake: she asked Monika which country she came from, and Monika got a bit weird and said, 'Romania. I am bad EU immigrant who everyone hates.'

Freda knew that this was about the Brexit thing that everyone went on about all the time, and she felt she'd been tactless to ask Monika where she was from, so she tried to think of something else to say. 'Are the strawberry pickers from Romania, too?' she asked, but that seemed to make Monika cross, too.

'From Bulgaria,' she said. 'Is next door Romania but completely different country.'

And that was that. Freda helped to clear the table and then wandered off to the playroom. She found that *University Challenge* was on, and had to swallow a great lump of homesickness because Mum and Ben liked to watch it and she could sometimes hear them, from her room at home, shouting out the answers. She flicked channels for a bit and then thought she didn't much want to be alone up in her room and now could be the time to try the watershed thing, and then text Charlie about it. She waited until nine o'clock and then, feeling quite scared, she flicked to BBC One and found something with police in it. She thought they were investigating a murder, and kept ready to close her eyes if there was a really gory corpse, but there was nothing like that – and not much swearing either, although people shouted a lot – and the only reason for her not to watch it, really, was that she couldn't understand what was going on. It was disappointing, and there was nothing to tell Charlie, so she went to bed.

So that was yesterday. Now here she was the next morning, and she had to worry all over again. She had slept quite well – Jasper had been quiet – and Mum's text just before eight o'clock woke her up: *Op this morning. Nico wants to know if you still have your eyes crossed xxxxxxxxx Mum*

She went downstairs, hoping that Lavender or Monika might have a plan for the day that would occupy her enough to push the worrying back a bit, but she knew, before she got to the bottom of the stairs, that no-one was thinking about her this morning. There was a hubbub coming from the nursery. She considered ignoring it and going straight to the kitchen for breakfast but, as she crossed the hall, Lavender popped out of the nursery and said, 'Freda, come in here.' She sounded cross and Freda had a panicky feeling that she had done something wrong. Had she somehow broken the TV last night? Had Lavender found out that she had been watching after nine o'clock? She went in cautiously and saw that most of the noise was coming from Hubert. He was sitting on Monika's lap, beetroot red in the face, covered in tears and snot, howling. Monika was crying too, and trying to comfort him, but he was beyond comfort, she could see. She could also see that Arthur was deliberately not looking at him, but sitting at the other end of the room, with his back to everyone, reading – or pretending to read – a book.

'Freda,' Lavender said, 'I did lock the garden gate when we came back from our walk yesterday, didn't I?'

Freda was totally confused. What had the garden gate to do with Hubert crying? 'I don't ... I ... which garden gate?' she stammered. 'You locked the big gates, I think.'

'No, no.' Lavender sounded snappy, not like her usual self at all. 'The gate in the wall. Did we lock it?'

*We?* Was Freda going to get blamed for something? Instinctively, she went for the standard defence they all used at school.

'I don't know,' she said.

'Oh, don't be silly, Freda. You must know. Did we or didn't we?'

'I don't know,' she said, and then ran out of the room because she really couldn't cope with this, not this particular morning.

She went into the kitchen, hoping to have it to herself, but found Grandpa there, eating his breakfast. He was reading the paper and didn't look up, so she slid onto a chair at the opposite end of the table and poured herself some cereal, which she tried to eat very quietly. Eventually, he put down the paper and looked at her over the top of his glasses. 'I would say I'm in the dog house,' he said, 'only it would be a bad joke in the circumstances.'

Freda had no idea what he meant, but the mention of a dog made her realise that there was no sign of Jasper. He was neither under the table, waiting for bits of fallen food, nor chewing at one of his disgusting bones, nor scrabbling at the door from the scullery. Was he still outside? If so, why wasn't he demanding to come in?

'Where's Jasper, Grandpa?' she asked.

He gave an odd sort of laugh. 'That is the question,' he said. 'Where is Jasper? Nobody knows where Jasper is. Jasper is missing.'

Then Lavender appeared. 'Hubert is inconsolable,' she said. 'I don't know what we're going to do with him.'

'Well, I'm sorry but if you'd locked the gate – '

'And if you'd checked that it was locked!' Lavender was very pink in the face. 'It's your job – as the man of the house – to check last thing at night, to keep us all safe. My father always used to – '

Grandpa stood up. 'I don't want to hear what your bloody father used to do,' he said.

Freda sat very still. She wondered if this was going to turn into a real row.

'I'm going to call the police,' Lavender said.

'Lavender, you can't.'

'I can, and I will. He is a valuable dog and he has been stolen. The police should be dealing with it. Why shouldn't they be able to recover him?'

'Because as soon as the police come round, they'll spot the encampment across the field, see that those Romanians are the likely culprits and haul them in for questioning. And then, in no time, the *Daily Mail* will have a story about the bleeding-heart human rights lawyer who has had his thousand-pound dog stolen by the very migrants he's always sticking up for.'

'They're Bulgarians, actually,' Freda said, and the words were out of her mouth before she knew she was going to say them.

'What?'

Grandpa looked furious, but she said, 'They're not Romanians, the strawberry pickers – they're Bulgarians.'

Grandpa stared at her. 'You spend too much time with your grandmother,' he said. 'And who told you they were Bulgarians?'

'Monika did.'

'Friends of hers, are they?'

'I don't think – '

But he wasn't listening to her. He turned to Lavender. 'There you are,' he said. 'There's your answer. An easy inside job.'

'Andrew, no. Monika would never – she loves the boys. She would know how upset they would be.'

Freda hadn't thought she could feel any more terrible this morning but now she did. Now, she seemed to have got Monika into trouble. She spoke.

'I'm sure Monika didn't do anything,' she said. 'She's a very kind person.'

'You,' Grandpa said, 'should be somewhere else.' And he stormed out of the room.

Upstairs, after she had cleaned her teeth, she thought she couldn't bear to go back down to all the shouting and crying, but she couldn't sit up here, either, where she would just worry about Nico. She looked out of the window at the bright morning and wondered whether she would be allowed to go out for a walk on her own. At home, since she became ten, she had been allowed to walk into town with Charlie, as long as she had her phone with her and came back when she said she would. She wasn't sure if Lavender would have any rules about her going out on her own, but everyone was in such a state this morning, she thought it probably wouldn't be a problem. The trick was to sound grown-up. She picked up her phone, put a jumper on and went downstairs.

Things were a bit quieter in the nursery. Lavender was no longer there, and Hubert was on Monika's lap, watching TV and sucking his thumb. Freda put her head round the door. 'I'm just going out for a walk, Monika,' she said. 'Will you tell Lavender?'

She thought that sounded convincing, just the sort of thing a grown-up might say. Out in the garden, though, going through the unlocked garden gate, she started to feel nervous. This wasn't like walking into town – this was walking into woods and empty fields. She thought, for a moment, that she would have an excuse for going back inside, because the big gate out from the play garden was locked and she couldn't turn the key. She stood and looked at it, thinking about someone stealing Jasper. The row seemed to be all about the door in the wall from the flower garden, and the key to that door had been in the lock, she had noticed as she came through. Yesterday, when she had gone through it with Monika and the boys in the morning, Monika had unlocked it, but she was sure she hadn't locked it again when they went back inside at lunch time, and it had been open when Freda and Lavender had gone out for their walk in the afternoon. So, probably Lavender hadn't locked it when they came back from their walk, and anyway, Ted had still been working in the garden, so wouldn't it have been his job to lock up? Why didn't Grandpa blame him? But there was this big gate now. She considered it and thought that a man could probably climb over it, because, although it was high, it was made of iron, with curls and whirls on it, where you could put your feet. But nobody could lift Jasper over it, could they? There would need to be more than one man for that.

She pulled up her T-shirt and wrapped the bottom of it round her hand to get a better grip, and then tried again to turn the key. She found that if she lifted the gate a bit with her other hand, the key ground round, and she could get out. Then she didn't know what to do. Yesterday, Lavender had relocked the gate from the outside and taken the key with her, so she supposed that was what she had better do. With a struggle, she got it locked and then put the key in her jeans pocket, where it was heavy and awkward as she walked, but she dared not carry it in her hand in case she dropped it and lost it in the grass.

She took the route they had taken yesterday afternoon, and she was relieved to find that dog walkers were here this morning, and she wasn't scarily alone. She swung along, trying to look as though she strolled around the countryside all the time, and mostly people ignored her. She thought of telling them about Jasper, because that was what you were supposed to do, wasn't it? People put up pictures of lost dogs and cats and asked for help in finding them. Nobody at Grandpa's house seemed to be doing anything, so maybe she should, but all those warnings she had been given over the years not to talk to strangers, from Mum, from teachers, even from a police woman who came to talk to them at school, weighed heavily on her and she couldn't quite bring herself to do it.

When she got to the strawberry pickers' camp, there seemed to be no-one there. They were all at work, she supposed. Then she noticed a girl, sitting on the ground with her back to one of the caravans. Freda was going to walk on by, but the girl waved and called, 'Where is your dog today?'

It would be rude not to answer, Freda thought, and anyway this wasn't a stranger. She had met her yesterday and Lavender had spoken to them all, so what harm was there? And besides, she might be able to find out if Grandpa was right.

'He's lost,' she said. 'You haven't seen him, have you?'

She watched for signs of guilt, but the young woman just looked surprised. 'Lost?' she said. 'Did he run away?'

'No, we think he was stolen.'

As soon as she had said it, she could see it was a tactless thing to say. The girl's face changed. 'Well, we didn't steal him,' she said.

Freda felt herself blushing. 'Oh no,' she said, 'I didn't mean...' and she heard Monika saying, *I am bad EU immigrant who everyone hates.* Then she looked at the girl, sitting there beside the caravan as though she was guarding something. Could Jasper be in there? Surely he would be barking, wouldn't he? Unless they had drugged him or something.

'The thing is,' she said, 'whoever took him probably walked him away, because there is no proper road by the garden, where he was.'

This had only just occurred to her, but she knew it was right. The thieves might have walked Jasper away, and it was quite likely that they had come past here, and unless it was the real middle of the night, the Bulgarians would probably have been sitting around outside. 'He's quite a valuable dog, 'she said. 'I think there would be a reward for information.'

The girl got up and came towards her. 'We work hard, little child,' she said, 'and we earn plenty. We don't need reward money, and we don't need to steal dogs, but I will ask if anyone has seen.' She lifted up her hand, which was wrapped in a handkerchief. 'I don't work this morning because a bee stung, but I ask the others at the break. Where do you live?'

Freda had a panicky feeling that she shouldn't say where she lived. This didn't make sense, because if they had stolen the dog, they knew, and if they hadn't, they weren't thieves and it didn't matter, but all the same it didn't feel right. She said, 'I could give you my mobile number – that might be best.'

'OK.' The Bulgarian girl got a phone out of her pocket – a much better phone than Freda's – and punched Freda's number in. Then Freda turned back for the house with a dizzy sense that she had done at least three foolish things: she had talked to a stranger, she had offered a reward, and she had given the stranger her phone number. She could be in so much trouble, but she really didn't care because Nico was having his operation and she had had no message yet from Mum, and that was all that she cared about really.

When she returned, she looked again at the big gate to the garden and imagined Jasper being hoisted over it. Beyond, she could see Monika sitting by the sandpit, and she watched as Hubert came running towards her. 'Jasper's still gone,' he said, and Freda decided, there and then, that she would find out what had happened to Jasper, because then Nico would be all right. It was a deal – not with God, because she wasn't sure about God – but with Fate, or something. In a way she couldn't explain, she knew that if she could find Jasper and stop Hubert from being sad, then Nico would be all right.

# Chapter Seven

## INTELLECTUAL PROPERTY

*Tuesday 26th July 2016*

The human brain is a remarkable organ. It is, I have discovered, capable of being completely absorbed by two quite different concerns at exactly the same time. Thus it is that I give my paper at the conference with all my usual prima donna bravura, while never losing sight of Nico, nor of Ellie's and Ben's wan morning faces. My eye on the clock simultaneously checks my forty-five-minute deadline and the probable progress of surgery, rescheduled for nine o'clock this morning.

Does anyone here guess that half my brain is somewhere else? Actors in long West End runs claim that they can make mental shopping lists or compose emails while playing love scenes. I am not attempting anything so acrobatic, but I do give quite a performance.

My subject is *Cross-Cultural Pragmatic Failure*, which just means the way you can understand the words people speak without understanding what they really mean. It is all about implicature and different cultural norms, and I start with an example of pragmatic failure by an Arab student of mine, who, in his letter of application for an MA course, wrote, *I am an excellent student and if you do not accept me you will be sorry*. This gets a good laugh and gives me my ice-breaker as I move on to a brief survey of Herbert Grice's Cooperative

Principle, and its four maxims: *Quality* (speak the truth); *Quantity* (be as informative as is required); *Relation* (respond relevantly); *Manner* (avoid ambiguity and obscurity). It is immediately obvious, of course, that we all flout these maxims on a regular basis, and conversation would be extremely boring if we didn't. This is the problem with the dialogue in most language learning text books – it sticks to the rules in a way that prepares students quite inadequately for real-life conversation, which is full of half-truths, evasions, non-sequiturs, ambiguity, terseness and prolixity. In my limited experience, soap opera dialogue – which most overseas students rely on as an aid to conversational English – doesn't really do the job, for the same reason; it is too linear, too structured, too rule-bound. What students need, I tell my audience, is to read Pinter, Albee, Orton and Caryl Churchill, whose characters lie, evade, obscure, and play power games with language on an epic scale. Their dialogue is great for actors to speak, but the devil to learn, because it is not linear. Your cue to answer a question will not be the question itself; that will have been three speeches back, when you avoided answering it. Pinter is famous for his silences, but equally idiosyncratic is his characters' propensity for breaking into lengthy speeches, only tangentially related to the topic in hand. The effect is disorienting, and often threatening, even if the speaker is only talking about London bus routes.

I move into real performance here, giving them snippets from *The Caretaker, Entertaining Mr Sloane* and *Top Girls,* displaying the gamut of accents at my disposal, and generally showing off. (I should tell you, at this point, that we are on something of a diversion here, so do feel free to skip this bit, if you want to. On the other hand, if you are interested, you can find my chosen excerpts tucked up in an appendix to this story.)

I start with the opening scene of Pinter's *The Caretaker*, in which Aston has brought a tramp, Davies, back to his house.

Davies asks whether Aston has a spare pair of shoes, but then spins off in all directions – the *bastard monks* at the monastery, the soap in public conveniences, some paranoid racism – and forgets about the shoes. Quality? Quantity? Relation? Manner? Davies breaks all the maxims – he is untruthful, irrelevant and obscure, and says both too little and too much – while Aston sticks doggedly to the shoes, the ostensible subject of their conversation. The effect is both comic and unsettling, but Davies is not trying to unsettle Aston; he breaks the rules, it seems, because he doesn't know how to follow them.

Most of us don't do this. We know the rules, but we flout them for effect: we exaggerate, insinuate, obfuscate, avoid questions we don't like and change the subject, and we expect our flouting of the maxims to be noticed. That is the point. We want our hearer to notice that they have raised a topic that we don't want to discuss, that we are being less than frank in order not to be unkind, that we are glossing over unpleasantness with euphemism, that we are making a drama out of a small event in order to entertain.

Here I move on to Joe Orton and *Entertaining Mr Sloane*. Orton's characters are ostentatiously unreliable: they exaggerate, fantasise, deviate, and contradict themselves without apology, and there is a tacit understanding between them that no-one is to be trusted or believed. I choose, in a nice parallel, another scene in which someone welcomes a stranger into their home. In *Entertaining Mr Sloane*, middle-aged Kath is welcoming Mr Sloane, a young man – her new lodger. In the opening minute, Kath tells him first that she had a son who was killed 'under tragic circumstances', then that she was widowed young, and finally that she was an unmarried mother. We see Kath and Sloane recognising one another as fellow fantasists and watch the development of the fantasies, first Kath's and then Sloane's. They ignore contradictions and implausibilities in one another's stories, and each of them reaches for well-worn clichés from fiction and drama – for Kath, the young lovers thwarted by their parents, the boyfriend's 'duty to his family', the last letter. She signals the end of her turn by asking about his preferences in pillow fillings, and Sloane takes over with his tale of life in an orphanage, his parents' suicide pact, and the visits to his parents' 'tomb'. And Kath helps him along with her inspired contribution, 'You have the air of lost wealth', which Sloane immediately seizes on. The fictions are shameless and understood between them. Just a few lines later, Sloane is telling Kath that he needs 'understanding', and Kath is admiring his 'delicate skin'. We understand that this exchange of untruths, this outrageous flouting of conversational rules, is a courtship dance, or foreplay.

So, this is fun to perform, including Sloane's shifts of accent and register – from the strict grammatical accuracy of lines like 'By whom?' for example, to the downmarket, 'I never had no family of my own', as he goes for his orphan scenario.

Then I finish up with Caryl Churchill's *brio* monologue for nineteen-year-old Shona in *Top Girls*. Shona, with no job experience of any kind, blags her way quite effectively into an interview for a job as a sales rep, because this is a world where exaggeration of one's experience and skills, and even straightforward lying, are taken for granted.

It is not until Shona is asked the fatal question, 'So just describe your present job for me,' that she uncoils the rope and hangs herself with it. She manages some stock sales jargon, but then starts to babble hopelessly about selling a lot of fridges in the summer because of the heat melting the butter. She is much happier describing the lifestyle of the saleswoman on the road – the stuff of her fantasies – the fast car up the M1, the nights in hotels, the gin and tonic at the bar, the dinner. It is not until she gets into the detail of her favourite menu, including her dislike of tomatoes, that Nell interrupts her.

*NELL: What jobs have you done? Have you done any?*

*SHONA: I could though, I bet you.*

And we are inclined to believe her.

Half the audience enjoys it. The other half, I suspect, would like to slap me for showing off, but I get a good round of applause. You, of course, may wonder why I am telling you all this. Well, what I have been talking about is deceit, evasion and fantasy, sometimes with the willing co-operation of the listener. I am in the process of telling you a story, a story about – among other things – a mysterious death. I feel you should know that, in my professional life, I am an expert on the ways we can use language to deceive, withhold and mislead. I just thought you should be warned.

It is coffee time after my session, and I go outside to switch my phone on. I really believe that there will be a message this time. My post-performance high tells me that this is the moment when all will be well, but my inbox is stubbornly inert. I could drown in disappointment. Looking around for some sort of buoyancy aid, I spot a group of smokers gathered by the door, and a craving for nicotine sets me jangling. I gave up smoking eight years ago, when Freda was a toddler and I couldn't keep leaving her while I dashed out into the garden for a fag. I thought I was quite past any cravings, but at this moment only a cigarette will do, so I walk up shamelessly to this group of strangers and beg for a smoke. They are very kind. They praise my performance and offer me a choice of brand. I accept something tipped and mild, and even that makes me slightly dizzy. It does restore me, though, as does some linguistic chat, and, after one more fruitless inspection of my phone, I go back inside, ready to fret my way through the rest of the morning. Then, as I nip into the loo before returning to the lecture theatre, Ellie's message arrives. I could easily have switched my phone off already, but had decided to leave it to the last minute. The message is not packed with information but it says enough:

*All done and ok so far. N is awake but sleepy. See you later xx*

It is fortunate that I am in a loo cubicle because I am able to have a brief weep before facing the world. The only problem is that I emerge to find a queue has formed, and accusing eyes are turned on me for overstaying my allotted time. I decide not to apologise.

The rest of the day passes well enough. I coast through on automatic pilot, applauding, smiling, greeting, and looking deeply interested as required, but I turn down dinner. I yearn for quiet. I am bone-tired. I head for home, hoping that Ellie and Ben are both with Nico. A drink, a shower and bed are all I ask. Is that too much?

Apparently, it is. My phone rings before I reach home. It is Annie.

'Didn't Ellie ring you?' I ask, without bothering with greetings.

'Oh yes. Bless Nico. He's been asking for his tea, apparently.'

'That's our boy.' I wait. If she hasn't rung for news, then she wants something.

'Are you busy tonight?' she asks.

'Bed,' I say. 'And a large drink. I am shattered. I gave my paper today, and what with the stress over Nico...'

I peter out. She pounces.

'Oh well, if you're too tired, then don't bother.'

'Bother with what?'

'Coming to rehearsal. Only you did say you would and I thought...'

'Does it have to be tonight?'

76

'Well, no, but it's the Claudio scene tonight, and that's the one I'm worried about, and we won't be doing it again for ages. But if you're too tired, then...'

She says *too tired* as though I had said I was washing my hair, and I capitulate, of course.

'What time?' I ask.

'Half seven.'

'Where?'

'I'll meet you outside my chambers at twenty past.'

I am just noticing that she hasn't thanked me when she says, 'You're an angel, Ma,' and rings off.

At home, I have the shower and the drink and change my clothes – not into sloppies but into silky trousers and a top which I believe to be flattering. If I'm going to spend the evening with the young, I need to keep my end up. I make a bowl of tuna salad, take some for myself, and leave the rest in the fridge for Ellie and Ben, together with the wine I've opened. My wine rack, I notice, is looking depleted. Anxiety is an expensive business. I leave a note, pick up a cardigan, and set out to walk. It's about a mile and the Tube will be stuffy.

The walk along Gray's Inn Road is hot and smelly. The heat bounces back at me from the pavement, and the ethnic restaurants, though excitingly cosmopolitan, belch out a series of searing, steamy blasts. I arrive feeling hot, and stickier than I would like, but I cool down as I wait for Annie in the shade of the august building that houses her chambers. It is an extraordinary thing to step inside the enclave that is Gray's Inn – much like stepping into an Oxford college, but on a larger scale. The traffic subsides, the temperature drops, the paintwork and brass plates on the buildings gleam. The place speaks of order, of history, and of a great deal of money. I spot an ancient notice, inscribed on a wall, which tells me that the servants of the Inn are charged to remove hawkers and any persons causing a nuisance. I am standing, pondering what sort of nuisance I could cause in order to give the servants of the Inn a bit of a run-around, when Annie arrives.

She leads me to a grassy square surrounded by more august buildings, and we find a group gathering under a tree. I have wondered, on the way here, how Annie is going to explain my presence. The answer is that she isn't, really. She presents me to the director, Tom Yeoman, whom I do remember from an ill-fated student production of *Hamlet* which Annie got me involved in a few years ago. Tom, who was a fair, baby-faced youth then, and who doesn't look much older now, was a good Horatio – a natural, straightforward, good chap – but I wonder whether he has what it takes to direct this cynical, complicated, ambiguous play.

'You remember Gina – my mum?' Annie says. 'She'd like to sit in, if that's all right?'

I would like to protest that it hasn't been my idea, but Tom is so charming that I am disarmed, and then, before we start, he gathers everyone round and says, 'This is Gina, everyone – Marianne's mum.' This reminds me, with a jolt, that I am supposed to call Annie *Marianne* outside the family circle. 'Gina is a Shakespeare buff,' Tom continues, 'and a super-sleuth. In a production Marianne and I were in together, we had a killer in the company, and Gina tracked him down.'

Eyes which have slid past me without interest are suddenly turned my way. I give an awkward little wave and feel foolish. Rehearsal starts.

I see quite quickly that the Claudio is giving Annie problems. His name is Piers, which immediately makes me antagonistic – my inverted snobbery at work. He is a pretty young man, with floppy blond hair and a spoilt droop to his mouth, which quite suits him for Claudio, but he is not really an actor. The rest of the cast are off books; Piers, on the other hand, clearly knows his lines, but is holding on to his book, not so much as a safety net, but as an excuse for not really acting. He is intelligent enough – he makes sense of the lines and phrases them appropriately – but he is just sketching in the emotions. It is a highly emotional scene – some might say melodramatic. Claudio is in prison, sentenced to death by Angelo for getting his betrothed wife pregnant. Isabella has come to the jail to tell him that her attempt to persuade Angelo to show mercy has failed, and that Angelo will pardon Claudio only if Isabella agrees to sleep with him; Claudio must, of course, see that this is impossible. Claudio's decent, civilised self does see that it is impossible, but the cornered, animal self, facing extinction, is not so sure. Shakespeare has written for him an extraordinary evocation of our human terror of annihilation:

*Ay, but to die, and go we know not where:*
*To lie in cold obstruction, and to rot;*
*This sensible warm motion to become*
*A kneaded clod; and the delighted spirit*
*To bathe in fiery floods, or to reside*
*In thrilling region of thick ribbed ice;*
*To be imprisoned in the viewless winds*
*And blown with restless violence round about*
*The pendent world; or to be worse than worse*
*Of those that lawless and incertain thought*
*Imagine howling – 'tis too horrible!*
*The weariest and most loathed worldly life*
*That age, ache, penury and imprisonment*
*Can lay on nature is a paradise*
*To what we fear of death.*
*Sweet sister, let me live:*
*What sin you do to save a brother's life,*
*Nature dispenses with the deed so far*
*That it becomes a virtue.*

Isabella's response to this is the elephant trap line, *O you beast!* It has become an impossible line for us to take seriously because of its jolly-hockey-sticks, *Mallory Towers* echoes, but Isabella means it literally. Claudio is reacting like a trapped beast, the human constructs of decency, loyalty and honour swept away by his animal terror. The violence of Isabella's response feeds off the intensity of Claudio's fear, and there is no way of parsing that speech of his that allows for playing it cool. The fear is naked, and the actor must express it. Piers, I'm afraid, is a long way from that. Spoilt and entitled as I suspect he is, I wonder if he has the imagination to go there at all, let alone the willingness to expose it to an audience. I glance at Tom Yeoman. I can see that he is not happy with the scene, but I'm not sure if he sees where the problem lies or what he can do about it.

Things improve, however, with the arrival of the Duke. Roderick Gillard is terrific. He is word-perfect and, with a week to go, he gives a performance that is, in effect, audience-ready. Annie doesn't really have much to do in her scene with him, but I can see her relax. The Duke is a really tricky role to get a handle on. You can play him as a scheming control freak, manipulating people's lives and emotions, or as a moral force, exposing hypocrisy and corruption, and dispensing justice to all. Or you can play him as a complex mixture of the two. At the beginning of the play, he announces that he is going away and leaving Vienna in the hands of his puritanical Deputy, because he blames himself for the state the city is in – young people full of vice, the suburbs full of brothels. He has been too lax, he says. It is time for someone else to clean things up. But he doesn't go away. He disguises himself as a friar (the cowl is useful) and lurks about in the shadows, intervening only to construct elaborate schemes to prevent Angelo's most savage decrees from taking effect and to build up a case against him, leading to his final exposure, humiliation and punishment. So, do we assume that he never trusted Angelo? Why else would he hang around, spying on him? On the other hand, the Vienna we are presented with is a city of vice, so does the Duke want it cleaned up or not? When the libertine, Lucio, calls the Duke *the old fantastical Duke of dark corners*, he gets punished for slander, but that is the Duke we see in the play, so what is the truth? And what are we supposed to feel about the Duke, as fake friar, hearing the last confessions of condemned men in prison? In the end, the Duke sheds his disguise and becomes a figure of justice, dispensing measure still for measure, but we can hardly ignore the murkiness of his own earlier behaviour.

Well, Roderick Gillard seems to be able to embody all of this with no trouble. He presents a kindly, protective, moral figure in his friar persona and, at the same time, as he unfolds to Isabella his cunning plan for saving Claudio and thwarting Angelo, he is a wily schemer, enjoying his own cleverness. I am impressed. Never mind Annie having a crush on him; I could have one myself.

When it starts to get dark, Tom calls a halt. I am not sure how much has been achieved beyond giving people the chance to run through the scenes and consolidate the lines, nor am I sure what I'm going to say to Annie beyond assuring her that anything that is wrong with the Claudio scene is not her fault. We move on to a nearby wine bar, where the young order food, as well as drink, and Roderick Gillard buys me a glass of prosecco. We sit at a table of our own, while the others tuck into their food, and I feel we are like adults at a children's birthday party, though I don't say this to him, as he may think me weird. I am alarmed to find that I care whether he thinks I'm weird, just as I hesitated over what to have when he offered me a drink, and he chose the prosecco for me. I want to make a good impression on him. This is worrying; I can't remember the last time I wanted to do that

– not even in the early days of my relationship with David, I think.

We chat easily – he is very good at making one feel comfortable – and I tell him I admired his interpretation of the Duke, avoiding anything gushy. We discuss the difficulties of the Isabella and Claudio scene, and I give my view that Piers needs to work on imagining terror. 'After all,' I say, 'we are none of us immune from *timor mortis*. Even the young. You lost someone from this group. That ought to bring it home.'

He looks blank.

'Isha Anand,' I say.

'Oh. Yes. Terrible business.' He looks momentarily stricken – a man of quick sympathies. I like that.

'Did you know her?' I ask.

'No. And I had forgotten that she was going to be in the play.'

'The nun,' I say.

He looks startled.

'Maybe she was going to play the nun in the convent with Isabella at the beginning. Or Mariana. Or pregnant Juliet.' I nod towards the young woman at the other table who has been rehearsing Juliet this evening. 'Was she always going to play Juliet?'

He looks across. 'I don't know,' he says. 'I'm not s – '

'Don't tell me the young have all started to look alike to you,' I say, and he laughs.

Then he turns his attention back to me, and he looks into my face in a way that I have given up expecting any man to do. He has the good taste not to say *Older women are so much more interesting*. Instead, he says, 'Tell me about your sleuthing.'

So, I tell him about the *Hamlet* episode – entertainingly, I hope – and then more. I wasn't intending to tell him about the other murders I've been involved in solving, because of not wanting to seem weird, but he buys me another drink, and questions me with forensic skill, and we end up talking long after the others have left. Annie gives me an inscrutable look as she leaves, and I send her a bland smile in return.

In a taxi, going home, I tell myself that the fact that he is not wearing a wedding ring does not mean that he is unattached. There is probably a partner; there is certainly baggage. Do I feel up to this? A generally fluttery sensation tells me that I do, but this may just be the prosecco talking.

# Chapter Eight

## FREDA

*Wednesday 27th July 2016*

'So ... do you ever get a day off, Monika?' Freda asked. Monika finished a mouthful and then said, 'Friday. Friday is free day.'

'Right.' Freda buttered her toast with great care, going right to the edges. That way she could avoid looking Monika in the eye, which was not all that easy, as they were sitting opposite each other at the kitchen table. The boys had eaten their breakfast and were watching cartoons; Grandpa and Lavender would be down at any minute. This was her chance. Freda was forming a plan, but Monika must not know it. 'Do you go somewhere nice on your free day?' she asked.

'Sometimes London,' Monika said, and Freda felt sure she must have seen her jump. *London.*

'On the train?' Freda asked.

'Yes, train.'

'Is there a station near here?'

'Not near. Marlbury.'

'Does it cost a lot, the train fare?'

Monika put down her knife.

'Why you ask so many questions today, Freda?'

*Why indeed?* Freda looked up at her, making her eyes as wide and innocent as she could manage. 'I just thought, it seems so in the middle of nowhere here, it must be lonely for you,' she said.

'Is half an hour only to Marlbury by the bus. Not so far.'

Freda made herself go on eating, and then, when she had chewed her last crust, she picked up her plate and cereal bowl and said, as she took them over to the dishwasher, 'So are you going to London this Friday?'

'No. Not this time.'

'Why?'

The question escaped before she could stop it, and she was sure Monika would be suspicious, but she simply said, 'Is too expensive. I go to Marlbury only. Buy birthday present for my mother.'

*To Marlbury.* Freda bent her head into the dishwasher and took a long time arranging the crockery. Marlbury was better. Getting Lavender to agree to her going into Marlbury with Monika if she was planning to go on to London would have been difficult, but going in with her to do some shopping would surely be all right, and then it should be easy enough for her to slip away and go to the station. She felt quite shaky with the daring of it. The only problem was that she wasn't sure if she had enough money. She risked one more question.

'So … the train to London costs a lot, does it, Monika?' she asked, starting to rearrange knives and spoons in the cutlery basket. 'How much?'

'Twenty-five pounds about.'

'Wow!'

Freda slammed the dishwasher closed and slid past Monika and out of the kitchen before she let her disappointment show. She had twenty pounds in her purse, which Mum had given her before she left. It was all she'd had in her wallet, but she'd said Freda wouldn't need money really, because she was sure Grandpa and Lavender would give her treats. Well, there had been a shortage of treats so far, and a train ticket to London wasn't the sort of treat Mum was thinking of. As she plodded up the stairs to her room, she thought about the twenty-five pounds It might not be as bad as it seemed. For a start, Monika would be talking about a return ticket, wouldn't she? Whereas Freda just needed to get there. Because she must get there. A message had finally come from Mum yesterday, saying that Nico's operation had been fine – but he had had the operation in the morning, and it was nearly teatime when Mum's message arrived. No-one seemed to realise how much worrying she was doing. And he would be coming out of hospital soon – probably at the weekend – and everyone would be together at Granny's, and she could not bear it – she really couldn't – being stuck here, where she didn't belong, and where, truly no-one cared about her.

Upstairs, she sat on her bed and calculated. Would a one-way ticket cost half as much as a return? That would be twelve pounds fifty and she would have enough for the bus fare into Marlbury, too. And then she would have a child's ticket, wouldn't she? So that would be less, too. She couldn't ask Monika about any of this; she would need to talk to Charlie, because Charlie had a smartphone and could look stuff up. Communication with her had been disappointing in the past few days. They had sent text messages, but Charlie was all wrapped up in her holiday and even she didn't seem to understand how worried Freda had been about Nico, or how much she hated being here. Now she was going to have to risk using up her phone credit, and actually speak to Charlie. She punched in her number.

'Hi Freddie!' Charlie sounded a long way away.

'Hi Charlie. Are you still having fun?'

'It's ace here. You have no idea – we – '

'Sorry, Charlie. I've got something to ask you and I'm worried about running out of credit. So, can we – '

'Chill, Freddie You sound all stressed. Nico's all right, isn't he?'

'He's fine. It's just – I'm going to run away.'

'Really? Wow! Where are going to go?'

'London. To my granny. I'm going to get the train, but I need to know if I've got enough money. Can you look up the fares for me? A child's ticket, one way? Text me when you've got it.'

'Freddie, are you sure? I mean – '

'I'm sure. I can't stay here. I'm going nuts. Can you just, please – '

'OK, OK, I'm looking right now. Do you want to go to St Pancras or Charing Cross?'

'I don't – whichever one is nearer to Great Ormond Street Hospital.'

'Well, I don't know that. I haven't got like a map here.'

'OK. Charing Cross. That's where I went with Mum, when we went to the theatre.'

'OK, so Marlbury to Charing Cross … one child … single …eleven pounds fifty but you have to go off-peak for that.'

'What's off-peak?'

'Not rush hour, I think.'

'That'll be OK. Eleven pounds fifty Thanks Charlie – you're ace.'

'You're brave, Freddie.'

'I hope so. Thanks, Charlie. Love you loads.'

Done. She sat on the bed, her stomach turning over with nerves and guilt. She had promised herself that she would find out what had happened to Jasper, and now she had only two days to do it. She had to do her best in those two days, and if she hadn't tracked him down by Friday, then she would have to ask Granny to help.

She was starting to gather together the small pile of belongings that she thought she could reasonably get away with taking on a shopping trip to Marlbury when she heard urgent feet on the stairs. Monika appeared in the doorway, tearful and red-faced.

'Have you got Hubert here?' she demanded.

'Hubert?'

Monika was in the room now, pulling aside the curtains, flinging the wardrobe open, patting the duvet and, finally, dropping to her knees and looking under the bed.

'Have you seen him since breakfast time?' she demanded, and then, without waiting for an answer, she strode out, and Freda listened to her slam in and out of the bathroom and then go into her own room, where doors and drawers were yanked open.

Freda went out to her. 'What's happened, Monika?' she asked, feeling scared and stupid.

'He is gone!' Monika cried. 'I just clean up kitchen while boys, I think, are watching TV. Then I think is very quiet in nursery – no fighting – so I go to see, and Hubert is gone.'

'But Arthur's there?' Freda asked.

'Ach! Arthur!' Monika growled. 'That boy!' And she started back down the stairs. 'Come!'

Freda followed her down to the nursery, where Lavender was kneeling in front of Arthur, who was staring stubbornly at his feet. She looked up as Monika and Freda came in.

'No?' she asked.

Monika shook her head. Lavender turned back to Arthur. 'Arthur, darling,' she said, 'you must tell us where Hubert went. Did he say he was going to hide? Monika has looked in all the rooms and she can't find him. Hiding was a good game for him to play but it is time for him to come out now.'

'Don't know,' Arthur muttered, eyes still on his feet.

Lavender let him go, and stood up, but Freda watched him, and saw his eyes slide to the French doors. She went over, tried the doors, and found them unlocked. She pushed one open.

'Have you been out into the garden to look for him?' she asked.

Lavender said, 'No, he can't have got out of the house. We keep –' and then she turned and looked at the open door.

'They weren't locked,' Freda said.

Lavender gave a terrible wail. 'He's been taken!' she shouted. 'First the dog and now my baby! Somebody wants to blackmail us. I told Andrew we should have gone to the police.'

Suddenly, she turned back to Arthur and gripped him hard by the shoulders. Then she started to shake him. 'You must tell me what happened!' she shouted. 'Did someone come in and take Hubert? You must tell me!'

Freda watched Arthur's face turn red and crumple into tears, but all he said was, 'I was watching TV.'

She stepped out into the garden. Why wasn't everyone out here? Either Hubert had wandered outside or someone had taken him. Either way, this was where they should be looking, not talking to stupid Arthur, who was, she thought privately, quite capable of doing serious harm to his brother. Hubert couldn't have reached up to open that door, but Arthur could. Had he pushed Hubert out into the garden? Or could he have opened the door to let a kidnapper in?

She went straight to the gate that led through to the boys' play garden and found it open. How come? Weren't they all supposed to be extra careful about keeping that gate locked after Jasper had been taken? Was there someone who had a key and who had taken Jasper and now Hubert? She pushed open the gate, willing Hubert to be playing there, swinging in his little swing seat, pleased with himself for coming out on his own, but the swing was empty and still.

She went down to the big gates and checked that they were locked. If someone had been able to lift Jasper over the gates, then they could certainly have lifted Hubert over. She turned to go back, and then saw that Ted was in his shed, which stood near the gates. Maybe he was the one who had unlocked the gate through into the flower garden. She could see his van was parked outside the main gates, which was surprising, because there was no real road out there – only a track – so, he must have come in that way and gone into the flower garden to see what needed to be done. Now he was sitting in his shed, smoking a cigarette, but the horrible thought came to her that Hubert might be in that van. Hubert would have gone with Ted, wouldn't he – just as Jasper would have done? They both knew Ted, and trusted him. No need to lift Hubert over the gates. He could have unlocked them, stashed Hubert in the van, and come back in again. She stood at the gates, listening hard. Hubert would cry, wouldn't he, if he was shut in the van? And then she had a picture of him with a gag round his little face, and she was contemplating this when a voice behind her said, suddenly, 'And what are you looking at, young lady?' She started so violently that she was sure she actually jumped off the ground, and she felt her face turn hot and red. She put her hands over it as she turned to face Ted, hoping to look as if she were crying.

'Hubert's missing,' she said, 'and the door was open from the nursery. Auntie Lavender's terribly worried.'

She kept her hands over her face and watched through her fingers to see what his face did, but he looked disappointingly unguilty.

'Little beggar's hiding somewhere, I expect,' he said. 'He'll not have gone far. I've been out here half an hour, and I'd have seen him. Let's have a look through here. If he's trampled on his mum's flowers he'll be in trouble.'

And then he led her round the garden, sending her in to tread carefully in the flowerbeds and look behind shrubs. Finally, when they reached the patio outside the kitchen door, he said, 'Well, he's not out here and he's not got out of the gates. You can tell your auntie that. He'll be in the house somewhere. Big place like that, plenty of spots to hide. They've probably got him by now.'

Ted turned away and went back in the direction of his shed, and Freda thought she would go into the house by the kitchen door, to avoid whatever scene might still be going on in the nursery. She didn't blame Lavender, though, for shaking Arthur and shouting at him; someone should have done that a long time ago, she thought. As she went past Jasper's empty kennel, with the bowls of water and biscuits still outside it, she thought she heard a snuffle from inside. For a wild moment, she thought, *Someone's done a swap. They've brought Jasper back and taken Hubert instead.*

Getting down on her knees, she looked into the kennel, saw the curled shape inside and knew it was not Jasper.

'Hubert?' she said. 'What are you doing in there?'

Hubert uncurled himself and looked at her. 'I'm waiting for Jasper,' he said. 'For when he comes home.'

It took some persuading to get him out of the kennel, but he was eventually swayed by the promise that he would be able to return to the kennel as soon as Mummy had had a chance to give him a cuddle (here Freda was gambling on Lavender's response being cuddle rather than slap), and they went inside.

In the hall, Lavender had the front door open, and was watching the drive. She glanced over her shoulder and said, 'I've called the police. They said fifteen minutes.'

'He's here, Auntie Lavender,' Freda said. 'Hubert's here.'

The ensuing scene, Freda thought, was really well beyond the way normal people ought to behave. Lavender screamed and swept upon Hubert so wildly that he screamed too and clung to Freda's legs. Then Monika appeared from the nursery and burst into tears and incomprehensible Romanian, and Arthur, coming after her, decided to cry too, simply because he wasn't going to be outdone by Hubert. Freda tried to suggest that they should ring the police to put them off coming, but no-one was listening, so it was she who let the two policemen in a few minutes later, when everyone else had gone into the kitchen to celebrate with ice cream and another round of tears.

The police were very good about it, she thought, as she sat on the stairs and listened. They didn't blame anyone for the false alarm, and when they were leaving and saw her sitting there, composing a text to Charlie, one of them asked if she was the young lady who had found Hubert. 'Very good detective work,' he said. 'You should come to us for a job when you're older.'

Suddenly bold at this praise, she followed them out to their car. 'Actually, I wanted to ask,' she said. 'I mean, did Lavender – Mrs Gray – tell you about the dog?'

'Dog?'

They were in a hurry, she could see, already getting into the car.

'The dog was stolen, two days ago, in the night. That was why we thought Hubert had been stolen, too. And I know you're too busy to look for lost dogs, but I'm trying to find him, and I wondered – I think he's quite valuable, so if someone wanted to sell him, how would they do it?'

'Could have been stolen to order,' the one in the driver's seat said.

'Or eBay,' the other one said, 'if they've got the nerve.'

And then she watched the car as it roared away.

# Chapter Nine

## PRIMA FACIE

*Wednesday 27th July 2016*

I wake early, feeling headachy and sweatily embarrassed. It is a mild version of the mornings of painful regret that I can remember from student days more than thirty years ago. What was I thinking last night? Well, obviously I wasn't thinking at all. I let a good-looking man ply me with drink and, though I don't remember anything clearly, no doubt I behaved absurdly – going on at length about my life as a sleuth, and probably showing too much cleavage. He is undoubtedly laughing at me at this very moment. I will be an embarrassment to Annie, and I will never live it down. I roll over onto my face, pull the duvet over my head and try to remember what exactly happened. I do remember that I came home, quite chastely, in a taxi, and it has just come back to me that he asked for my phone number as we parted, so my behaviour may not have been as dire as I feared, when the phone rings. My clock radio says it is 7.35. My heart somersaults. What else can this be but a call from the hospital? Ben spent the night there and he must be ringing to say something is wrong. I struggle out of the duvet, put out a shaky hand and croak, 'Yes?'

'Too early?' David asks.

It's a trick I have played on him in the past, ringing him in the early morning, before he has had a chance to start thinking straight, but today I swell with righteous indignation.

'You know Nico's in hospital, David,' I say. 'Didn't it occur to you that a call at this hour would be alarming?'

'Sorry,' he says. 'Is he all right?'

'As far as I know.'

'Good. So, look, I'm ringing now because you were more than usually pressing about info on Isha Anand, and I've got a full-on day and won't be free to get back to this again until late tonight, so – '

'Oh, all right,' I say. 'Spare me the stuff about what a busy and important man you are. You asked me to take this case on, remember? I'm actually doing your job for you.'

'I did not ask you to take any case on, Gina. You are not a police officer. I just wanted – '

'Oh, don't give me that. You know, and I know, what you wanted, so just tell me what you've got.'

'Well, since you ask me so nicely, all right. I don't have everything, but I do have the post-mortem report and the results of the initial investigation. Isha Anand was strangled. She was not sexually assaulted. There was no evidence that she struggled – no defence wounds, nothing under her fingernails. It appears that she was taken by surprise, and the scarf was thrown round her neck from behind.'

'Scarf? Have you seen the scarf?'

'It's with the evidence. A long, silk scarf in an Indian design. The investigation report says it's a make readily available in the UK, rather than in specialist Asian clothes shops, so that's not helpful.'

'Did they establish whether it was Isha's own?'

'None of her friends could swear it was hers, but they said she often wore that sort of thing, though she basically dressed in Western-style clothes.'

'What about her phone? What did they get from that?'

'The tech guys say the sexting photos were doctored – internet images with photos of Isha's face blended in. That

94

could have been done on a computer or a smartphone, but they weren't done on Isha's phone – they were texted to her phone. There was no evidence of them on her computer, or her brother's computer, or his smartphone.'

'But if they were texted to her phone, then you must have the number they were texted from.'

'An unregistered mobile.'

'Bugger!'

'Exactly.'

'And there's nothing you can do to track that down?'

'No.'

'It's interesting, though, that you found her phone at all, isn't it?'

'Interesting in what way?'

'Well, there's not much doubt that the person who concocted the photos, and sent them, was also Isha's killer. He – or possibly she, I suppose, if the strangling was done from behind, as you say – set up the photos to draw attention to the idea that this was an honour killing, which it probably wasn't. So why didn't the killer just plan to take her phone away after he had killed her? Then he wouldn't have had to bother with getting hold of the unregistered mobile.'

'Two answers to that. One is that the sexter and the murderer aren't necessarily one and the same. It's still possible that someone set out to ruin Isha's reputation – for whatever reason – and someone else believed the photos were genuine and believed she had been dishonoured.'

'But if that wasn't her brother, then who would it be? Her father is dead, and her uncle is in India. It would have to be someone who had hoped to marry her, wouldn't it? Did your colleagues try to find out anything about that?'

'I don't know. There's nothing in the investigation report. I don't know if they drew a blank or never pursued that line. But there is one more thing: there are photos of Isha's body as it was found, in the area outside her flat. You can see that the scarf is round her neck, but the end of it has been wrapped around her head and across her face, so it looks like – '

'– a hijab.'

'Exactly.'

'Except that Isha was a Hindu, not a Muslim.'

'Yes.'

'So, it means – what?'

'That whoever killed her didn't know her, or didn't know her well?'

'You mean,' I say, 'that we go back to Brexit xenophobia. Someone attacked her because she was a *Paki*, and then wrapped the scarf round to show that was why they'd done it?'

'Maybe.'

'Except this is Bloomsbury, and there are the photos.'

'Yes.'

'You still don't believe it was random, do you?' I ask.

'No.'

'So, what are you going to do about it?'

'I can't see – '

'You have to find out who sent those photos. There must be a way. Clarissa would know what to do.'

'And this is the real world.'

'Well, I'm going to investigate Hinduism and head-covering. I'm sure I've seen Hindu women with scarves over their heads – not tightly wrapped, but draped over. I'm not done yet, even if your lot are.'

I feel this is the line on which to finish the call, but he does a throat-clearing thing and says, 'I was wondering, actually, if you fancied going to the theatre on Friday night. *Macbeth* at The Globe? I'd be happy for you to give me a tutorial on it beforehand, over dinner. And we could think about fictional murders and not talk about real life at all.'

Under normal circumstances, this would be an appealing offer, but I hear myself saying, 'Actually, I've got a date on Friday night.'

This is not true, but I have hopes that it may be. When Roderick asked for my phone number last night, I – in a witless effort to impress him – gave him one of my cards. These are produced for us by the Development Office at the university. They don't, of course, have our private numbers on them, so Roderick has only my work phone number, and I shall not be in my office to answer any calls. However, he also has my work email and, in the fullness of time, when he has had a chance to realise how much he would like to see me again, I shall check for messages there. Friday, I think, would be the perfect day to see him again.

David, of course, does not believe in my date. You don't get to be a DCI with the Met without recognising a lie when you hear one.

'OK,' he says. 'Well, if the date falls through for any reason, I'll have the tickets.' And he rings off.

I drag myself into the shower, put on a third set of respectable clothes and have breakfast with Ellie before she goes back to the hospital. She is looking much better; but then she is still young enough for a burst of relief and one good night's sleep to wipe out most of the ravages of days of anxiety. And she has her appetite back; she is loading butter and honey onto thick slices of toast, while I confine myself to coffee and half a grapefruit. When she has gone, I set off for UCL, but without a spring in my step. It's not just last night's drink. I'm tired of this conference now, and I realise that I haven't given enough thought to the discussion panel I'm on this morning. My paper was the key thing, and now here I am, one of four *distinguished practitioners in the field of English for Academic Purposes*, and I have no idea what topics will be raised. We'll be responding to questions from the audience, so I suppose it's anyone's guess, but I wish I were feeling sharper.

Had I been more on the ball, I would, of course, have anticipated that most of the questions would be, in one form or another, about making a career in EAP. We are *distinguished practitioners* and the eager young EFL teachers want to know how to get to where we are. They are looking for an escape from the often murky and insecure world of TEFL, and we tell them how to get more qualifications, be picky about where they work, develop specialisms and keep networking, but we all, I suspect, want to add, *and be brilliant, like us.*

It's a rather uncomfortable hour, but it passes quite quickly, and then I am out and ready to cut and run. I switch on my phone as I leave the building, and I find that I have just missed a call from Annie. I decide not to ring back – I feel certain she will be wanting to berate me about my tête-à-tête with Roderick last night and I'm not prepared for that. However, a couple of minutes later a text comes through:

*How about lunch? My treat. Want your feedback on rehearsal. xxx*

This may be a trap, but neither of my daughters has ever taken me out to lunch, so I don't feel I can refuse.

*Lovely. Where? When?* I text.

*Fetter Lane, Le Bistro,* comes the reply. *12.30?*

It takes me a while to locate Le Bistro. I know roughly where Fetter Lane is, but I get lost in Chancery Lane and go around in circles for a bit. As a result, Annie is already there when I arrive. She is sitting at a corner table, looking cool in a white shirt, while I am damp and crumpled. I sink down onto the chair opposite her with a puff of relief, and see that I am annoying her already. I glance around and note that the clientele is almost entirely young and in legal attire. Even in my conference jacket, I look like the embarrassing mother up from the country. *Well, you're not up from the country,* I tell myself. *You live in Bloomsbury.* But at the same time, in the stale air of this oppressive little eatery, I feel a sharp pang of longing for the easterly breezes of my Kentish beach shack.

We order. I choose modestly, since Annie is paying – a salade niçoise and a sparkling water – and she chooses something with crayfish. Then she leans back in her chair and says, 'Well?'

This throws me, because I don't know if she is asking about the rehearsal or about Roderick Gillard. 'The rehearsal was interesting,' I say guardedly. 'There are some good performances.'

'And?' she leans forward, searching my face.

'Well, you're very good, of course,' I add

She looks at me, pleased but sceptical. 'But does the Claudio scene work?'

'Piers isn't making it easy.'

'Really? I don't feel that.'

'I just thought he wasn't giving you enough terror, not enough for you to feed off anyway.'

'Oh, we talked about that.' She leans back again, dismissive. 'Piers doesn't want to ham it up. We thought cooler was better.'

'Except that his words aren't cool – nor are Isabella's.'

'It's just the *O you beast* speech that's the problem, really. The foul things she says to Claudio.'

Our drinks arrive at this point, and once we're settled with them I say, 'There's something you could try with that speech. Try playing it as though she's so cruel because she is actually afraid he might persuade her to do it – to have sex with Angelo to save him. I could imagine her saying those lines with her eyes closed and her hands over her ears – staving him off.'

She sips her drink. 'It's worth a try,' she says. 'And what about Roderick?'

'He's very good,' I reply. 'An excellent Duke. A really subtle performance.'

'And what did you think you were doing last night?'

'Doing?' I ask, feebly.

'Doing. Getting him to yourself, knocking back prosecco, staying on after the rest of us left. He's the head of my chambers, Ma. I can't have you embarrassing me – having some sort of thing with him, just to get back at David.'

'What has David got to do with this?'

'Oh, come on, Ma. You and David. You can't stay together, and you can't stay apart, and that makes you a menace to everyone.'

'Are you sure,' I ask, cross enough now to be reckless, 'that you haven't got a crush on Roderick?'

'Don't be ridiculous.' She has gone very pink. 'Anyway, there's an etiquette. A head of chambers wouldn't ... '

'Is he married?' I ask.

'Divorced.'

'Children?'

'Yes. Grown-up.'

'Hmm,' I say.

'What's that supposed to mean? You're divorced with grown-up children. Does that make you a bad person?'

'It makes me a tricky prospect for a relationship.'

'Well, that's you.'

We drink in silence. I wish our food would come. Finally, I ask, 'Jon's due back at the weekend?'

'Yes.'

'A bit of an adjustment for him, I imagine, after Uganda.'

'An adjustment for both of us.'

'Yes.'

Conveniently, our food arrives, and we eat in silence for a bit, until I say, 'Last night was a non-event – really. We chatted, he wanted to know about the *sleuthing* Tom had talked about.

It was a warm evening, the prosecco was nicely chilled, and I possibly drank a glass more than was necessary, but we left the wine bar soon after you did and I took a taxi home – end of story.'

*Except he has my card.*

'Did he say anything about me?' she asks.

'Not a word.'

This probably disappoints her, but it has the virtue of being true.

'I'm happy to come to rehearsal again,' I say.

'We're doing the two scenes with Angelo tomorrow.'

'Would you like me to come?'

'Roderick isn't in those scenes.'

'No. But you are, so I'll come.'

'OK. Thanks.'

We part outside. I thank her for lunch and head for home, reflecting that lunching out has its pitfalls and I might do better to confine myself to sandwiches in the garden for a while.

Then, although the prospect scares me more than I want to admit, I go to Great Ormond Street to visit Nico.

# Chapter Ten

## FREDA

*Thursday 28th July 2016*

What was she supposed to do with herself today? The question rang in Freda's head as soon as Lavender's pretty, flowery, fluttery window curtains let in the early morning light. What she should be doing was pursuing the hunt for Jasper, but things had happened that made that difficult. For a start, she was waiting for a message from Charlie. After the policeman had mentioned eBay, she had texted Charlie, asking her to see if she could find any Labrador Retrievers for sale on eBay, but there had been no reply, and she had got sick of checking her phone and finding it blank. She had even checked it in the middle of the night. But that wasn't the worst of it. The worst was what had happened with Grandpa yesterday.

It was before supper, when he had just come home from work, and Freda had been out in the garden, looking again at the big gates and wondering whether even two men could have lifted Jasper over them, or whether – and she got down on the ground to try it out – he could have been pushed or dragged underneath. Grandpa had been in Ted's shed with him, chatting, and as he left the shed he had called to Ted, 'So, the nine-fifty in Norwich,' and Ted had said, 'Right you are.'

Freda had no idea what they were talking about, and wasn't even interested, but Grandpa had spotted her there, crouched by the gates, and had shouted at her, 'For God's sake, Freda! Have you got nothing better to do than lurk around listening to adults' conversations? Is this how you behave at home?'

The shouting, and the mention of home, coming both together, had been about enough to sink her, and she had just had to make a run for it before she started crying – which she wasn't going to do in front of him. She had run straight past him, through the garden, through the house, flapping away Monika, who had tried to say something to her, and up to her room, where she had slammed the door, dived on her bed and howled until she felt better. She had called to Monika, through her closed door, that she had a stomach ache and didn't want any supper, and then she had had a bath, got into bed and finished *The Ghost of Thomas Kempe.*

Now she was starving, and thought she would go downstairs and get herself some breakfast while it was early and there was no chance of seeing Grandpa. She knew he was going to be at home for the day – yesterday, when he had come home, she had heard him tell Lavender that his case had *settled*, and that he could take the rest of the week off. She was just going to have to avoid him, and tomorrow she would go off to Marlbury with Monika and get the train to London, to Mum and Granny and Ben and Nico, to people who loved her.

She put on the clothes she had pulled off and left in a heap on the floor yresterday and then slipped quietly down the stairs and into the kitchen. Once there, she couldn't help looking into the utility room, and then into the kennel outside, in the silly hope that Jasper might have magically returned, but he had not, of course, so she poured herself some cereal and a glass of orange juice, and sat in the kitchen, which was not silent, you realised when no-one was talking, but full of chatter of its own – the fridge humming, the pipes murmuring, the clock clicking its tongue.

She contemplated how she was going to spend her day in hiding. It was a pity, really, that she had finished *Thomas Kempe*; the only other book she had with her was *Minnow on the Say*. This was another of Granny's choices, but it looked like a boys' book to her and she wasn't sure she was going to like it. Granny had said it was an excellent mystery story, though, so she would do her best.

She thought she could risk a walk round the garden, which would be good if she was going to be spending the rest of the day stuck in her bedroom, so she stepped out of the kitchen door onto the patio, and then onto the grass, where she kicked off her flip-flops so that she could walk barefoot in its cool dampness. The air was warm with the promise of a really hot day, and she thought wistfully of Nico's paddling pool, which he didn't mind her taking a splash in when Ben got the hosepipe out and everyone ended up soaking wet. Feeling homesickness – and it really did feel like sickness – knot in her stomach, she did two handstands and a cartwheel, because she found that being upside down somehow took her out of herself. Then she went back into the kitchen, put a slice of bread, a piece of cheese, two tomatoes and an apple onto a plate, added a chocolate biscuit, poured herself a glass of water, and went cautiously back upstairs. She would have to carry on with the stomach ache excuse to avoid lunch, but she couldn't starve, could she? She just hoped Lavender wouldn't want to dose her with some horrible medicine for the stomach ache, or – worse – think she had started her periods, like Kylie Archer in her class at school had.

Safely upstairs, she cleaned her teeth, made her bed, opened the window as far as it would go, checked her phone – just a *Good Morning* from Mum – and settled down with her book. It was only seven o'clock. This book was going to have to be really enthralling.

It was actually pretty good, in spite of its being about two boys and also a bit old-fashioned, and she was quite absorbed in it when she suddenly realised that there were heavy feet coming up the stairs. She listened, hoping that it was Monika and that she would go on by to her room, but knowing, really, that these feet were too loud to be either Monika's or Lavender's. Then there was a knock at her door, and she lay frozen. The knock came again. She knew she ought to say, *Come in*, but somehow she couldn't say anything, so she got up, went slowly to the door, and opened it just a bit. Her grandfather stood in the doorway, blocking it completely. There was no way of getting out of the room, so she found herself retreating into it.

He stood there, with a weird smile on his face. 'Do you mind if I come in?' he asked.

Freda still couldn't speak. If she opened her mouth, tears would come, she knew, so she just shook her head and backed off further to let him in. He closed the door behind him, and he seemed to fill the little room, his head nearly hitting the sloping ceiling. Her knees were wobbling, so she sat down on the bed, hoping desperately that he wouldn't come and sit beside her.

He didn't. He sat down on the little stool by the dressing table, which didn't look strong enough for his weight. He looked quite odd on it, but less scary.

'I came to apologise,' he said. 'I shouted at you yesterday, and I shouldn't have done.'

Freda had no idea what to say, even if she could trust herself to speak, and she couldn't just sit and stare at him, so she kept her head down, and suddenly got very interested in her feet, examining them as though they were quite new to her.

She heard her grandfather shift uncomfortably on the stool. 'I was embarrassed, you see,' he said, 'because you'd heard my conversation with Ted. You did hear it, didn't you?'

She managed a nod.

'The nine-fifty in Norwich,' he said, and he smiled in a way that wasn't really a smile. 'Do you know anything about betting?'

Still dumb, she shook her head.

'Well, I like a bit of a bet on the horse races, Freda, and your auntie disapproves. She worries that I spend too much money on it. So, I get Ted to place my bets for me, you see, and that's what we were discussing yesterday – only of course I wouldn't want your auntie to know about it.'

She should say something now, she knew, but her teeth seemed to have been glued together. Helplessly, like a puppet, she nodded again. He was waiting for more, she could see, but when he didn't get it, he stood up.

'So, we're friends, are we, Freda, and not a word to Auntie Lavender?'

With a huge effort, Freda unlocked her tongue. 'Yes – I mean, no,' she whispered, and he came over and dropped a kiss on the top of her head.

'Good girl,' he said.

When he had gone, she sat looking at the door he had closed behind him. 'Pathetic,' she said. 'You are pathetic, Freda Gray. And if he thinks you are a complete dappo, you have only yourself to blame.'

Now it was impossible to get back into her book, into the long, slow summer days on the river that she had been enjoying. She felt all jangled up. Grown-ups were so puzzling. Even Mum and Ben were sometimes. Why ever would Grandpa have to keep his horse bets a secret from Lavender? You only had to be in the house for an hour or two to see that Grandpa made the rules, not Lavender. Like not letting her ring the police about Jasper, and no-one being allowed into his study. So why couldn't he spend his money however he liked? She did think she could remember Granny saying something about Lavender being rich, and that this was how she and Grandpa could afford to live in Aren't-We-Grand Hall, but she also knew Grandpa had an important job as a lawyer, so he must earn money too, mustn't he? She had thought about the *nine-fifty in Norwich* and had wondered why Grandpa hadn't liked her hearing that, but she had thought it sounded like a train time, and he and Ted might be going on a secret expedition – except that then he would have said 'at Norwich', wouldn't he? As Granny kept telling her, it was the small things that made English such an interesting language.

After a bit, she had calmed down enough to get back to her book. She could go downstairs now, of course, or out in the garden, but for the moment she felt happier here – and she was still waiting for a message from Charlie.

It was nearly twelve o'clock when the message finally came, and then it was not what she had hoped for.

*Soz for delay. Up a mountain looking at a monastery. Boring and no signal.*

*Soz cant do ebay. Children not allowed.*

Freda sat looking at the message, feeling miserably let down. Charlie didn't really care, did she? Furiously, she typed,

*Use some gump, Chas. Doesnt your mum go on ebay? Hack in or wtvs.*

Getting no reply, she threw her phone down on the bed, and stomped downstairs, easing off on the stomping when she got to the main stairs because she needed to play sweet now. If Charlie wasn't going to help, then she needed to get her help from somewhere else. Maybe Lavender had a computer? Surely she emailed her friends? Maybe she even did Facebook, which Freda wasn't allowed to do. And Monika? There was a good chance that Monika had a smartphone. They both wanted to find Jasper, didn't they?

Why shouldn't they go on eBay and see if anyone was selling him?

Fixing a cheery smile to her face, she strolled into the play garden, where she found Lavender and Monika sitting together by the sandpit, keeping a wary eye on the boys. Neither of them asked whether she was feeling better – Lavender because she hadn't even noticed that Freda hadn't been at meals, probably, and Monika because Freda shook her head at her when she opened her mouth to ask. Freda sat down between them on the warm, knobbly garden bench and looked at Lavender. Trying to sound as business-like as possible, she asked, 'Do you use a computer, Auntie Lavender?'

Unexpectedly, Lavender laughed. 'Goodness, Freda, how old do you think I am? Of course I do. Where would I be without online shopping?'

Freda felt herself blushing. 'Sorry,' she said. 'It's just I haven't seen one in the house.'

'I use my little tablet, darling, and that's usually in my bedroom. Why did you want to know?'

'It's just, there's something I need to look up on the internet, and I wondered – '

'Oh, darling!' Lavender's face went into a worried look that was so extreme that Freda almost wanted to laugh, except that she could see she was going to be turned down. 'I can't let you go on the internet, darling,' she said, 'not at your age. There are parental controls and things, you know, and I would feel dreadful if you got onto something unsuitable.'

'It's nothing like that. The policeman who came to the house said that whoever took Jasper might try to sell him on eBay, and I thought we could have a look to see.'

Lavender's face went from worry to panic. 'Oh, no,' she said. 'No, we're not doing that. Jasper's gone now, and Hubert's getting used to it, and we don't want any trouble.'

'But if we can find Jasper on eBay, we can tell the police, and – '

'No!' Lavender jumped up. 'We can't risk it. When I thought someone had taken Hubert, I ... Don't you see, Freda, whoever took Jasper knows where we live and how to get in. If we put the police onto them, they'll be angry with us, and they might come for the boys next. No! Don't argue – I don't want to hear any more about it. Monika, don't take your eyes off them. I'm going inside. I'm getting a headache.'

Freda and Monika watched her go. 'That's crazy, isn't it?' Freda said.

Monika shrugged. 'Is all crazy here,' she said.

'If you've got a smartphone,' Freda said, 'we could have a look.'

Monika shook her head. 'If she say no, then no,' she said. 'I don't interfere.'

Freda stood up. 'That is just so wussy,' she said, and went indoors.

On her way upstairs she hesitated outside Lavender's bedroom, wondering if she dared go in and look for the tablet, but she told herself that it would too risky, as well as rude. Climbing the stairs up to her room, though, she thought that she might go on a hunger strike when she got back home, and stick to it until someone – Mum, Ben, Granny – bought her a smartphone.

# Chapter Eleven

## COMPROMISE AGREEMENT

### *Thursday 28th July 2016*

There should be a special name for them, these mornings when you emerge into consciousness, your brain groping for the obligations, challenges and horrors lurking in the day ahead, and find that it comes up with – nothing. Nothing! A blessed, empty, wonderful day that demands nothing of you at all. Annie calls it a *one-day fun-day*, but that sounds altogether too energetic – fun, I find, can be exhausting. And it's not a duvet day, either – because that's a day when so much is being demanded of you that you decide to blank it all out. The trouble is that this works only for a limited time, and then guilt kicks in, and you're left with a common or garden self-blame day, and that's no fun at all. When I ran away to the seaside, I had demand-free days all the time; the most that was asked of me, generally, was to walk the dog in the rain. It got boring, though, to tell you the truth. A bit of stress is said to be good for us, and I'm inclined to believe it. However, I have earned today – this day that asks nothing of me. It is my day of rest, and I intend to enjoy every empty minute of it.

I get up late, vaguely surprised that I haven't been woken by Ellie going off to the hospital. She has obviously slept in too, I think, and I start to put out plates and mugs for a leisurely breakfast for the two of us. Then I see the note on top of the coffee machine. Even without my reading glasses, I can detect the agitation in Ellie's writing:

*Ben rang. Nico has an infection. In ICU. Will ring if any news. Pray if you think it will do any good*

*xE*

'Oh Christ,' I say as I sink into a chair, though I don't think this is the sort of praying Ellie had in mind. I look at the clock. It is ten past nine. I have an empty day ahead, and all there is to fill it is panic.

I think about making coffee, which was where I was heading when I found the note, but my stomach heaves when I open the coffee tin, so I decide on a bath instead. I don't go in for therapy baths, with scented candles and aromatherapy oils, but a soak in some hot water never did any harm.

Out of the bath and wrapped in a towel, I go to my laptop and google *hole in heart surgery, post-operative infection*. Unhelpfully, I learn that this is rare; more helpfully, I read that early and aggressive intervention with antibiotics is generally effective, and I have to be content with that. I keep remembering Nico as he was yesterday, when I found him sitting up in bed, cheerfully surrounded by bits of Lego. I remind myself, feebly, how quickly children go from well to ill, and how equally quickly they get better again, but this isn't 'flu we're talking about, is it?

I put some clothes on and make another move to the coffee machine, deciding, when I get there, that I need camomile tea instead, in spite of its cat's pee aroma. I take this, together with a slice of toast and marmite, out into the garden, where the air is already growing soupy. I sit on the peeling rustic bench and repeat to myself my mantras for the day: *Great Ormond Street is the best place he could be; they are doing all the right things; he is a well-nourished child; it will be all right.* My phone rings, and I rush indoors to answer.

'Ellie?'

There is silence.

'Ben,' I say, 'is that you?'

'It's me,' a voice says. 'Why did you think – '

'Annie?'

'Yes. Why shouldn't it be me?'

'I thought it would be Ellie. Nico's worse. Did she tell you?'

'No. But I'm not surprised. Nobody in this family tells me anything. My mother talks about me secretly with her ex-boyfriend, my sister doesn't tell me that my nephew is seriously ill. My father doesn't return my calls. Nobody considers – '

'Annie, shut up!'

I think I hear a sharp intake of breath, but she is silent.

'Take a moment, will you?' I say. 'You really can't be the centre of the drama today.'

Another silence.

'OK' she says. 'Sorry.' And then, 'It's just – '

'No!' I say.

She sighs. 'Tell me about Nico,' she says.

'I don't know much. Ellie just left me a note. Ben stayed at the hospital with him overnight, and he rang Ellie at some point to say that Nico has an infection and is in the ICU. She went straight there, and I haven't heard any more.'

'Will you let me know when you do hear anything?'

'Of course.'

'Has anyone told Freda?'

'I think I'd better leave it to Ellie to decide about that.'

'She'll be angry if she's kept in the dark.'

'Yes.'

We are silent, and I realise that, since she rang me, she must want something, but now she can't find a comfortable way to segue into her request.

'Did you want to ask me something?' I say, eventually.

'Well, I was just wanting to check that you're still coming to rehearsal tonight, but obviously if Ellie needs you to be there, then ...'

'I can't promise. We can't know how things will be. If Ben and Ellie are both at the hospital still, then I might as well come, but otherwise ...'

'Yes.' I can hear the deep breath she takes, and feel the effort as she says, 'You have to put them first, obviously...'

We hang up.

It is 10.30. I have texted Ellie, but I don't expect to hear back any time soon. She has probably had to turn her phone off, anyway. I need to find a way to fill the day. I start with a walk to M&S in Tottenham Court Road, where I browse the clothes aisles and buy a couple of summer tops, which are too young for me and no doubt will be returned in due course. Then I stock up on food, deliberately including Nico's favourites, because I tell myself that he will be ready for them soon, won't he? I replenish my wine stock, too, and get a taxi home. The taxi driver wants to talk about Brexit. He is, fortunately, a Remainer, but I am not strong enough even to share his pain. I let him talk, murmuring agreement noises, but I contribute nothing substantive. All he wants is a sounding board, after all.

Back home, when I have put away the food and drink, I decide to reorganise the kitchen cupboards. Last weekend I unloaded the removal firm's crates in a hurry, and I now think everything is in the wrong place, so I haul it all out, pile it up on every surface, and start again. The new arrangement may not be any better, but the activity lasts me till well past lunchtime, and it strikes me that my London life is insufficiently challenging domestically. Down by the sea, I shopped at the Co-op and heaved my provisions home on the bus. I grew my own vegetables and sweated over the peeling and chopping and cooking. Here, I have not quite resorted to ready meals, but I am only just short of that – I buy vegetables washed and trimmed, tomatoes pureed and jarred, fish filleted and floured, salads washed and bagged. Some heavy domestic labour is just what I need.

The other advantage of this task is that I haven't listened to the radio. I have been making too much noise for doing so to be worthwhile, so I have spared myself the endless post-Brexit analysis, speculation and catastrophising. The media embrace disaster with indecent glee.

Mid-afternoon, I finally get a text from Ellie:

*Nico is responding to antibiotics but still very drowsy. Staying here. Don't make supper for us. xxE*

I text Annie to say I hope to be at rehearsal, and I take a quick look through the two scenes between Isabella and Angelo, to give myself some ideas that might help Annie. They are wonderful scenes, actually. In the first, Isabella argues passionately and cogently for mercy, against Angelo's equally passionate defence of the primacy of upholding the law. I love the fact that Shakespeare puts his most powerful arguments for mercy into the mouths of two female characters – Isabella and Portia. That women should be arguing for mercy is not in itself surprising – women are supposed to be softer-hearted, after all – but the surprise is how powerful mercy is in their mouths. There is nothing soft or weak or yielding about it: for Portia, *'Tis mightiest in the mightiest. It becomes/ The thronèd monarch better than his crown,* while Isabella turns the concept round, denouncing the mere humans who use their petty authority to play God in judging and punishing:

*Could great men thunder*
*As Jove himself does, Jove would ne'er be quiet*
*For every pelting, petty officer*
*Would use his heaven for thunder,*
*Nothing but thunder!*

There is nothing of the weeping, kneeling supplicant in Isabella's appeal – which is a good thing for Annie, because that would hardly play to her strengths.

The second scene is more complicated. Angelo wants to put his nasty bargain to Isabella – her brother's life in return for sex – but can't find a way to say it; Isabella is still focused on pleading for Claudio; Angelo seizes on Isabella's excuses for Claudio's sexual lapse as justification for her potential lapse in giving in to him; Isabella, unworldly as she is, doesn't understand what he is talking about. Finally, exasperated, Angelo has to spell it out: *Plainly conceive, I love you*. But that's not plain at all, because it's not love he's talking about, but plain old lust, and this is not a prelude to a marriage proposal, but a demand for what might be called consensual rape. The scene culminates in Isabella's ringing cry of defiance:

*I will proclaim thee, Angelo, look for't.*
*Sign me a present pardon for my brother,*
*Or with an outstretched throat I'll tell the world aloud*
*What man thou art.*

Except that it's not as easy as that, of course, because, as Angelo says, who will believe her word against his? The abuser's perennial trump card. So, later in the play the disguised Duke has to step in to save the day with a clunky bed-switch plot, which depends on the hard-to-swallow premise that, to a man, all women are the same in the dark. Take this seriously and everything falls apart, doesn't it – courtship, marriage, love even?

But, whatever the plot failings, these are great scenes for Isabella, and I hope Annie relishes them. If I can't truthfully tell her she is doing them justice, then I'm in trouble.

The hot, muggy weather is edging towards thunder as I walk towards Gray's Inn in the early evening. I have texted Ellie but have had no reply. I hope I will find either her or Ben back in the flat when I get home. *No news is good news,* my feet tap out on the pavement as I walk, and a mocking little laugh echoes in my head as I say it. I should have had something to eat, but without the need to cook for the others I couldn't be bothered. I stop at a newsagent's and buy a bar of Fruit and Nut. It is the taste of childhood, and it threatens to make me cry.

If I look peaky when I arrive at the rehearsal, no-one notices. The play opens next week, and they are at the obsessive stage of preparation. Again, Annie doesn't quite introduce me to anyone, but Lyle Fenton, playing Angelo, introduces himself. He is thirty-ish, I suppose – a bit too young for Angelo – striking, with dark auburn hair swept back from his high pale forehead, and clear, rather penetrating, hazel eyes. He is smoothly charming, assuring me that Annie is going to be terrific. I reserve judgement on how terrific he will be.

Actually, he is pretty good, and so is Annie. In fact, their first scene is stunningly good – enough to raise a smattering of applause from the other actors. Most importantly, they generate a personal chemistry that makes it absolutely believable that Angelo could be seized by unexpected pangs of lust. There is something very sexy about arguing. I should know; it is the basis of my relationship with David, and it was the fun part of my relationship with Andrew in the early days, before he took it up professionally and could outsmart me. Anyway, Annie and Lyle know how to do it, and Shakespeare sets it up beautifully by having sleazeball Lucio there, egging Isabella on. Lucio is a friend of Claudio's, and it is he who hauls Isabella out of her convent and persuades her to go and plead with Angelo. Lucio stands for all that is wrong with the Duke's permissive Vienna. He is promiscuous, cynical, irresponsible, a user of people, and a liar, but he also understands men and women; he can see exactly the power that Isabella's combination of purity and passion can exert over a deeply repressed man like Angelo. At the beginning of the scene, when Isabella is inclined to give up in the face of Angelo's absolute insistence on the primacy of the law, Lucio urges her on, telling her she is *too cold,* and then continues to encourage from the sidelines as she grows more passionate in her arguments. And he judges exactly the right moment for her to make her exit, leaving Angelo poleaxed by lust and self-loathing:

> *What dost thou, or what art thou, Angelo?*
> *Dost thou desire her foully for those things*
> *That make her good?*

To which the answer, of course, is *Yes.*

The rehearsal of the second scene is marred by rumbles of approaching thunder. The scene will be fine, I think, but they rush through, just getting to Isabella's final soliloquy as the heavy, preliminary drops of rain plop through the branches that are sheltering us. We break off and make a dash for the wine bar, arriving soaked and breathless. I catch sight of us all in the mirror behind the bar: the young look bright-eyed and flushed; I look dotty, with my hair flattened to my head, and my mascara running. I buy the first round of drinks, to compensate.

Tom Yeoman gives a few notes as we wait for our food. He is fulsome in his praise, and I can see that Annie and Lyle are high on their achievement. I see, too, what an attractive man Lyle is, smiling at Annie, his eyes almost green in the candlelight, and how well he knows it, and I wonder what Annie feels about him. And I see that, though Tom Yeoman praises the two of them, it is Lyle he actually looks at, hardly giving Annie a glance. Something is going on there, and I don't know what it is. I think, too, that he could have given more credit to the Lucio, who played his scene with just the right level of sleazy knowingness. The actor is sitting next to me, so I turn to him.

'I like your Lucio very much,' I say.

'That's very kind of you,' he replies

'We haven't been introduced. I'm An – Marianne's mum – Gina – just here to offer moral support, really.'

'Ah, yes. Very important at this stage. Good for all of us, actually, to have an audience.'

He looks Indian, and his accent is classic public school, with just a touch of extra care. He puts out a hand.

'It's good to meet you, Gina. I'm Asmil Anand.'

He must see the confusion on my face as he says this, because he gives a slight smile that is almost apologetic. 'You probably heard about my cousin,' he says.

I am flustered. I feel my face getting hot. 'Isha?' I ask.

'Yes.'

'I'm so sorry,' I say.

'Yes.'

He has deep, liquid brown eyes and he is looking at me as though he is trying to convey something unspoken. I look round at the others. No-one is paying attention to us, and the general level of noise in the place means that you can only hear a conversation that you are actually taking part in. Annie and Lyle are deep in talk; Tom and the chap who is playing the Provost have a text open and are poring over it. I turn back to Asmil.

'Were you close?' I ask.

He gives the slightest of laughs. 'You could say that,' he says.

'Did you grow up together?' I ask, remembering that Isha and Bimal were brought up by their uncle.

'No, no. When I say cousin – we were second cousins, actually.'

'I see.'

I realise how ignorant I am, and how much my idea of Indian middle-class life has been picked up in bits and pieces from novels. I picture an extended family of cousins, living in a sprawling compound of white buildings with cool courtyards and running fountains, presided over by a bevy of aunts who command daily life in a flurry of gorgeous saris. It's Blandings Castle, only twenty degrees hotter and with different clothes.

Asmil is still looking at me with that intent look. 'At one time we hoped to marry,' he says.

'Really?' I say faintly. Why has David not told me this? Does he even know?

'At one time?' I prompt, almost in a whisper.

'It was understood that we would marry, and then there was a falling-out.'

'Between the two of you?' I am being unforgivably nosy, but he doesn't seem to mind.

'Between my father and my uncle.' he says.

I risk one more intrusive question. 'But you and Isha would have liked to marry?'

He does not answer immediately. Then he says, 'I certainly would.'

And then our food arrives. We have ordered several sharing boards – Italian and Greek, vegetarian and meaty – and the conversation becomes disjointed and general as we pass these around and concentrate on scooping hummus, spearing olives, and tearing at the charcuterie. Everyone appears to be starving. I pick and nibble at things as the boards swoop past me, and I drop out of the conversation to reflect on the implications of what I have just heard. One of our main reasons for dismissing the honour killing scenario has been the absence of an obvious male relative, once Bimal has been excluded. Now, suddenly, here is an almost too perfect candidate on the spot, a cousin who was also a would-be husband, a man who had wanted to marry Isha, but who wouldn't commit himself as to whether she wanted to marry him. And the most puzzling thing of all is that I believe he wanted to tell me about his relationship with Isha. That look he gave me as he introduced himself; I can see now that it meant, *Hear the name, make the connection, ask me about Isha.* Why? Did he kill Isha, and does he now have a terrible urge to confess? In which case, why choose me? Simply because he doesn't know me? Or because he does know me – or knows about me? I don't remember if he was there at the beginning of the rehearsal the other night, when Tom introduced me to the company as a super-sleuth, but he was certainly there later on, because they rehearsed his scene with the Duke. Is Asmil doing a David on me? Is he trying to hook me in, to get me interested in finding out the truth about Isha's death? Well, the moment has passed for talking to him about it now. If he wants to tell me more, he will have to seek me out.

I go home on the Tube, unable to get a cab because of the rain, and I get wet again from my dash to the Tube station. As soon as I am on my own with my thoughts, fears about Nico come swarming back. There is no message from Ellie on my phone, so I text her once again. If I get no reply, and she and Ben aren't at home when I get there, I shall ring the hospital and demand information. Sleep seems an impossibility.

The flat is just as I left it. Ellie and Ben have not even been back for refuelling. Panic rises in me. I pick up the phone. I have to call directory enquiries for the hospital number and I can hear my voice shaking as I ask for it. I misdial on my first attempt at ringing the hospital, and I am just trying again when the front door opens. Ben stumbles in and slumps into a chair.

'Ben,' I say. 'Tell me.'

'He's doing all right,' he says. 'He's – 'and then he starts to cry in that way that some men do, as though the sobs are being racked out of them, as though fighting the tears is more urgent that the emotion that provokes them.

I stifle the urge to ask him if he has had anything to eat, and instead go into the kitchen and pour him a glass of grappa – a Christmas gift to me from his parents. It steadies him, and he starts apologising. I shut him up and ask how Ellie is. He looks at me with a kind of awe.

'She is amazing,' he says. 'British stiff upper lip, you know, it goes all the way through.'

'Can she stay the night in the ICU?'

'In a room next door.'

'And has she had anything to eat?' There we are – I couldn't resist for long.

'A sandwich,' he says.

'And how is Nico, really?'

'His fever is down. He woke up for a while, and now he's sleeping again. They want to keep him in the ICU for another twenty-four hours, then move him back to the ward, if all is well.'

'Has Ellie told Freda?'

'She decided not to – not to worry her if he's going to be all right.'

I look at his empty glass, and wonder if I should have some grappa too. I feel far too wound up to sleep, and it might help. Wine won't do the trick, unless I drink a whole bottle. I go into the kitchen and decide, prudently, to root about in a box that holds packets of herbal teas. I buy them for their health-giving properties and then ignore them. I select one that is actually labelled *Sleepy Tea* – a concoction of camomile, lavender, liquorice, and linden flowers. It tastes pleasant with a dollop of honey, but I have no faith at all in its power to knock me out.

And I am quite right. I lie wide-eyed in the semi-dark (I never did get a blind on my study window), and the only way I can block panicky thoughts of Nico is to worry away at Asmil Anand. The thought that comes to me is the veil – the scarf that was wrapped around Isha Anand's head and face. If Asmil had killed her, what would he have meant by using that scarf? I need to know about Hindu women and veils, and if I'm not going to sleep, I might as well do something constructive. I get out of bed and switch on my laptop. Out of habit, I take a quick look at the day's emails and see that there is nothing from Roderick. He seems to have failed the initiative test. Too bad. I google *Do Hindu women wear veils?* and get what looks like a sensible website. I learn that some Hindu women (together with Sikhs and Jains) wear a *ghungat* after marriage, usually formed from the end of the sari and pulled over the head, and sometimes the face. I learn that there is nothing in Hindu doctrine to support this, but rather it reflects Muslim influence. Nowadays, it is worn in poorer, more traditional areas of India. Whether or not a woman wears the ghungat after her marriage, it is a traditional feature of a Hindu wedding.

So, this is very interesting. Isha Anand was not a woman who would have expected to wear a ghungat, because she wouldn't have worn a sari – except for a traditional Hindu wedding. If the person who killed her was a Hindu, they would have known this. Asmil Anand had expected to marry Isha. Could the veil have been symbolic of his claim on the woman who refused to marry him? If he killed her, why does he want me to be interested? If he didn't, why does he think I can find out who did?

# Chapter Twelve

## FREDA

*Friday 29th July 2016*

It was like the feeling you had on the mornings of SATS tests, but times ten, she thought. She sat up and reached for her backpack, which was sitting ready on the end of the bed. She checked the contents again.

She couldn't take much, or Lavender and Monika would be suspicious, but you couldn't set off for London with nothing, could you? Her purse and her phone were there, safely in the zip pocket. Then her book, pyjamas and toothbrush, the chocolate biscuit and apple that she had taken yesterday, but not eaten (she hoped that didn't count as stealing), a spare pair of pants and a clean T-shirt. She would wear a jumper, but there was room for it in the bag if the weather got hot. At some time in the future, she would have to collect the rest of her stuff, but she wouldn't think about that now. Maybe Mum would do it for her. Or maybe she would make her come back and apologise to Lavender and Grandpa for running off. You couldn't tell – it could go either way.

On her bedside table was the note she had written for Lavender. She had decided to leave it in her room, because then it wouldn't be found until Monika raised the alarm, and by that time she would be on the train. She wasn't happy with the note. She'd had no paper with her, so she had torn a blank page out of the back of *Minnow on the Say,* and it had had rough edges, and she had puzzled for a long time about what to write, because she did feel bad. Monika and Lavender had both been so nice when she had asked if she could go with Monika into town. 'A girls' outing,' Lavender had said. 'What a good idea, isn't it, Monika?' And Monika had smiled and said, 'Like sisters,' so Freda had felt herself go scarlet with embarrassment about deceiving them, and nothing she could put in a note would make up for that. In the end, she had written:

*Dear Auntie Lavender,*

*I am sorry I left without telling you, but I need to go and see Nico as I am very worried about him.*

*Thank you very much for having me. I liked my room and enjoyed collecting eggs and other things.*

*Will you please say thank you to Monika for being kind to me?*

*I hope you find Jasper.*

*With love from*

*Freda*

She read it through again now, and added:

*PS Monika did not know I was planning to go to London, so please do not blame her. It is not her fault.*

That was better. She imagined Lavender reading it. Would she be mainly cross, or more upset? She wondered if she should leave her mobile number, so Lavender could ring and check that she was all right, but her phone credit was nearly all gone, and she didn't want to arrive in London with a dead phone, so she decided not to.

It was seven-thirty. She and Monika were catching a nine-thirty bus into Marlbury, once Monika had given the boys their breakfast. Freda thought about Lavender managing the boys for the day. She wasn't very good at it, which meant she

124

would be in even more of a flap when she found that Freda was missing. Well, it couldn't be helped. Her plan was to part from Monika when they got to Marlbury, having arranged to meet up somewhere later. She would explain, quite truthfully, that she was allowed to be in Marlbury without a grown-up, now she was ten, but not say that Mum's rule was that she and Charlie had to stick together. She would suggest to Monika that they should swap phone numbers, and then she would send her a text once she was on the train. She was sorry to be tricking Monika, and sorry that she would be spoiling her day off, but she would call her when she got to Granny's, explain everything and say she was sorry. Monika would understand, wouldn't she? After all, didn't she want to run away, too?

Downstairs in the kitchen, Monika had breakfast out on the table, and the boys were already eating. Freda poured herself a sprinkling of cornflakes and sat with it, forcing down very small mouthfuls. She knew it would look suspicious if she didn't eat, but her stomach felt as though it had a great big lump in it, with no room for food at all. When the boys had finished, she volunteered to sit with them while they watched a DVD, so that Monika could do some clearing up and get her things together for the shopping trip. The boys were quiet with her. Sometimes, after breakfast, they were quite wild, full of morning energy, charging around and finding things to bash each other with, but today they sat watching the TV, Hubert with his thumb in his mouth, Arthur alternating between looking at the screen and looking at Freda. She couldn't help an irrational feeling that he somehow knew she was planning to run away. It was stupid, of course, but he was such a weird boy that you just couldn't be sure.

Eventually, Lavender appeared, with an especially bright smile on her face, assuring the boys that they were all going to have a *lovely* day together. Then Freda realised that the boys had been quiet with her because they were biding their time. Once there was only their mother to deal with, then they would go mental, probably. What would Grandpa do? Stay shut in his study, she guessed, and leave Lavender to cope.

Monika was as keen as she was to get out of the house, so they were ready to go ages before the bus was due. They were hanging about in the hall when Ted came through from the kitchen and put his head round the nursery door, to tell Lavender that he was going to be out for the day.

'I'm taking the van,' he said, 'and I'll pick up some bags of compost from the garden centre. I'll be in again on Monday morning, as usual.'

Lavender came out into the hall, looked at Freda and Monika standing there, all ready to go, and said, 'You could give the girls a lift, couldn't you, Ted? If you're going into Marlbury?' But he more or less turned his back on her, and headed for the door.

'I'm not going into the town,' he said, 'only to the garden centre. I don't want to get snarled up in town traffic,' and he stomped back through the kitchen, slamming the door behind him.

Lavender's face had gone quite pink, but she laughed as though it didn't matter. 'Well, he's an old grump this morning, isn't he?' she said. 'You probably wouldn't want a drive with him anyway, would you, even if it did save you the bus fare?' Then she went back into the nursery, and they heard her shout over the boys' din, 'All right, Arthur, if you're going to rush about like that, the garden's the place. Come on, out we go.'

Freda and Monika looked at each other and, without saying anything, made for the front door.

The bus was late, and they stood at the stop for a long time without talking, Freda because she was afraid her voice would be wobbly, and Monika because she was looking at her shopping list and counting the money in her wallet. On the bus, though, Monika started to chat about her mother's birthday, and what she was planning to buy for her, and Freda decided that now was a good time to broach the idea of their splitting up once they got to Marlbury.

'I haven't got much money for shopping,' she said, 'but I thought I'd go and look at the Roman mosaics. It's free to get in for children, and I really love them, and the coins.' She tried to sound convincing about loving the mosaics. She did quite like them, but she had seen them lots of times, so it was hard to sound really enthusiastic. She just hoped Monika wouldn't say that she would love to see them too. She didn't think she would, because she had a lot of shopping she wanted to do, but, just in case, Freda added, 'I need to see them again for a school project, but you wouldn't be interested, and it's really expensive for grown-ups.' She was becoming such a liar, she thought. Could you go back to being truthful, she wondered, once you had learnt how to be a liar?

Monika looked doubtful. 'Would your mum allow you on your own?' she asked.

'Oh yes,' Freda said airily. She had practised this in her bedroom. 'Mum always said that when I was ten I would be allowed to go into town without her, as long as I had my phone with me. I can give you my phone number and you give me yours. Then we can keep in touch. And we can meet up later on. I'd really like you to help me buy a present for Nico.'

'OK.' Monika got out her phone and they entered one another's numbers.

Freda sat back in her seat. With that hurdle over, she felt much more relaxed. She looked at Monika, feeling suddenly extra fond of her. 'I hope you find something lovely for your mum,' she said. 'Have you got any ideas?'

'I am thinking a scarf,' Monika said. 'It's easy to send, and English scarves are good quality.'

127

'Go to Fenwicks,' Freda said. 'It's really posh in there. Charlie and I go in just to smell the perfumes.'

Monika looked at her. 'Charlie is a boy friend?' she asked.

'No! Girl. She's Charlotte, really, but she doesn't like it. She calls me Freddie.'

Monika smiled. 'Freddie,' she said. 'Suits you.' And Freda felt bad all over again.

At the bus station, Monika went over the road to Fenwicks, and Freda turned towards the High Street and the Roman museum. She had no intention of going inside. It was quite interesting, but every year at school their class teacher had decided that a trip there would be a good idea, and since it was only ten minutes' walk from the school, it was a good idea for the teachers, but not, she thought, for the pupils who wanted a coach trip and a picnic lunch and the exciting possibility of getting lost. She walked straight past the museum, past the library, past the road down to her school and on to the station, weaving her way through the clumps of tourists, and their shrill-voiced guides, who filled the area between the city walls and the abbey. She wondered what they were looking for. This was just a shopping street, after all.

There was a queue at the ticket window at the station. There were four people before her, and a woman at the front was taking a long time, so that those behind were beginning to sigh and look at the clock. Freda looked at it, too. Her train wasn't until eleven o'clock, so she had plenty of time. She was glad, in fact, to have one or two people before her, because she wanted to hear what they said when they bought their tickets. Out in the street, she hadn't felt conspicuous on her own, but here, standing in the queue, she felt noticeably small, although she was actually quite tall for her age, and she thought she saw some people looking at her a bit oddly.

When she came to ask for her ticket, she wanted to sound as though she did this all the time.

By the time she got to the front, she had heard a woman buying a three-month season ticket, which wasn't any help to her, but she had also heard the man in front of her say, 'Return to Charing Cross', so she stood up on tiptoe, and looked the ticket man in the eye, and said, 'Single to Charing Cross, please,' quite loudly. At first, he seemed just to look over her head, but then he did look at her.

'On your own?' he asked.

'Yes.' What else could she say?

'How old are you, love?'

'Twelve,' she lied, firmly.

'And you're going to London on your own?'

'Oh. No,' she said, realising that she should have had a plan for this. *Lie, lie,* a voice in her head told her. 'I'm not travelling on my own,' she said. 'Just buying the ticket on my own.' She opened her hand, in which she was already holding the right money. 'My mum gave me the money,' she said.

'So where's your mum, love?' he asked.

'She went to the toilet,' Freda improvised, 'with my little brother.' And then, with a brilliant stroke of inspiration, she added, 'She doesn't need a ticket – she's got a season ticket.'

The man nodded. 'All right,' he said, as he pushed the ticket across to her. 'Platform two. You go and find your mum, love. OK?'

'Yes. Thank you,' she said, scrabbling to pick up the ticket with sweaty fingers, and she walked through to the platform, feeling that every eye was on her. Just in case anyone was following her, she did go to the toilets, and spent some time washing her hands. In the mirror, her face looked odd, she thought, flushed and sweaty, and a bit excited, like you would look after a netball game. She splashed some water on it.

129

On the platform, she found a mother with three girls a bit older than her, dressed up for something special. She thought they might be going to a matinee of a musical, maybe. Perhaps it was someone's birthday. Whatever it was, she decided to stay near them – not too close so they got suspicious, but near enough to look as though she might be with them. She followed them onto the train, and when they sat down at an empty table, she tucked herself into a window seat across the aisle from them, hoping she looked like part of their group to any grown-up going by, but wishing she was looking a bit smarter, to be convincing. *Just don't get noticed,* she told herself, so she got out her book, put her head down, and tried to be invisible. Then a message pinged through on her phone.

She got the phone out, and realised, with a guilty jolt, that she hadn't texted Monika. The message, she could see, was from Charlie, but that would have to wait until she had sent the other one. She found Monika's number and typed:

*Really sorry to trick you but I am on a train to London. I need to see my brother and my mum. I left a note for auntie lavender and told her you didnt know I was going so you wont be in trouble. Love freda.*

It wasn't very good, but she couldn't think what else to say. She turned to Charlie's message. She didn't have much hope that Charlie had found out anything about dogs for sale; she felt a bit ashamed now that she had told Charlie to hack into her mum's eBay account. After all, it wasn't Charlie who had made the promise to find Jasper. She clicked on and read:

*Couldnt get on ebay but found another site homes4pets. Golden lab retriever for sale with marlbury phone no! £1000! 01217 763758 or 07740291611. Go miss marple! xxxxxx*

Freda stared at her screen. Charlie sounded more excited than she herself felt. When she had got onto the train, she had felt that life at Nettlebourne Farm had slipped away from her, like waking up from a dream. It had been horrid, and she had failed to find Jasper, but now she was looking forward to seeing Nico and Mum, and she didn't want to think about anything else. She looked again at the message. It was quite possible, wasn't it, that the dog was Jasper? If it was, then it certainly wasn't the Bulgarians who had taken him, because there was a landline number. The numbers danced about in front of her. The obvious thing to do was to ring and find out more, but she couldn't afford to use up her phone credit, and whoever had the dog probably wouldn't speak to a child, and she didn't want to attract attention by talking on the phone. She typed:

*Thanks Charlie, Great work!* and put her phone away.

It wasn't possible to concentrate on her book, though, now that she had all these new thoughts in her head, and it seemed to take forever for the train to get to London. As they came to the outshirts of London, it got more interesting, because the train ran behind the backs of houses, and she could look at the gardens and try to imagine the lives of the people living there. All sorts of dramas could be going on, couldn't they? And the train just went chugging by, with nobody caring.

When they stopped, eventually, at Charing Cross, and she got out, she almost wished she were back on the train. It had felt safer there. Everything here felt so huge, and so noisy, and so confusing. She had been here with Mum several times, and it had felt all right with her there, but now it felt scary, and she realised that she hadn't really thought through this part of her plan. She didn't know Granny's new address, so her plan had been to go straight to the hospital, but she had no idea how to walk there. She followed signs to the Underground, and was almost swept along by the mass of people going the same way. She found one of the big maps with all the stations on it, and even managed to find Charing Cross, but there was nothing that said Great Ormond Street. As she stood staring at it, a woman touched her on the shoulder, and she jumped, her heart pounding.

'Are you all right, dear?' the woman asked. She was quite old, Freda thought, and worried-looking.

'I'm fine, thank you,' she said, as firmly as she could manage.

The woman bent down and put her face close to Freda's. 'Did someone bring you here, dear?' she asked.

'Yes,' Freda said. The lie came automatically; her experience with the man in the ticket office had taught her that being on her own was considered a bad idea.

'But you ran away?' the woman asked.

Freda stared at her. She actually felt her mouth drop open. How could this woman possibly know that she had run away? It flashed through her mind that she might be a detective. Could Lavender have reported her running away to the police?

'No,' she said, beginning to back away.

The woman put out a hand to stop her. 'It's all right,' she said. 'You're safe now. I can take you to an office here and you will be safe.'

Freda wrenched her arm away. 'Are you the police?' she asked.

'No, no, dear,' the woman said. 'But I can help you.' She put out her arm again, but Freda dodged out of the way.

'I'm fine,' she shouted, and took to her heels, racing back towards the station concourse, dodging and weaving her way through the oncoming crowd. Out in the station, she fumbled in her bag for her phone. There was only one thing to do now. She found the number and pressed.

'Hello, Granny,' she said. 'I'm at Charing – ' and then her phone went dead.

# Chapter Thirteen

## DUTY OF CARE

### Friday 29th July 2016

I am quite interested in dreams. I don't believe, for a moment, that they predict the future, and I'm not sure that they are even a reliable guide to one's psychological state, but I love their obliqueness, their sidelong quality. I like the way people you knew thirty years ago – and weren't much interested in, even then – suddenly make a guest appearance in your head in the middle of the night. The absurdity of it. Of course, some dreams can be quite crudely metaphorical. A friend of mine, whose son wanted to be a professional musician but was having a hard time establishing himself, kept dreaming that she and her husband were trying to push a grand piano up a steep slope. Each time they got nearly to the top, they would lose control, and the piano would come crashing down again. It was somewhere between the torture of Sisyphus and a Laurel and Hardy sketch; tragedy and comedy, as Shakespeare knew, are only a hair's breadth apart. My dreams are nothing like as solid as that. They are full of anxieties, it is true, but I am much more likely to have an anxiety dream when I haven't anything to worry about (except global warming, Brexit, refugees drowning in the Mediterranean, human trafficking and an unbalanced narcissist becoming leader of the free world). I have a theory that, when my days are not filled with things to worry about, I build up a surfeit of worry which has nowhere to go, and that this waits for the night when my defences are down and takes me up ladders which fall away beneath me, to yawning precipices from which I cannot back away, to chasms, pits, gulfs and hiatuses of all kinds. These bring me shuddering awake, my stomach churning and my heart hammering with the terror of the fall. As a variation, I am quite often at the wheel of a car. I am not a driver in my waking life, though I did drive once upon a time – until my car-obsessed husband left me and I decided, for reasons I don't quite remember, that I could shame him by becoming a pedestrian. In my dreams, I sit competently at the wheel, and I steer and signal with aplomb; what I can't do, though, is stop. Sometimes, my car has no brakes; sometimes, I seem simply to have forgotten how to use them. So, I drive on, trying to slow down, looking with increasing desperation for a place where I can safely run the car to a standstill. The metaphors are not difficult to interpret: a life out of control, you would diagnose, and a settled belief that disaster lurks in the very ground beneath my feet. Well, maybe. There is a character in a Carol Shields novel – *Happenstance*, I think – who says she always has anxiety dreams about food when she is away from home on her own. In these dreams, she has a house full of people, and nothing to feed them with – the fridge is empty, the cupboards bare. Her theory is that she has had years of daily responsibility for feeding her family, for planning, shopping and cooking, for taking account of food allergies and intolerances, for coping with teenage whims and the likelihood of unscheduled guests at her table. She believes that when she is released from all of that there is a food-planning programme in her brain that has nothing to work on and so defaults to nightmare. Dreams as a way of using up what you don't need – that's an interesting idea. A nocturnal putting out of the bins.

All this is by way of a prologue to telling you that last night I dreamt that Annie fell off a boat, and I have no idea whether this means I am worried that she is on some self-destructive course (Jon gets back this weekend, and she won't talk about it), whether she was a dream stand-in for Nico, who obviously worries me, or whether it is Isha Anand who is on my mind, and the vulnerability of young women in general, and my own daughter in particular. Actually, I think it probably is Nico anxiety taking over, because, you see, the Annie in my dream is a toddler. We are on a boat, she and I. Andrew is there too, possibly, but there is no doubt that she is my responsibility. We are on the deck – it is a large boat, a ship, even – I turn for a moment to speak to someone, and when I turn back it is to see Annie flying over the deck rail and plunging into the sea. There is, I think, a bit more after that, but I wake with that image in my head, sick and sweating with the horror of the plunge. It is only when my breathing starts to calm, and my heartbeat slows, that I think how odd it is that, in the dream, Annie was wearing pink, and I never, ever, dressed my girls in pink.

Whatever the meaning of the dream, it manages to wreck my night. I try getting up and making tea, I try listening to the World Service on my laptop, I try letting Martin Jarvis's soothing tones take me to Blandings Castle, but none of it works. The tea sends me on several trips to the loo, the radio only batters me with the multiple places in the world where people's lives are insupportable, and – perhaps because of this – the Wodehouse world loses its charm and seems just outrageous – the rampant genetic privilege of the rich and stupid.

At six o'clock, I wrap myself in a dressing gown and go out to sit in the garden. It is morning now, so I am allowed coffee, but I make it milky, smooth and gentle – I am wired enough without a jolt of pure caffeine. Out here, birdsong competes with the burble of city sounds, but it offers a kind of peace, and the instinctive, deceitful optimism of a fresh day. I actually have nothing planned for today. I could go into my office and pretend to do some work, but exams are done and dusted, and I'm not in the mood for forward planning for next year. The appropriate task would be a bit of schmoozing – emails to people I met at the conference – *Great to meet up again. Such interesting work you are doing. Lovely presentation – one of the highlights of the conference. Love your idea of our collaborating on a book – must get together* et cetera. Only for that you have to have at least a modicum of the milk of human kindness washing around in you, and I'm all dried out this morning.

Eventually, I go and shower and I wash my hair because, to be honest, I did have a plan for today, though it does not seem to be working out. With no real justification, I had convinced myself that, by now, Roderick Gillard would have tracked me down and proposed something delightful by way of an evening meeting. I turned down David's offer of dinner and *Macbeth*, you may remember, on the grounds of my phantom date with Roderick, and now I am tempted to ring David, and tell him that I am free after all, because I am miserable and I can't face an evening here on my own with my misery. But the necessary chunk of humble pie involved in ringing David sticks in my throat. He knew I didn't really have plans for this evening, and if I ring him, he will let me know that he knew; I shall be able to hear him smirking over the phone. I try out a few possible gambits, but I know that none of them will get past his well-calibrated lie detector. It is all very disappointing, but I shall wash my hair, anyway, because it would be really annoying to find myself with a last-minute invitation and bad hair.

Showered, blow-dried, and dressed, I make toast and coffee for Ben, who is heading back to the hospital, and then I do go into SOAS. I will write those emails and, after all, this is where Roderick can contact me, so why not be there?

My office feels stuffy and smells unused, although I have been away from it for only a week. I open the window to let in the warm city air, and I switch on my computer. There is a knock at the door. Maria from Reception puts her head round.

'I thought I saw you come in,' she says, and hovers on the threshold. 'Thought I'd have a word before you get busy.'

She looks uncomfortable.

'Come in,' I say, moving my bag off a chair.

She sits down, perched on the edge. She is a little, neat woman, and she looks rather childlike, pulling her skirt over her knees.

'The thing is, Gina,' she says, 'I think I might have done the wrong thing.'

'Not you, Maria,' I say. 'Never!'

She blushes. 'Well, I hope it doesn't matter, but I gave someone your phone number.'

'Really?' My heart has done a little flip. 'When was that?'

'Yesterday. He came in, this man, very smart, nicely spoken, and he said he needed to contact you urgently. He showed me your card which you'd given him, but he said he knew you weren't going to be in this week, and he really needed to talk to you about your daughter. He gave me his card – he's a lawyer – and he said he knew your daughter through their work.'

I take the card. It is Roderick's, of course, and my first reaction is disappointment, because it needed so little initiative on his part to get my number – just some good clothes, an authoritative manner, and nice, mumsy Maria, who fell for a possible problem with a daughter. My next position is anxiety: perhaps there really is a problem with Annie. What if that wasn't just a ploy to see my fascinating self? What might he want to tell me? That he and she are having an affair? That he thinks she is in the wrong profession? That she is in trouble?

Well, he has had my number since yesterday, and he hasn't called yet, so it's not all that urgent, is it? For the moment, I'm going to assume that it's me he's after, but I will ring Annie later, to make sure she's all right. She will be snappy because Jon is due back tomorrow and she is nervous, but that's too bad.

I turn to Maria. 'Which number did you give him?' I ask.

'Your new landline number – not the mobile.'

'Fine,' I say. 'That's all right. I know him. He's not a stalker or anything.'

She gets up. 'I thought he was all right,' she says. 'Mind you,' she adds, as she goes out, 'there'd be worse people to be stalked by.'

*How true, Maria.*

The news that Roderick has my home number cheers me up, and also hurries me up. There's no point in his having my home number if I'm not actually in my home, so I race through the post-conference emails, tightening the cords of my little professional network, polishing my credentials as a good colleague and scattering rash promises about collaborations and consultations, like sprinkles of fairy dust, as I go.

I am just done, and thinking that I will go home for lunch, when my phone rings. I grab it, hoping it will be Ellie with good news, but FREDA appears on my screen.

'Hello, darling,' I say. 'How are –' but she interrupts me.

I hear her say, 'Hello, Granny. I'm at Charing –' and then there is silence. I call her back, but get a message telling me that the phone I am calling is switched off. What the hell is going on? I'm at Charing. There is a place called Charing in Kent, but it's not near Marlbury, and there is, as far as I know, nothing of interest there. I can't believe that Lavender has taken the children on an outing to Charing. So, it must be Charing Cross we're talking about, but what can she possibly be doing there? And why, why, did her phone cut off in that sinister way? I try to be logical. If she is at Charing Cross, then someone – Lavender? Andrew? – has brought her there. But why? Would they have brought her on an educational or cultural trip to London? Without the little boys, who would be a nightmare on any such trip? It is possible, I suppose, but if this was a planned trip, why didn't they contact Ellie or me to arrange to meet up? And why, even now, was it Freda who rang, rather than one of them? And why is her phone now switched off? What I begin to think is more likely is that there has been a falling-out. They are pissed off with Freda, for some reason, and have brought her to London to return her. I can't imagine why anyone would be pissed off with Freda, whom I find excellent company, but she has developed a sort of stringency of late – she speaks her mind. I can't think where she gets that from.

All the time my mind is turning over possibilities, my body is ahead of it. I am shutting down my computer, putting my phone and keys in my bag, checking my wallet for money, and running down the stairs. By the time I have concluded that Freda has indeed been brought here for unceremonious dumping, I am out in the middle of the road, waving like a lunatic at an oncoming taxi.

'Charing Cross,' I gasp as I climb in. I don't add, *And step on it,* because, even when frantic, I do retain some control over the ridiculous.

On the taxi ride, my speculations grow darker. It's that turned-off phone. If Freda turned the phone off herself, it could only be because she was ringing illicitly and had to abort the call. Why? If Andrew or Lavender is with her, they need to contact me, or Ellie, don't they? I can't see why they wouldn't ring themselves, but they would certainly not have a reason to stop Freda ringing. So, my mind unwillingly asks me, suppose she is not with one of them? Suppose someone else has charge of her. *Trafficking.* Utterly illiberal images come to my mind of swarthy foreign men with their hands on Freda. And yet, how could she possibly have been snatched from the Kent countryside and brought to London?

All the time I have been thinking, I have been trying Freda's phone, although I know it is hopeless. When I get out of the cab, I look at my watch. It is twenty minutes since she called. Is she still here? I have a plan – I will find a help desk, or anyone who looks official, and I will get an announcement put out, calling for Freda to come to – where? It used to be the stationmaster's office, I remember, when I used to go to school by train. Is there such an office here? Should I just cut to the chase and call the police?

I barrel through the crowds, looking for anyone who looks official, anyone in a uniform. I think I am crying. And then I see her. She is standing by the departures board, a tiny figure with a little rucksack on her back. I swoop down on her to enfold her in a tearful hug. She seems all fragile bones, and she is trembling hard. She feels like a bird does when you rescue it from a hunting cat. When she says, 'My phone ran out of credit. I didn't know it had till you didn't say anything, so I didn't know if you heard anything I said,' I can hear her teeth chattering. I am so angry with Andrew and Lavender that I actually can't speak. Instead, I steer Freda towards a nearby Caffè Nero, and, as we go, she asks, 'Did you hear me? Did you know I'd be waiting under the clock?'

'I didn't get anything except, *I'm at Charing* – ' I say, and she looks up at me with her eyes shining in her white, pinched, little face.

'But you knew I would be under the clock,' she says, 'because that's where people always meet in books – under the clock.'

I don't tell her that this time it was blind luck that I spotted her, because I would like her to keep her faith in the power of books; I just give her an extra hug.

At the café, I order a milkshake and a slice of lemon drizzle cake for her, and a double espresso and an almond croissant for me. It is lunch time, but I think we both need treatment for shock, and sugar is the quickest remedy. I add sugar to my coffee, and then I ask the question I am bursting with. I stir my coffee, trying to look casual.

'So, who brought you up here?' I ask. *And how the hell could they just dump you – a ten-year-old – here on your own?* a voice hisses in my ear.

She slurps some milkshake, and then says, 'No-one brought me. I came on my own.'

'You mean Grandpa and Lavender just put you on a train and left you to come on your own?' Now I'm not even trying to keep the outrage out of my voice.

She shakes her head. 'They didn't know,' she says. 'I just came.'

I look at her, and her face is somewhere between embarrassed and defiant.

'You ran away?' I ask.

'I had to see Nico,' she says, and now, for the first time, I see tears. 'It was horrible there and nobody cared about him at all.'

So, Ellie must have decided to tell her that Nico was worse, after all. I put out a hand and squeeze her arm. 'He's going to be all right, sweetheart,' I say. 'It was scary when he got worse and had to go into Intensive Care, but he's getting better now, and he'll probably go back on the ward later today.'

Her face, which has been defiant, seems to crumple. She pushes her plate and glass away, puts her head down on her arms, and sobs. I drag my chair round next to her and put an arm around her shoulders. She is speaking through her tears, but it is difficult to hear what she is saying. I bend my head close.

'All my fault ...' she seems to be saying, '... promised ... find Jasper ... all my fault.'

I let her cry, stroking her back until she calms and looks up. She grabs a paper napkin and wipes her face. 'We have to make a phone call,' she says.

With some prompting, she comes out with a story of sorts: I hear about a kidnapped dog, some Bulgarian fruit-pickers, Hubert hiding in a dog kennel, a promise to find the missing dog, a policeman, a friend with a smartphone in Croatia, and, finally, online pet sales and a Marlbury phone number.

'And if only I had a proper phone,' she wails, in conclusion, 'none of it would have been so difficult. I would have found Jasper by now and Nico would be all right.'

It is a confusing tale, but I like to think I'm quite good at untangling a tricky plot and I believe I get the drift. I certainly get the deal – the bargain – the belief that she could somehow make sure Nico was all right by getting Hubert's dog back for him. We make deals like that all the time, don't we, though we may not want to admit it? I never used to let either of my girls leave the house without a kiss and a warning not to speak to any strangers, and to take care crossing the road. Even when Annie wasn't speaking to me (and there were many such times) she had to submit to the kiss and the mantra, because I knew that disaster would befall her if I failed to say it, and it would be my fault. And prayers? I am no expert here, but aren't they essentially deals with God? So, I do understand the deal, and, with a little prompting, I understand Freda's story enough to say, finally, 'So we need to phone that Marlbury number, and see if the dog is Jasper, don't we?'

She nods, but when I say, 'Have you got the number?' she pulls her blank phone out of her pocket, and almost throws it onto the table.

'It's in there,' she says.

I know nothing about pay-as-you-go phones. I would never have one precisely because they will always run out of credit just when you most need them. Isn't that the whole point of them?

'So how do we put more credit on it?' I ask.

'There's a number to ring, and Mum pays for more.'

I see a snag. 'But you have to ring on that phone, and that phone is dead?'

She nods. 'Sometimes Mum does it at a cashpoint,' she says.

'OK.' I stand up. 'Are you finished with that milkshake? Let's go and find a cashpoint.'

We find one, with the little green top-up symbol, which I must have seen numerous times, but never registered, and the procedure turns out to be quite simple, since Freda knows what to do, and my part is only to produce my credit card. When the phone springs into life, Freda retrieves the landline number, and we find a bench to sit on while I ring it. I get a standard not-at-home answer, and when I ring the mobile number that she has also retrieved, I get another message, this time a personal one. *This is Ted Warren,* it says. *Leave a message and I'll get back to you.*

So, I leave a message, *My name is Gina Sidwell. I'm interested in the Labrador Retriever you have for sale. I'd be glad if you'd ring me back,'* and I give my number. 'So,' I say to Freda, 'that's all we can do for the moment. We'll get a taxi home, in case he rings back right away. There's no signal when you're on the Tube.'

She looks appalled. 'We can't go home,' she says. 'We have to go straight to the hospital. I have to see Nico.'

'I don't think you can, darling,' I protest. 'He's in the Intensive Care Unit. I don't think children are allowed. Mum didn't even want me to go in.'

She gets up off our bench. 'I have to see him, Granny,' she says. 'If you won't take me, I'll go by myself. I came up here by myself, and I can go to the hospital by myself.' Then she shoulders her rucksack, and says, 'If you'll just tell me the name of the Tube station I need.'

*Dammit.* I can picture exactly the scene that will ensue: nurses will be kind but adamant; Freda will be stubborn and tearful; Ellie will be flustered and upset, and everyone, in the end, will blame me. 'All right,' I say. 'We'll go in a taxi. Come on.'

Then, as we are crossing the concourse, my phone rings. 'Ted Warren here,' a voice says. 'You called me about a dog.' The accent is quintessentially Kent; the tone is brisk and not particularly friendly.

'I did,' I say.

'Well, it's gone,' he says.

'Gone? You mean it's run away?'

'No!' He sounds defensive. 'Why would it run away? It's sold. I'm on my way up to Norwich to deliver it now. You just caught me. I just stopped for a break.'

Now he says this, I realise that much of the chatter I can hear is at his end. He is in a motorway service station.

'Well, that's really disappointing,' I say. 'Do you have any others?'

'I don't breed them. I'm just selling this one for a friend. There's plenty more on the website. You'll find another easy enough.'

He is about to ring off, but I get in one more question. 'Just so I've got an idea,' I say, 'would you mind telling me how much you're getting for the dog?'

'Nine-fifty,' he says, and he is gone.

*Damn.*

I put my phone back in my bag, thinking hard. 'The dog's sold,' I say to Freda. 'And I do think it might be Jasper. There was something about the way he reacted when I asked if the dog had run away. And he said he was selling it for a friend – that's always dodgy.'

'Then we have to ring the police,' Freda says. 'We have to. We've got the man's phone number. Do you think the police can find someone from their phone number?'

'I'm sure they can, but I know his name. It was on his answerphone message. Ted Warren.'

Her eyes open wide. '*Ted!*' she says. 'Lavender's gardener is called Ted. I always thought it might be him who took Jasper.'

'Well, you're brilliant.' I am as excited as Freda by this time. 'So, what we need to do is ring Lavender and tell her that her gardener stole her dog. Then she can ring him, and tell him he's not going to Norwich, he's going to bring the dog straight home. Job done!'

It is only at this point that it occurs to me that Lavender ought to be frantic about Freda by now, since she has been AWOL for several hours.

'Have you let her know where you are?' I ask.

'I left a note to say I was coming to London. And I sent a text to Monika.'

'Monika?'

'She looks after the boys. She's Romanian. She was nice to me. She understood about Nico.'

Well, a note and a text are hardly enough reassurance that a ten-year-old in your care is safe and well, are they? I feel furious with Lavender and Andrew all over again. Why haven't they been on the phone to me if they knew Freda was heading for London? I can only think that they have been ringing Ellie, whose phone will be switched off in the ICU. I hope to God they haven't got through to her when she's got as much anxiety as she can cope with already, but she would have rung me, if so, wouldn't she?

I get my phone out again. 'I think we make a call to Aren't-We-Grand Hall right away,' I say, and I scroll down for the number. Then I think again. 'We'll do it in the taxi,' I say. 'There'll be less noise, and I can shout at your grandfather without people thinking I'm a mad woman.'

As we walk to the taxi rank, I say, 'This man, Ted, said someone was paying nine-fifty for the dog. That can't be nine pounds fifty, can it? So, it's nine hundred and fifty. Nearly a thousand pounds for a dog. That's grotesque. Especially when I think that Caliban came for free.'

Installed in the taxi, I warn the driver that I am about to shout at my ex-husband, and I dial the number. Lavender answers. Is that a tremor of anxiety in her voice?

'Lavender,' I say. 'Gina here.'

'Gina!' she says. 'I'm so – Have you – ?'

'Have I got Freda here, Lavender? Yes, I have. And you only had to pick up the phone to find out.'

'I've been trying to ring Ellie,' she says. 'But she's not answering. I've kept trying but … We've been terribly worried.'

'She's not answering, Lavender, because she is in Intensive Care with Nico. He's very poorly.'

'Oh, yes. Oh dear. I didn't realise he was so poorly. I – '

'No. You didn't realise because you didn't bloody well ask, did you? But at least you've got some excuse – he's not your grandson, after all, so I won't shout at you any more. Get me Andrew, will you?'

'Well, he's in his study and – '

'Just get him!'

Andrew comes to the phone after some delay, and he is all primed for blustering. 'I should have known you'd be involved in the child's ridiculous escapade,' he says, by way of greeting. 'She obviously thinks she's the heroine of some adventure story. You have no idea how much trouble – '

'Shut up, Andrew,' I say. 'None of this is Freda's fault. You were a crap father, and now you're a crap grandfather. Your grandson is in Intensive Care after a serious heart operation. How many times have you asked after him? Your granddaughter has been staying with you, worried out of her mind about her brother. What have you done to reassure her or make her feel better? What the hell is the matter with you? No! Don't interrupt. I haven't finished. Because it turns out that you're a crap employer, and a crap dog-owner, as well. So – '

It is not Andrew who interrupts me at this point, but Freda. She is in a state of great agitation and is gesturing at me to break off the call. I am reluctant, now that my invective juices are flowing, but she is urgently insistent, so I say, 'I'm going to call you back. I have an emergency to deal with. Don't go anywhere. I'm not finished,' and I end the call.

'What on earth's the matter, Freda?' I ask. 'I was just getting going with Grandpa.'

'That's the thing,' she says. 'I think he might be even more crap than you thought.'

*Oh God. I really must modify my language choices in front of Freda.*

'I think it's very unlikely that he could sink further in my estimation,' I say.

'Well, I think he's the one who stole the dog,' she says.

'Stole his own dog? I don't think that's logically possible, Freda,' I say. 'It's a definition of steal that what you take belongs to – '

'Just listen, Granny,' she interrupts, shaking my arm. 'You said Ted was taking Jasper to Norwich, didn't you? And you said the price was *nine-fifty*?'

'That's what he said.'

'Well, listen.'

And then she tells me a story about hearing Andrew tell Ted something like, *we'll go for the nine-fifty in Norwich,* and then shouting at her because she had overheard him.

'And then you say he came and apologised the next day?' I ask.

'Yes, and he said he was talking about the time of a horse race in Norwich that he wanted Ted to bet on for him. Only I thought it didn't make sense, because he said it had to be secret from Lavender, because she would be cross with him for wasting money, but Lavender is never cross with him – except once, when he wouldn't ring the police about Jasper. Usually Grandpa does what he likes, and Lavender doesn't argue.'

'That sounds about right,' I say. 'He had a trial run with an argumentative wife and didn't like it. Anyway, I'm pretty sure there isn't a race course in Norwich. And they certainly don't have races at nine-fifty in the morning – or at night, for that matter!'

'So, I think Grandpa got Ted to take Jasper, and then he put him up for sale on that website, and he was telling Ted to sell him to the person in Norwich who offered nine hundred and fifty pounds. The price was a thousand pounds, but I expect the Norwich person bargained.'

'But why, Freda? Grandpa can't be so short of money that he needs to sell the dog. He has a good job, and I know Lavender's got money. Unless he really does have a gambling problem. Maybe he's lost thousands betting on the horses.'

'He doesn't like him,' Freda says.

'Who doesn't like whom?'

'Jasper. Grandpa doesn't like him. He made him stay in the kitchen, because he chews things. And then he said he had to be outside in a kennel at night. I thought it was mean. He's only a puppy.'

'How old is Jasper?'

'Six months, I think.'

'Well, he just needs training properly.'

'Like Arthur and Hubert,' Freda says. Then she frowns. 'The trouble is,' she continues, 'I don't see why Grandpa had to get rid of Jasper secretly. Why didn't he just say he had to go? Cos, like I was saying, he makes the rules. He said Jasper had to go outside and everything, so why couldn't he just say he was a nuisance, and he didn't want him?'

I consider this. 'The thing about Grandpa,' I say, 'is he wants people to like him and admire him. He likes to be the good guy, at the same time as doing exactly what he wants to do, and that's tricky to pull off. He obviously didn't like living with Jasper – he probably wouldn't want any dog – but he knew Hubert would be very upset if he got rid of Jasper – and Lavender would be upset if Hubert was upset – and he didn't want them not to like him. So, he came up with this crazy idea, because he's a devious bast – man. And if you hadn't been there, he would have got away with it.'

'Yes,' Freda says. Her face has become rather solemn, but she gives herself a little shake. 'Grandpa won't like me at all, after this,' she says, 'but he didn't like me much, anyway.'

'He doesn't like me, either. Join the club.'

'The trouble is, he's the only grandfather I've got.'

'Well, there's Nonno. Won't he do?'

'I suppose.' She looks at me. 'Mum thinks you should have married David. He would be a cool grandfather.'

'Mum should mind her own business,' I say briskly. 'Now, what are we going to do about Jasper?'

'Grandpa has got to ring Ted and tell him to bring Jasper home. Ted could pretend to Lavender that he had just found him or something, couldn't he?'

'Probably. Lavender is dim enough to believe it, I expect.'

'Can you persuade Grandpa?'

'Watch me,' I say, and I dial the number.

'Hello, Gina.' He picks up on the second ring, knows it is me, and no doubt is ready for a fresh attack, only he doesn't know what's coming.

'Andrew,' I say, 'do tell me if I'm wrong, but can it be that you are so benighted and delusional that you thought it would be a good idea to have your own dog kidnapped, and sold on the internet?'

He blusters. 'I have no idea what you're talking about, Gina, and I thought we were discussing the way Freda has behaved.'

'It was Freda who worked out what you've been up to, Andrew. Your cunning plan was rumbled by a bright ten-year-old. Doesn't that embarrass you?'

'You're talking nonsense. That child thinks she's in an Enid Blyton story.'

'No. You're the one who thinks that. It's insulting how easily you thought you could deceive your nearest and dearest. Nine-fifty in Norwich? A horse race? Bollocks! Even Freda knew it was bollocks. I've spoken to Ted Warren. He's driving that poor dog up to Norwich as we speak. Will he get the nine hundred and fifty for himself? Is that his payment for doing your dirty work?'

'Look, Gina – '

'No, you look. Get Ted Warren on the phone, now, and tell him to bring the dog home, or I ring Lavender, and tell her what you've done. You could try to lie your way out of it, of course, but I think Lavender will know the truth. She's not the brightest bulb in the box, but she must know something about you by now. You'd be unwise to risk it.'

'This is ridiculous, Gina. It's nearly all over. The dog will have a good home, and the boys will soon get over it. Children do.'

'Really? In your vast, hands-on experience of children that's your expert view, is it? And how do you know Jasper will be in a good home? Have you talked to the buyer? Inspected his new home? Do you trust Ted to care about where he's leaving him? And what happens when Lavender starts talking about getting a replacement for Jasper? How are you going to get out of that?'

'And how am I supposed to explain Ted bringing Jasper back?'

'Well, Famous Five Freda has managed an answer to that. Ted turns up with him, and says he's found him wandering in all that countryside you've got around you. OK? Suck it up, Andrew. Get Jasper properly trained, and let those you're supposed to love enjoy him. Try being a proper father. I'm ringing Ted in ten minutes. If you haven't rung him by then, I'm ringing Lavender. It's up to you.'

I click off, and put my phone away. Freda is gazing at me. 'Wow!' she says.

'Never let a man bully you, Freda. It's the first rule of life.'

'OK.' She thinks. 'More important than being kind to other people?'

'Well, you need to be strong if you're going to help other people. If you're being bullied, you can't be strong.'

She nods. 'OK,' she says.

I feel a bit bad about her easy acceptance of this number-one rule, which I have only just formulated. 'Of course, there are other views,' I say. 'You don't have to take my word for it.'

'No,' she says.

I check my watch when we are dropped at the hospital. Andrew's ten minutes are up. I get out my phone to call Ted but, as I do so, a message comes through. *On way back to kent with dog dont ring me again,* it says.

'I think we've won, Freda,' I say. 'Jasper's on his way home.'

'Good,' she says. 'Then let's go and see Nico.'

I want to tell her that nothing she does, or has done, will make any difference to what Nico's heart is doing, but she knows that, really, doesn't she? It's what she feels that matters, and I can't change that.

We go inside, and Freda loves the murals, and the bright colours, and the generally hopeful air of the place; she doesn't seem to suffer from my instinct that fear and loss have permeated the jolly walls, the funky floors, the animal-shaped chairs. She is almost skipping along as we follow the signs to cardiac ICU, and I feel I have to say, once again, 'You know they may not let you in to see Nico, don't you?'

'Yes, they will,' she says. 'Look, this way,' and she marches on ahead of me.

When we get to the closed door of the unit, Freda presses the bell, but I speak to the young male nurse who opens up. I try to sound authoritative and polite at the same time, but I don't think I do very well. 'We'd like to see Nico Biaggi,' I say. 'I'm his grandmother, and this is his sister.'

He shakes his head. 'Sorry, he can't have visitors at the moment,' he says, and panic surges in me.

'He's not worse, is he?' I ask, and I can hear a horribly pathetic pleading note in my voice.

'No,' the nurse says, but his face looks alarmingly solemn to me. 'Nico's doing fine, but it's not visiting time, except for parents. Three-thirty is visiting, so you've got an hour or so to wait. I'd suggest going to the café.'

I am wobbly with relief that Nico isn't having a crisis, and I am ready to head off meekly for the café, but Freda is having none of it. She steps forward between me and the nurse and says, 'I can't wait for an hour, I'm afraid. It has been really hard for me to get here. I had to come secretly, and travel on a train by myself, and people tried to stop me, and a woman nearly kidnapped me, and my phone ran out of credit, and now I think you could just let me in to see my brother, even if my granny can't come in. I will be very quiet.'

He looks at her, and then at me, and says, 'Wait here.'

Freda smiles at me triumphantly. 'There you are,' she says, 'I didn't let the man bully me, did I?'

We wait. A couple of minutes later, the door opens again, and Ellie emerges, looking flustered and quite cross. She hugs Freda, but it's me she talks to. 'What the hell do you think you're doing, Ma?' she asks. 'What's this story about Freda going on a train on her own? Why's she here?'

Suddenly, I am just too tired for any of this. The pile-up of worry about Nico – not just mine, but Ellie's and Ben's, as well – the sleepless nights, the panic after Freda's phone call, the drama of the dog, the shouting at Andrew, have all done for me. I am close to being ambushed by tears.

'Ask Freda, Ellie,' I say. 'I've just been trying to pick up the pieces. I don't mind, but I don't want to be shouted at. I'm going out for a walk. You talk to Freda. I'll be back at three-thirty. If you need me, I've got my phone.'

In my agitation, I walk the wrong way and and it takes me an age to escape from the building. When I do get outside, I take deep breaths of the city's exhaust fumes as though they were pure mountain air. Then I consider how to spend this hour I have given myself. I could get some more coffee, but I need sedation rather than agitation. I could find a pub, and dose myself with alcohol, but that doesn't always work out well; I can get aggressive when I'm upset and have a drink inside me, and I might make a scene. A walk is what I need, I decide, a soothing stroll in a green space. This is perverse, since I am standing in the middle of one of the biggest cities in the world. I set off, however, in search of a park, and I don't have to go far to find one. *Coram's Fields,* the sign says, and I think vaguely of Tattycoram, in *Little Dorrit,* and foundlings, and nineteenth-century philanthropy as I approach the wrought iron gates, through which I can see an elegant pagoda-style building, and a lot of grass, and children playing. It looks charming, but when I get closer, I see the notice on the gate: *No adults unless accompanied by a child, no dogs, glass bottles, alcohol or bicycles.* I do a double take. *No adults unless accompanied by a child?* Can it really say that? It can. This is a safe place. In theory it is a place where unaccompanied children can play unmolested. I should celebrate this as an excellent idea, of course, but I am hurt to the heart to be shut out of this grassy paradise, pressing my face to the bars and denied entry. I feel like taking a leaf out of Freda's book. I want to find someone in a uniform and plead my case as a mother, grandmother, teacher and general all-round good egg, who has never harmed a child in her life, but even as I think this I can hear Annie, Counsel for the Prosecution, making the case against my claim of innocuousness. So I turn my back on the green fields, even when I discover that there is, in fact, a park next door to this one that is open to all, and commit myself instead to The Brunswick Centre, an urban ziggurat which I find further along the road. It is a city fantasy, composed of tiers of gleaming white apartments, each with its own glazed balcony overlooking an adult playground of shops, cafés, pubs and cinemas. It must be any singleton's dream, I think – your own luxury pod to hide away in, and a world of food, drink, retail and entertainment laid out below you, if you can afford to buy anything once you have paid your enormous mortgage. I don't want to live here, but, exiled from Eden, I accept this as a temporary demi-paradise, and buy myself a cheese and ham panino and, recklessly, a glass of prosecco at a cheerful bistro. It feels odd to drink prosecco on my own, but it lifts my spirits all the same.

When I get back to the hospital, I find Freda sitting outside the closed door of the ICU, absorbed in an intricate game of cat's cradle with Ben, and apparently perfectly calm. 'Have you seen Nico, then?' I ask.

'No,' she says, without taking her eyes off the web of string that she is removing from Ben's outstretched fingers, 'it's not three-thirty yet, but Ben is getting quite expert at this. It's because he's a pianist. He's got manual dexterity.'

I look at Ben, who shrugs and starts to take the cradle back from Freda. I sit down. A nurse comes out from the ward.

'Well done, Freda,' she says. 'You've been very patient. Do you and your dad want to come in now?'

Freda goes a bit pink and looks at Ben. I see him give her the very slightest wink. 'Yes,' Freda says. 'Come on – Dad.'

'We don't allow more than three people in at a time, I'm afraid,' the nurse says to me.

'Do you want to go in, Gina?' Ben asks. 'I can wait.'

'No, you go in,' I say. 'Enjoy being the four of you. I'll just sit here and be an unaccompanied adult.'

Three surprised pairs of eyes turn to me, but I lean back in my chair and close mine. 'I'll have a rest,' I say.

# Chapter Fourteen

## INTERIM PROCEEDINGS

### Saturday 30th July 2016

We are getting ourselves sorted out. Yesterday's air of crisis has been largely dispelled by some proper food and a decent night's sleep. After Freda's visit to Nico, everyone came back to the flat for an early supper, while Nico was being transferred from the ICU back onto the ward. Ben spent the night at the hospital again, but it will be his last there; Nico is due to be discharged on Monday, and space is needed for the parents of newly-admitted children. So, the plan for this evening is that Ben will take Ellie out for dinner, and then they will both sleep here. Last night, Freda slept with Ellie, so I didn't have to sleep on the sofa. I slept the dreamless sleep of the truly exhausted, and I emerge, this morning, with my ravelled sleeve nicely knitted up.

Ellie and Freda are snuggled up on the sofa in the sitting room, watching a cookery programme, when I go in and Ellie says, 'We fancy pomegranate muffins with a streusel and almond topping for breakfast, don't we, Freda?'

'Toast and jam is the closest I've got,' I say. 'And I could manage a smoothie.'

'We'll help,' Ellie says, and she sets the table and makes toast while Freda and I pile fruit into the blender. Ellie rattles drawers and complains that my kitchen cupboards are very strangely organised.

'It was an experiment,' I say. 'Therapy.'

'You're not doing feng shui, are you, Ma?' she demands.

'Certainly not. This was an invention of my own.'

'Well, it's nuts.'

'I may reconsider.'

The smoothie mixture comes out looking discouragingly grey, and tastes mainly of banana, but we congratulate ourselves on its health-giving properties. We are discussing the possibilities of the day ahead when Ben comes in. Nico is doing well, he says. He is sitting up and making something complicated with Lego, and he is expecting to see Ellie later. Ben goes to make himself some toast, accepts my offer of scrambled eggs and, when he is settled at the table with these, he says he will take Freda somewhere for the morning.

'Where shall we go?' he asks. Freda considers. 'Not a museum,' she says. 'Somewhere to charge about. I feel all squished up since yesterday, and Granny's garden's too small for running.'

'I know the perfect place for you,' I say. 'Ben will be allowed in too, but only if he sticks with you.'

When they are gone, and Ellie too has departed for the hospital, I think about putting my kitchen cupboards back to their status quo ante, but then decide that can wait. I put clean sheets on the study bed so that Freda can sleep there tonight – my turn for the sofa again – and then I have the coffee that I didn't have at breakfast, sit down with the paper, and find myself thinking, once again, about Isha Anand. I can't escape the feeling that Asmil Anand was urging me to try to find out more about her murder, and that – just like David – I think he knows more than he has told me so far. What is the matter with these men? Why can't they do their own investigating? What do they want from me?

What we need, I decide, is to know much more about Isha's life. The initial investigation hardly seems to have covered that at all. There were a few interviews with people who received the sexting message, but that was all. This was a young woman who had grown up without parents, living half a world away from most of her family. Her relationship with her second cousin, and putative fiancé, was complicated, and her brother was too young to be a real confidant, so who did she talk to? Surely there was someone? A work colleague? Did she have a mentor at work? Cressida Long? We know she was in her chambers, and Isha worked on the defence case that led to Cressida Long's harassment. If Cressida was Isha's mentor, she may not have had much spare energy for that role once the harassment started, and then there was the police investigation, and the court case. If she had been Isha's main support – possibly a listening ear – and had then got overwhelmed by her own concerns, that would have left Isha stranded. I grab the shopping list pad from the kitchen and start writing:

*See Cressida Long – Isha's work life, future plans. Anything about her personal life?*

*Talk to Annie again (?!)*

*Talk to Asmil again*

*David? Records of police interviews with friends?*

I write *Monday* against Cressida Long's name, since it is the weekend now, and I can't expect to find her in her chambers until then, and I write *???rehearsal* against Annie, because Jon is due back today and I'm leaving them to sort themselves out. After a bit of thought, I put *?rehearsal* against Asmil's name, as well. I haven't been scheduled to attend any more rehearsals, but I don't think Annie will turn me down if I offer myself. Against David's name, I write *Now*, and I pick up my phone.

He is not answering. His terse request that I leave a message is the same as it ever was, and it makes me nostalgic and irritated in equal measure.

*Ring me back,* I say, without introducing myself. *I need more information from your half-baked investigation. Soon.*

Then I make more coffee, skim my *Guardian* – averting my mind from the Brexit grief – and fidget until Ben and Freda return. Freda is in bouncingly good spirits, all traces of yesterday's trauma apparently forgotten. Or maybe not. Maybe she is a bit high, a bit frenetic? Well, she has won a famous victory, after all, defeating her grandfather, who – he would have us believe – is one of the finest legal minds of his generation. I know how she is feeling; I just need to be ready for the fall.

We have croque-monsieur, followed by cherries, for lunch, and then Ben goes off to the hospital and I promise to bring Freda around later. Freda and I watch *Little Women* on DVD. I have two versions of it – not just the Winona Ryder and Susan Sarandon one, but also the Elizabeth Taylor and Peter Lawford version from 1949. I don't suggest this one for Freda, as I don't think she would appreciate the period charm, and the girls are all so very mature. (I chiefly like it for the absurdity of casting the glamorously Italian Rossano Brazzi as the scholarly German Professor, Friedrich Bhaer). Freda identifies with Jo, of course, but I begin to feel that I have made a mistake, as she gets quite upset by the episode where Amy falls through the ice. I am glad that we run out of time before the scene where Beth dies, and we abandon the film to go and see Nico.

Now that he is back on the ward, I can go in too, and I am so glad to see him looking so solidly there and himself that it is all I can do not to snatch him from his bed and hug him hard. I feel I should have brought him a present, but his bed is covered in toys, and my present would have been a book, which is not really his best thing. He wants to hear again Freda's story about Jasper, which she told him only in garbled form yesterday. The story has been sanitised – Grandpa is not identified as the master criminal in this version. This is Ellie's doing, I presume; she doesn't want Nico to see him as a villain, even if Freda does.

When patients' teatime comes around, we are tactfully edged away, with the suggestion that some quiet time is in order, so we depart. Ellie and Ben are reluctant to leave Nico for the night, but he seems unconcerned – more interested in his boiled egg and toast fingers. We walk back to the flat – Ben and Freda, Ellie and I – and Ellie asks if I can lend her something to wear to go out for dinner, since she has brought only hospital visiting clothes with her, and they are all sweaty and discouraged-looking by now. She is half a head taller than me, and quite a lot slimmer but, exploring my wardrobe when we get home, we find a long, sleeveless, vaguely ethnic top, which looks fine worn loose over her own leggings, and she manages to squeeze into some shiny sandals of mine, as well. Once she has showered and washed her hair you would hardly guess at the ordeal she has been going through. The strain shows more in Ben's face, I think, but he doesn't have the advantage of make-up.

When I have dispatched them for their evening, with injunctions to relax and make the most of it, I investigate the fridge for supper for Freda and me. There is some cold ham which is on its use by date, so I suggest ham and salad, followed by pancakes, and Freda is enthusiastic. We do our duty with the salad, and I have just got butter sizzling for the pancakes, while Freda rummages for lemons, sugar and honey, when the phone rings. Not my mobile – the house phone, which has rung only once since I moved in; on that occasion, a chap in India informed me that there was a problem with my computer which he could fix as soon as I had told him all my passwords. I asked him how it was that scammers could get hold of my phone number before my friends had it, and he hung up. The phone is in the kitchen, so I pick it up, and bark, 'Hello,' into it.

There is a silence before a voice asks, 'Is that Gina Sidwell?'

'Yes.' I am still brusque.

'This is Roderick Gillard. You may remember we met...'

Oh, the modesty of it – *You may remember we met.*

'Of course,' I say, reaching to take my butter off the heat. 'At the rehearsal. You were a very fine Duke of Vienna.'

He ignores the compliment. 'I enjoyed our conversation,' he says, 'and I know it's terribly short notice, and you're probably busy, but I wondered if you were free to go for dinner somewhere.'

'When?' I ask stupidly. 'Dinner when?'

'Well, now.'

'It's a lovely idea,' I say, 'but I have my granddaughter here.'

*Damn. Now he'll be adjusting his ideas about how old I am. Does he have grandchildren? Annie said he had children, but nothing about grandchildren.*

'We're making pancakes for our supper,' I say, aiming to turn his mind to the charming image of a young, fun grandmother.

'Lovely,' he says. 'Lucky granddaughter.'

'You're welcome to join us,' I say.

Why do I say it? Do I think for a moment that he will say yes? I really don't. I am just compensating for being a granny, still, polishing up a spontaneous, free-wheeling counter-image.

'Well, I do happen to be in Bloomsbury – you did say you lived in Bloomsbury, didn't you?'

Did I? Well, probably. I am embarrassingly proud of my elegant new address, and I had drunk quite a lot of prosecco.

'Well, then,' I say. 'I'll keep the pan hot till you get here.' And I give him the address.

'There's a man coming for pancakes,' I say to Freda, when I put the phone down.

'Yes,' she says. 'Is he going to be your new boyfriend?'

'No! What makes you think that? He knows Auntie Annie, that's all. He's another lawyer.'

'But he asked you out for a date.'

'Not really. He just happens to be near here.'

She looks up at me. 'I'm sorry if I'm in your way,' she says.

How does this child manage to be so knowing? Are all ten-year-olds like this now? When I was ten, I don't think I had any idea that older people had sex lives of any kind.

'You are not at all in the way,' I say, 'and I would much sooner have spent the evening with just you. Now it'll be boring for you, I'm afraid.'

'Maybe,' she says. 'Maybe not.'

I look round the kitchen and sitting room, glad that I did some tidying this morning. I am certainly not ashamed of my smart flat. My own appearance, on the other hand, has room for improvement.

'I'm just going to the loo,' I tell Freda, and dash to the bathroom to comb my hair and put on some lipstick. I consider putting on a different top, but I am still hovering in my selection when the doorbell rings.

Roderick is looking coolly elegant, of course, in a blue linen jacket, a shirt of a paler, toning blue and nicely cut cream trousers. Combined with thick, only-just-greying hair and pale blue eyes, the effect is impressive. How come he is at a loose end on a Saturday night, and bothering with me?

I usher him in, and he makes duly appreciative remarks about the flat as we make our way through. I explain that I've been here for hardly more than a week, and he says it's looking very lived-in already. In the kitchen, Freda is sitting at the table, waiting patiently for her pancakes. He shakes her hand, and she goes pink. I realise that I really should give him something else to eat beside pancakes; he was expecting to go out for dinner, after all. I survey the fridge and find it wanting. I have shopped mainly for snack food, to be eaten on the run by Ellie and Ben, and for Nico's favourites, ready for his return. There are pizzas and pasta sauces, neither of which is followed well by pancakes, and there is a chicken, earmarked for roasting tomorrow but no use to me now. I open a decent bottle of Valpolicella, pour us each a glass, and offer him a ham sandwich, since Freda and I didn't finish the ham, but did eat all the salad. The only bread I have is in the freezer, so I make him a toasted ham sandwich with plenty of mustard, and the end of a packet of rocket as an attempt at a garnish. He is suitably grateful.

'So, what brings you to Bloomsbury?' I ask, as I am making the sandwich.

'The Brit Mus,' he says. 'I wanted to see the Herakleion exhibition again, before it closes. Crazy to go on a July Saturday, I know, but later in the day the crowds have mostly dispersed, and I'm a member, so I don't have to queue.'

'I haven't seen the exhibition,' I say. 'Should I?'

'It depends on whether archaeology is your thing. It's a bit of an interest of mine.'

'You should meet my friend, David,' I say. 'He's an archaeologist manqué. He goes on archaeology holidays.'

'What does he do for a day job?'

'He's a policeman, actually.'

Why have I brought David into the conversation? And why, having done it, have I downgraded him to humble policeman, rather than saying that he's a senior detective with the Met? I look at Freda, who is watching us with acute interest. Is she wondering the same thing?

I start on the pancakes, and conversation moves to pancake preferences – lemon and sugar, honey or jam – and ways of folding them. Freda demonstrates how Ben folds his into a parcel. 'It's the Italian way,' she says. 'And that way you can put the lemon and sugar on twice – once when you fold the sides over and again before you fold the ends over.'

We try this, and I comment on the Italian gift for getting things right.

'Except politics,' Roderick says.

'And we, of course, are doing brilliantly,' I say, 'having just voted to cut our own throats. I think I'm giving up on democracy.'

*'The worst form of government except for all those other forms that have been tried from time to time.'*

'Did Churchill really say that, do you know?'

'I believe so.'

'But demagoguery – the Athenians knew all about that, even when they were inventing democracy. I'm sure Boris Johnson, that famous classicist, sees himself as another Cleon. What can you do about that?'

'I think you might be going to tell me.'

Is he laughing at me?

'Well, the obvious answer is to educate people better, so they can't be taken in by spurious arguments. But governments aren't going to spend money on that, are they? Not when it's in their interest for people to be easily conned.'

He opens his mouth to answer, but then his phone rings. It has a standard ringtone – nothing operatic or jokey, I'm glad to hear. He glances at it and then says, 'Will you excuse me? I should answer this.' Then he disappears into the garden.

Freda leans across the table towards me and asks, 'Is it all right if I ask to see his phone? I think it's a good one, and I need to do some research on proper phones.'

'It's probably a very expensive one,' I say, 'out of your league, I'm afraid.'

'Never mind. It's a start.'

Roderick returns and says, 'Family!' by way of apology, but I have the sudden conviction that he was supposed to be seeing another woman this evening and was putting her off.

'Do you mind if I look at your phone?' Freda asks him.

'Another pancake?' I ask.

He accedes to both, and he and Freda are soon deep into the technicalities of his very smart smartphone, which they continue to discuss while munching their way absent-mindedly through their fresh pancakes. I'm starting to feel excluded – and unusually embarrassed by my own Luddite attitude to new technology.

'You're very *au fait*, Roderick,' I say. 'I'm impressed.'

He smiles. 'You mean considering my advanced age?' he asks.

'No, I – '

'It's because of my advanced age that I have to be *au fait*. I'm the oldest person in our chambers. If I couldn't manage drop boxes and so on, they'd be encouraging me to spend more time with my garden.'

'Right.' I am uncomfortably conscious that, at work, I go to Maria for anything complicated and respond to anything odd my computer does with an immediate call to Mark and Jack in IT. They never seem to mind, but I think, now, that it's because they regard me as a helpless old biddy.

'Well, I'm impressed,' I say again, lamely. 'But you'd better warn Freda that a phone like yours is out of her league, even if her mum would approve.'

'There are good ones a lot cheaper,' he says to Freda. 'I bought a nice one for my grandson that didn't cost the earth.'

*Grandson.* Good. He's not younger than me, then. He is, however, deeply engrossed in his conversation with Freda, and I'm starting to feel pissed off.

'Coffee?' I ask. 'In the sitting room?' I would like this to be a signal for Freda to go to bed, but there is not much chance of that. When I go into the sitting room with coffee for Roderick and me, he and she are engaged in playing some game on his phone.

'I changed the sheets on the bed in my study, Freda,' I say, 'so it's all ready for you.'

'Thanks,' she says, her eyes riveted to the screen.

And then my doorbell rings. I am not used to this yet, and I feel unreasonably alarmed, but, when I open the door, I find David standing there. I probably take him by surprise with the warmth of my greeting, but I am actually delighted to see him. A good-looking younger man showing an interest in me is just what I need at this moment, to shake Roderick out of his complacency and prise him away from Freda and that bloody phone.

'David! How lovely!' I cry, loudly enough to be heard in the sitting room. Then I usher him through and make introductions:

'David, this is Roderick Gillard - he's acting with Annie in *Measure for Measure*. Roderick, this is David Scott, who is a DCI with the Met and who was, incidentally, responsible for all the DIY around here - curtains, blinds, mirrors. He is quite my hero.'

David looks startled, but shakes Roderick's hand, greets Freda, and accepts a cup of coffee. As we all sit here, I wonder what on earth we are going to talk about, and I offer grappa to supplement the coffee and oil the wheels. I need not have worried, though. Roderick moves smoothly into asking David about his work, and they find all sorts of points of contact, of course, since Roderick is a criminal lawyer. They are polite enough to invite me into the conversation from time to time, but actually I am quite interested in just listening to them. Freda is bored, though. She gets a book out of her rucksack, and curls up with it on a corner of the sofa.

Eventually, Roderick asks for directions to the loo, and David takes the opportunity to tell me what he has really come for.

'There's been a development,' he says. 'Well, two developments.'

'In the case?'

'Bimal Anand is on his way back here. He got on a plane in Delhi this evening.'

'Why? What made the family change their minds?'

'We gave them an assurance that there was no question of his being arrested, but that we needed him as a witness. So they agreed. They want to know who murdered Isha, after all.'

'When you say *we*, how are you involved, when it has been so emphatically not your case?'

'That's the second development. Hannah Smart, the DI who has been the nominal SIO on the case, has gone off on annual leave, and so has her DS, so I volunteered to keep an eye on it. The powers that be are very happy with it being dormant, of course, but they like to tick the boxes for procedural correctness, so they were happy to attach my name to it.'

'And you've woken it out of hibernation?'

'Just a bit. It seemed to me that Bimal was the key to a lot. If anyone knew what was going on in his sister's life he did – he was staying with her – so I contacted the uncle, and he was very reasonable. I was prepared to go out to Delhi to talk to Bimal, but I wouldn't have got clearance for expenses.'

'Is the uncle coming with him?'

'No. He can't leave his work, he says. But Bimal is used to looking after himself. He'll stay in Isha's flat. Apparently she employed a cleaner, who has been in and cleared the fridge and picked up mail and so on. We'll talk to Bimal tomorrow.'

'DCI Scott,' I say, 'I take back all the harsh things I have said about you.'

'Yes,' he says, 'until the next time.'

Then Roderick returns from the loo, and says he must be off, and David gets to his feet, too. There is a flurry of handshaking and then, suddenly, Freda and I are alone.

It is nearly ten o'clock, and I declare it bedtime for both

of us. Freda says she wants to sleep on the sofa, so I provide pillow and duvet while she goes to the bathroom, and then watch as she snuggles down. As I bend over her to give her a kiss, she asks, 'Who was Isha?'

'What?'

'David said she was murdered.'

What do I say? She really doesn't need to know about this, does she? Nico will be discharged from hospital on Monday, and then, I assume, they will all go home, so if things take off with the case, I shall be free – free to get as involved as David will let me.

As I'm preparing a brush-off answer, she says, 'And who is Bimmle?'

'*Bimal*,' I say automatically, and then I think that, really, she deserves something more for paying such acute attention while apparently reading her book.

'Isha was a young woman who was killed a few weeks ago, near here. She was a lawyer – Auntie Annie knew her. Bimal is her brother. He's in India, but he is coming back so that David can talk to him. He might be able to help to find out who killed his sister.'

'How was she killed?'

'I don't think you need to know that – not just before you go to sleep.'

'Is her brother younger or older than her?'

'Younger.'

'Well, in my experience,' she says, sounding terribly grown-up, 'little brothers don't know much about their sisters. We keep our secrets.'

'He's seventeen.'

'That's grown-up.'

'Sort of,' I say.

# Chapter Fifteen

## FREDA

*Sunday 31st July 2016*

This was what pure happiness felt like, Freda thought, as she lay on the sofa with the morning light filtering through from the kitchen. Granny was asleep just the other side of that wall, and Mum and Ben were asleep in the room behind her. She knew they were safely back from their restaurant dinner, because she had stayed awake until they got in. And Nico would be out of hospital tomorrow, and everything would go back to normal. And Jasper was back home, so Hubert would be happy too. She hugged her happiness to her. You ought to be able to tuck this feeling away somewhere, she thought, and take it out and look at it when things were horrible.

The bubble of her happiness was deflated slightly when she started to get dressed and realised that the only spare T-shirt she had brought with her, which she had worn yesterday, had drips of something on it – sugary lemon juice, probably – and that she would have to wear yesterday's pants again. But she discovered that today was just going to be a magical day when Granny took one look at her at breakfast time and said, 'After a person has made a jail break, Freda, she needs to go shopping. How about a trip to the West End for a really good shop?'

Freda grinned. 'Can we transform me, Granny? I am really manky to start with – look at me!'

Her grandmother looked at her. 'I was thinking we might make a few improvements before we hit the West End,' she replied. 'Most of the shops don't open till midday on a Sunday. If that's the only T-shirt you've got with you, give it to me, and I'll wash and tumble-dry it. And we'll wash your hair, too.'

'OK. Do what you like with me,' Freda said, and she leaned back in her chair and held up her arms in surrender, because she was so happy to have Granny taking charge and telling her what to do. Granny's bossiness was annoying sometimes, but after days of having to manage everything for herself, it was such a relief to be bossed.

So, after breakfast, when Mum and Ben went off to the hospital, Granny ran a bath, put all Freda's clothes in the washing machine, and shampooed her hair for her. Her mum usually did it, and Freda knew it was something she needed to practise doing for herself, but when she had tried it, the shampoo had run down into her eyes, and she hadn't rinsed it all out properly, so her hair was sticky and frizzy afterwards. Out of the bath, and draped in a towel like an ancient Roman, she let Granny have a go at her hair with her straightening tongs. She was amazed at how straight Granny managed to get her annoying curls. 'Your hair is so like mine, Freda,' she said, as she worked away at it. 'Aren't genes funny things?'

'But your hair isn't frizzy,' Freda objected

'Only because I spend a fortune on it. Don't you remember how it was when I lived by the seaside? Wild, I was.'

'I remember I thought you might be a witch.'

'So did a lot of people who didn't have the excuse of being only seven years old. There. How's that?'

They both looked in the mirror. 'Transformed!' Freda said.

'The straighteners aren't good for your hair, though,' Granny said. 'So, this is a one-off. When you're older you can ruin it if you want to, but not yet. Resign yourself to curls for a while.'

Dressed in clothes only slightly damp from the tumble drier, Freda walked with her grandmother to the Tube station, enjoying the feeling of her hair bouncing on her shoulders, when it was usually pulled back into an elastic band to keep it out of the way. She could almost feel what it was like to be one of those irritating girls who were always flicking their shiny hair about, and she wondered if your hair could change your personality. At the station, Granny explained the Tube map to her, and they joined the crowds of people who all seemed to be heading for West End shopping.

When they got out at Oxford Circus, Granny had a plan. 'Miss Selfridge,' she said, 'and Top Shop.'

The Top Shop proposal was a bit disappointing, because there was one of those in Marlbury, but this one turned out to be huge, with such an array of clothes that it was difficult to know where to start. Privately, Freda wanted to start with jeans and trainers – really good designer ones – but she knew, from shopping with her mum, that this wasn't what grown-ups meant when they offered to take you clothes shopping. They wanted to buy you dresses, and things with colours that matched. Pretty was what they liked, and there was nothing wrong with pretty, in its place, but jeans and trainers meant status – they said who you were, and it was hard to explain that to Mum, who would say, *Your own character and what you do says who you are, Freda. Clothes are just the surface. You can't be somebody just by buying expensive trainers.* And Granny would say much the same, she was sure, only she would probably be blunter about it.

In Top Shop, they prowled the rails, picking up armfuls of clothes, with Granny cheerfully saying, 'Try it in this colour as well,' and heaping yet another garment onto the pile in Freda's arms, and in the end, when they presented themselves at the changing rooms, the pile was so high that she could hardly see where she was going.

The assistant looked cross. 'Only six garments at a time,' she said.

So Granny seized some of them and said, 'That's all right, these are for me,' with a completely straight face, and they were let in.

Granny sat in the cubicle next door to hers, while Freda ran in and out to show her things, and every now and then Granny went and asked the assistant for a different size. 'She thinks we're just playing around,' she whispered to Freda, 'and that we won't buy anything in the end.'

Freda had a moment of anxiety. 'But we will buy something, won't we?'

'Absolutely. The whole, lovely lot, if you want.'

'Magic,' Freda said.

In the end, they bought some patterned cut-offs with two matching tops, a denim fringed miniskirt with two more tops, a pair of jeans that weren't quite as expensive as Freda had been hoping for but looked pretty good, and a pale green dress with shoulder ties and a short, swirly skirt, which Freda loved above all the rest. It was terribly expensive, and it was the only thing Granny hesitated over. 'There's only a month of summer left,' she said, 'and it won't fit you next year will it?'

'It isn't just for summer,' Freda insisted. 'I can wear it in the winter too, for special occasions.'

'But you'll freeze in it in the winter, darling.'

'No, I won't,' Freda told her, firmly. 'I'm young, Granny.'

'So you are,' Granny said. 'I'd almost forgotten what young is like.'

And it was added to the pile they picked up to take to the counter to pay for. 'We're taking these,' Granny said to the surly assistant, as they carried them away, 'so, we weren't wasting your time after all.'

When their purchases were being totalled and Granny had her credit card out, she said, 'Shut your ears, Freda. You don't want to hear the final sum.'

She wasn't sure if Granny meant it, or was just joking, but she did cover her ears, because it might be so much that it would be scary, and she would be worried about Granny not having enough money for food.

As they were on their way out, Granny stopped suddenly. 'Shoes!' she said. 'We haven't bought any shoes.' So they went on to Miss Selfridge, which Granny liked because she said she used to shop there when she was young, and there they bought some not very expensive but glamorous silver flip-flops, and a pair of trainers with flowers on them, which even Granny liked.

'I think,' Freda said, as they left the shop, 'that I may never be so happy again.'

'Oh, you will,' her grandmother said. 'You will need to be. You will be very unhappy sometimes – that's life – so you will have to be very happy when you can.'

They went to an Italian restaurant called Zizzi for lunch, and there Granny ordered fish in a very green sauce, and Freda had a bowl of spaghetti Bolognese, which tasted truly Italian – that was to say, more like it tasted when Ben's mum made it than it did when Freda's mum made it.

When she said this, Granny said, 'It's the good olive oil – and the fresh basil. My sauce tastes as though it's still growing in the ground.'

And then Granny's phone rang, and the day stopped belonging to Freda.

'David?' Granny said, and then, 'In Oxford Street. Why?' Then she said, 'Zizzi, but –' and, 'David, I've got Freda with me, I – ' before she took her phone away from her ear, put it away and said, 'It seems that David is joining us. He's got something important to talk about. It really is the limit for him to spoil our lunch.'

'I don't mind,' Freda said, 'if I can have salted caramel ice cream after this.'

David arrived a few minutes later, looking cross, not even glancing at Freda, and not even saying he was sorry to barge in.

'What were you doing in the West End?' Granny asked him, but he didn't answer until he had waved at a waiter and ordered a pizza and a glass of water.

Then he said, 'You weren't answering your phone, so I rang Ellie. She told me you were shopping.'

'You rang Ellie at the hospital? Really, David – '

'This is important, Gina. Just listen, will you?'

Freda looked at her grandmother. Nobody talked to Granny like that and got away with it, did they? But she just put her hands up as though he was pointing a gun at her, and said, 'Fire away. Freda, eat up your spaghetti and take no notice of us.'

Freda went back to her spaghetti, but she listened so hard that she was glad she was wearing her hair over her ears, in case they might be visibly swivelling, like Caliban's used to when he heard Granny opening a tin of dog food.

'Bimal has disappeared,' David said.

'In India?' Granny asked.

'No. He definitely got on the plane and got off at this end. He went through at Heathrow and picked up his luggage. Then he disappeared.'

So, it was a good thing, Freda thought, that she had asked Granny about Isha and Bimal last night, because now she had some idea of what was going on. Apparently engrossed in twirling her spaghetti, she listened in again.

'Did you have someone watching out for him?' Granny asked.

174

'No. And isn't it just like you to find the sore point and prod it? I didn't send anyone to meet him at Heathrow. I didn't want to scare him with an immediate police presence, and we didn't think anyone knew that he was coming back except us.'

'So, when you say he's disappeared...?'

'An officer went to his sister's flat an hour and a half ago and it was clear that he hadn't been there. We got the cleaner to go round there to look, and she said nothing had changed since she'd left it yesterday.'

'So, she was one person who knew Bimal was coming, because she had been asked to get the place ready?'

'She did.'

'But you didn't think of that?'

'Gina, give me a break, will you? I just took this case on. I didn't have all the – '

'OK, OK. Here comes your pizza. Eat up and don't get cross. I'll talk while you eat.'

'No!' He said it so loudly that Freda jumped. 'I don't want the bloody pizza anyway. I only ordered it to justify being here. Just listen and don't interrupt, and then I'll tell you what I want you to do.'

'How very masterful you are today. Do try to remember that I am not actually part of your team.'

'The boy is quite possibly in serious danger, Gina. Do you want to help or not?'

'Talk to me.'

Freda found she had finished her spaghetti, so she couldn't pretend to be concentrating on that any more. She got her phone out and fiddled about with it, although it couldn't do anything interesting.

'So, here's where we are. We are not able to track Bimal's phone – it's switched off. I've put in a request for his phone records to see who he called in the last forty-eight hours. We have already spoken to the woman who runs the cleaning agency Isha used. Their cleaners are mainly Eastern Europeans, and they vet them thoroughly. This is an upmarket agency, and the cleaners are going into houses full of expensive stuff. Of course, there's no guarantee that the cleaner wasn't involved. We're checking if she has a boyfriend, brother or other connection she might have talked to. I feel pretty sure that Isha's murderer was male. Now, what we also need to do is to track down Bimal's school friends. It is just possible that he has gone, quite harmlessly, to one of them, meaning to contact us later. Maybe he wanted a bit of moral support. Except the switched-off phone is worrying. That's where you come in. We don't know who Bimal's friends are. We might get leads from his phone records, but that's going to take time, and I don't really have the manpower – sorry, person power – to keep anyone on it. Remember, this inquiry is supposed to be dormant. And it's Sunday. All I've got is one duty DC today, and I've got other things I need him to do. I might rustle up more tomorrow, but we need to move faster than that.'

'What do you want me to do?'

'Mobilise Annie. Get her to contact Isha's friends and see if any of them know anything about Bimal. We know he spent a lot of time at Isha's flat – half terms, some weekends. If they met him, they just might be able to give us a lead. It's a long shot and I can't justify putting police resources into it, but – '

'– I've got nothing better to do, so why not send me on a wild goose chase?'

'I'm only asking you to talk to Annie. We've talked to the cabbies at Heathrow, and no-one remembers anyone resembling Bimal. If someone picked him up, he must have let them know he was coming, but we need to find out fast whether he is safe. Just because he let someone know, it doesn't mean that person isn't dangerous. Bimal knows something about Isha's life that relates to her murder.'

'Won't you get his contacts more quickly from his phone records?'

'Yes, if he used that phone. But it's quite possible that he contacted someone before he left India, and in that case, he is most likely to have used his uncle's landline, and not spent money on an expensive transcontinental call. Getting the phone records for the minister's private phone would be very difficult indeed, I think, and I don't want to – '

'You don't want to let his uncle know that he's missing unless you have to.'

'No.'

'Embarrassing, isn't it, getting him here and then losing him?'

Freda hadn't understood everything that they had said, but the way Granny said this made her laugh and the two grown-ups suddenly noticed her.

'Salted caramel ice cream, Freda?' Granny asked.

'Yes, please.'

'I think I'll have one, too. David, can I buy you one?'

'No – thank you.' He stood up, although he hadn't taken a bite of his pizza. 'Well?' he asked.

Freda looked at her grandmother, and she looked back at her. 'What do you think, Freda?' she asked. 'Should we go and see Auntie Annie? Jon is just back from Uganda – I don't know if we'll be very welcome.'

'You could give her a ring,' Freda said.

'I could.' She turned to David. 'All right. My assistant here says yes, so we'll do it.'

'Thank you,' he said, and then he was gone.

The salted caramel ice cream was good, but Granny hardly ate any of hers. She didn't talk either – just sat with what Freda recognised as her thinking face – and, as soon as Freda had put her spoon down, she summoned the bill, paid it, hustled Freda out and made her almost run, with the shopping bags, to the Tube station.

There, they consulted the map. 'Change at Warren Street,' Granny said. 'The blue line and then the black line.'

The trains were crowded, and it was hard to manage the bags without spreading into other people's seats. It was also very hot, and Freda was quite glad to find, when they emerged above ground, that it was starting to spit with rain, until Granny spoilt things by saying 'This will bring your curls back, I'm afraid.'

Freda had been a couple of times to the flat Auntie Annie lived in now. It was at the top of a house, and the kitchen was part of the sitting room, she remembered, so that the flat was mainly just one big room, with sloping ceilings, and a bedroom and a shower room leading off it. And it looked as though it would burst from all the stuff in it – books, CDs and DVDs, a sound system, a TV and a computer, plants, lamps and two sofas, Jon's piano and other musical instruments, and in the kitchen there were pots and pans hanging from racks suspended from the ceiling. Granny pressed a buzzer beside the names Gray and McIntyre, and Auntie Annie's voice, sounding all tinny, said, 'I'm coming down.' While they waited, Granny said, 'I probably should have phoned first, but too late now.' The door opened, and Auntie Annie stood there in shorts and a T-shirt, and bare feet. She looked not exactly not pleased to see them, but startled at the same time.

'What's all this for?' she asked, and Granny said, 'Freda's shopping. We've been on a spree.'

Auntie Annie said, 'Oh. Lovely,' and Freda wondered if she had thought they were bringing her presents. She didn't invite them in. She dropped a kiss on Freda's head and said, 'Nice to see you, Freedie,' but then she looked at Granny and said, 'Jon's asleep. He's exhausted. I don't want to disturb him.'

'Well, I wasn't proposing to shout,' Granny said.

'Really?' Auntie Annie said. 'That'll be a first.'

'Oh really, Annie,' Granny protested, and Auntie Annie said, 'There you are! You're shouting already. We'll go to the park. Give me those bags – you can leave them here. I'll get my keys and leave Jon a note.'

Then she left them standing on the doorstep, and Granny said, 'I hope you'll be kinder to your mother, Freda, when you're grown-up.'

Auntie Annie came back, with shoes on, and said, 'We'll just go to the little gardens on the corner.'

The gardens were quite pretty, but full of people, and there were no spare benches to sit on, so they walked around while Auntie Annie asked about Nico, but not about why Freda was in London, and Granny eventually said, 'I'm here on a mission, actually. Sent by David. Police business.' And then she explained about Bimal disappearing, and about wanting to contact Isha's friends to try to find Bimal's friends.

Auntie Annie said, 'I can try, but I doubt anyone can help. Isha was very private.' Then she said, 'People leaving a bench over there,' and sprinted across the grass to bag the bench. Sitting there, they watched as she tapped in a message and sent it. 'I can only contact friends we have in common, obviously,' she said. 'People in the play, and some work colleagues. Let's see what happens.' She waved her phone. 'Watch this space. Do you want an ice cream, Freedie, while we wait for replies?' Freda was about to say, 'Yes', because you always said yes to ice cream, didn't you? But Granny said, 'She had an ice cream for lunch,' and Auntie Annie gave Freda a *Grown-ups, what can you do with them?* shrug.

'Are we expecting replies right away, then?' Granny asked.

'Sunday afternoon? You bet. Nobody will be far from their phones.'

Freda surveyed her aunt's admirably smart smartphone and sighed. She would almost have sacrificed the green dress for a decent phone. Then the first message pinged in. Auntie Annie looked at it.

'Hmm,' she said. 'The negatives are likely to come in first, I suppose.'

They sat there, then, the three of them, in a row on the bench, looking a bit odd, probably. Anyone walking by and noticing them would wonder what they were doing, sitting there in silence, she thought. *The three wise monkeys.* She didn't know what those were, actually, but at break time, when she and Charlie and Sofia managed to get the best bench, and were just sitting there chatting, if Mr Chapman was on duty he would say, 'Ah, the three wise monkeys, I see,' as he walked by, as though it was a big joke. She didn't like Mr Chapman much, and she wasn't looking forward to having him as her teacher next year. People said he was a good teacher, but he always seemed a bit sneery, and people also said that he favoured the boys, and liked teaching maths best. She was trying not to think about it.

Then three messages came through in a rush, but Auntie Annie shook her head each time, and Granny started to get restless. 'This isn't going to work, is it?' she said. 'I don't know what David was thinking of. Why should Isha's friends know about her younger brother's friends?' She looked at her watch. 'Freda and I really need to go,' she said. 'We've been invited to a party this evening.'

Freda was startled. Was this true or one of Granny's jokes? 'A party?' she asked.

'Yes. Well I've been invited – my neighbours upstairs – just drinks – a sort of welcome – and if Mum and Ben are still at the hospital, I won't leave you on your own.'

'But I haven't been invited.'

'I'll sort it out with our hostess – Melissa, she's called. She seems nice. I'm sure she'll be happy for you to come. You can wear your new dress.'

A grown-up party, in London, and wearing her expensive new dress. She was imagining telling Charlie. This almost trumped a beach in Croatia, she reckoned.

Auntie Annie looked at her watch. 'Let's give it till half past,' she said, 'and then I'll walk you back to the Tube. I can let you know if anything comes in later.'

A couple more negative replies came in before they got up and returned to the flat to pick up their shopping. As Auntie Annie walked with them to the Tube, her phone pinged again and she looked at it. 'Tom Yeoman's brother,' she said. 'Rachel, who's playing Juliet in the play, says Tom Yeoman's younger brother, Harry, is a schoolfriend of Bimal's.' Then she stopped still and said, 'That's odd,' and scrolled back through her messages. 'I'm sure Tom replied, and said he didn't know anything – yes, here it is: *Sorry, never met Bimal and can't help.* That's a bit strange, isn't it?'

'Well –' Granny said, 'I suppose Isha could have mentioned to Rachel that her brother knew Tom's brother – when they were at rehearsal, for instance – but Harry Yeoman wouldn't necessarily have mentioned Bimal to Tom, and Harry probably didn't know that his brother knew Isha. I don't think we can honestly say that's suspicious.'

'That's because you like Tom. You think he's a nice young man.'

'Isn't he?'

'He's not particularly nice around women. He's a bit of a shit, in fact – sorry, Freda.'

'Really?' Granny asked.

'Yes, he uses that nice-boy, fresh-faced image of his to lure them in, and then he dumps them. And he's had a bit of a *droit de seigneur* thing going with the women in the cast.'

Freda didn't know what the French bit meant, but she was able to follow the rest of the conversation and understand most of it.

'Really?' Granny said again.. 'Has he tried it on with you?'

'Yup. Turned up at the flat uninvited one evening, with a bottle of wine, saying I must be lonely with Jon away. Very subtle.'

'Can I ask what you said?'

'I said I was working on a brief – which I was – and suggested he took his wine to someone who wasn't busy and felt like cheating on her boyfriend.'

'And he went?'

'Oh yes. I'm not saying he's a rapist, Ma.'

'Didn't it make it awkward – with the play?'

'Somewhat. He doesn't really talk to me. That's partly why I wanted you to come to rehearsal. I needed someone to comment on my performance because he never does.'

'He's probably embarrassed.'

'Mmm.'

'Do you know for sure that he's tried it on with the other women? Perhaps he's just got a thing for you.'

'He's definitely had a grope at Rachel, and he's pretty sleazy around Susie, who's playing Mistress Overdone.'

'What about Isha? Do you think he tried anything with her?'

'Probably. I think so. He definitely fancied her. She'd never done any acting – she didn't audition. He approached her to be in the play. '

'Which doesn't make him a murderer.'

'Of course not. I didn't say it did.'

On the Tube, under her pile of bags, Freda turned to her grandmother. 'Granny,' she whispered, 'can I ask you something?'

'You can.'

'You know Auntie Annie said someone was a shit?'

'Yes, well she shouldn't use words like that in front of – '

'Well, I've heard Mum say it anyway. But what I wanted to know is, can you call a girl a shit?'

Her grandmother considered. 'Well, women – girls – can behave shittily, but we don't usually call them shits. That's for men only, I think.'

'Why?'

'I don't know, Freda.'

Back in the flat, there was no sign of Mum or Ben. Granny said she was desperate for a cup of tea, so Freda left her to it and took her purchases into the sitting room, where she shook them out and spread them around so that she could enjoy looking at them. It would do no harm, she thought, to put the green dress on now, and be ready for the party. She was suddenly nervous that it wouldn't look the same as it had in the shop – that it would be all wrong. When she had it on, she couldn't see herself in either of the big mirrors on the wall. They were quite high up, so she could see only the top of her head. She went into the bedroom where Mum and Ben had been sleeping and looked for a mirror in there. She couldn't see one immediately, but then she remembered the big wardrobe in the room where she and Nico slept in Italy, which had a mirror inside the door, and she opened a cupboard door, and sure enough there she was – green dress and silver sandals, her hair a bit curly but not too bad. She twirled, so that the skirt of her dress twirled with her.

'Goodness! You gave me a shock. I didn't realise you were in here.'

Granny was standing in the doorway, and she had a funny expression on her face.

'You look so grown-up,' she said.

'I think I look like a fairy.'

'OK, Titania. Off you hop, and let me see what I can find to wear that won't disgrace you.'

While she waited, Freda took a couple of selfies – her phone could at least do that – but decided not to send them to Charlie until she could tell her about the party itself. Eventually Granny appeared from the bedroom, wearing a rather disappointingly plain blue dress and saying, 'I decided to leave all the glory to you, and I do, at least, feel slim in this.'

They had to go out of Granny's flat and ring the buzzer at the house's big front door to be let in to the flat upstairs where the party was happening. The woman who greeted them there was very blonde, and tanned, as though she spent a lot of time in the sun. She was wearing a white dress and a gold necklace, and made Granny look a bit dowdy by comparison. She was very nice when Granny explained that Freda was staying with her, and asked if Freda would like sparkling elderflower to drink. Freda said, 'Yes, thank you,' although she had no idea whether she would like it or not. It was actually rather delicious – like lemonade, but more flowery. The only problem was that this was a walking-about party, and Granny was taken around and introduced to people, with Freda tagging along and trying not to spill her drink on her dress. Each time they were introduced, people said 'Hello, Freda' quite nicely, but then they talked over the top of her head, so she thought she would sit down for a bit and finish her drink.

Looking for a quiet corner, she spotted a cat, asleep on a wide window ledge, so she went over and hoisted herself up onto the ledge, and sat there comfortably, stroking the cat, which didn't really wake up, but purred quietly. She realised that she hadn't thought at all about their own cat, Ariel, who was back at home in Marlbury. She had been Granny's cat when Granny lived by the sea, but she had come to live with them when Granny moved to London. Now she had been at home on her own for a week, with just Martha, their neighbour, going in to feed her. Freda wondered if they would get back to find that she had run away to find something better. She wouldn't blame her.

From where she was sitting, she could survey the party. First of all, the room, which was not cosy, like Granny's sitting room, but rather shiny, with glass coffee tables and a glass chandelier that seemed to be made of tiny bottles. Then there were the people. It was odd to watch people without being able to hear what they were saying – all those mouths opening and closing – and to see Granny, smiling and laughing with all these strangers, as though she knew them. She turned her attention back to the cat, and then noticed that Granny had come to sit on a sofa near the window. 'I have to take the weight off my shopping feet,' she said, over her shoulder, to Freda. 'Shouldn't have worn these shoes.' She leaned back and closed her eyes, and Freda could see, suddenly, how tired she was, and how her face slid downwards somehow when she wasn't smiling or laughing. And she only had a moment to close her eyes, because the next minute, a woman with red hair, wearing long, wide trousers, came and sat beside her. 'You've got the right idea,' she said, and when Granny opened her eyes and sat up straight, she added, 'I'm Beth. I live around the corner. You've got the garden flat here, I gather.'

Freda saw her grandmother put on her party face – as though invisible strings were pulling it upwards. 'Gina,' she said. 'Yes, I've got the garden, but it does mean I am, essentially, living underground.'

The woman laughed. 'I'd have liked the garden flat where we are,' she said, 'but it was too small. We still have teenagers living at home. We need as much space as we can get our hands on.'

Freda watched Granny lean forward and pick up a bowl of nuts and offer it to Beth. 'You live around the corner?' she said. 'Are you in one of those lovely houses in Russell Place?'

'Yes, Woburn Court. We were lucky to get it before prices really went crazy.'

'Isn't that where that awful murder happened? I don't remember the young woman's – '

'Isha,' Beth said, 'Isha Anand. Yes.'

So why, Freda asked herself, did Granny pretend that she didn't know Isha's name when she knew it perfectly well? When she was helping the police about her murder? She was being sly, somehow, but why?'

'That must have been terribly distressing,' Granny said, and Freda thought she sounded like an actress. Granny never normally said things like *terribly distressing*.

'It was,' Beth said. 'Still is, actually. I'm really surprised at how long it's taking me to get over it.'

'Did you know her?' Granny asked.

There was a pause while Melissa, the hostess, came by and offered a plate of little pancakes with smoked salmon on them. They each took one, as did Freda. She wasn't keen on smoked salmon, but she thought the cat would enjoy it. Then Beth said, 'I didn't know her, really. I hate the way people claim to know someone as soon as they're in the news. We used to say hello as we passed on the stairs, that's all. She was a different generation, not much older than my kids – though she did always seem very grown-up. No wild parties or anything like that.'

'The perfect neighbour.'

'Well, yes. There was just–' Beth stopped, swirled the drink in her glass round, and then swallowed it in one gulp. 'There was just one odd thing – only a day or two before she died. I have sometimes wondered if I should have told the police, but it was something and nothing, you know…'

Freda knew that her grandmother's ears would be pricking up, although she stayed looking perfectly casual.

'I can see it's bothering you,' she said. 'These things nag away, don't they?'

'They do,' Beth said. 'Absolutely.' She held out her glass as a man went by with a bottle of wine in his hand, and he refilled it. 'My husband says it was nothing,' she went on, after she had taken a good swig, 'but what it was – a package for Isha was delivered to me by mistake – slack postman, you know. I found it when I got back from work, but Isha wasn't home then, so I took it down to her later. She didn't answer when I rang the bell, but I felt sure she was in because I could hear a radio or TV on, so I rang again, and eventually she came to the door, but she looked terrible. She was usually very smart – very young professional, you know – but she was all over the place. That lovely, glossy hair was all dishevelled, and she had obviously been crying, and her mascara was all smudged I asked if she was all right and she said, 'Yes,' but then she just sort of crumpled to the ground. It was quite awkward, there in the doorway. I thought she could do with a stiff drink – or at least a cup of tea, if she didn't drink – I wasn't sure, you know, about her religion, and if … Anyway, I didn't think I could barge into her flat and start putting the kettle on, so I more or less hauled her up, and persuaded her to come to my place. Brian was out at a work do, and the boys were in their rooms – homework supposedly, but probably not – so I sat her down and offered her booze or tea and she opted for tea. I didn't ask her any questions, and she just sipped her tea. She was shivering, so I fetched a pashmina for her. Maybe I should have asked her what was wrong, but I didn't want to intrude, you know? So, we just sat there. She stopped crying, and shivering, and eventually she gave the pashmina back and said she felt much better, and she got up to go. I went down to her flat with her, and at the door she thanked me and said something about needing to declare something, and that she'd got it clear in her mind now. I didn't ask her what she meant – I felt she wasn't really talking to me. And then I went back upstairs and shouted at the boys about their homework – what do we pay the school fees for? I ask myself – and I didn't think about it again, until I heard that she'd been killed.'

'No wonder you're still upset,' Granny said, all sympathetic again. 'Did the police talk to all the neighbours – afterwards?'

'Yes. And they asked me when I had last seen her, and I told them about taking the package down, but not about her being upset. I don't know why not – it seemed private, somehow, you know, and not something to rake up now she was dead. And we all thought it was a random killing – racist, you know, with all the Brexit nastiness – so it didn't seem relevant, but I have been wondering whether I should go to the police about it, even now – only Brian says not. He's a lawyer. He says they could charge me with perverting the course of justice.'

Freda watched her grandmother thinking. The sympathetic expression stayed on her face, but she was very still. Then she said, 'As it happens, I have a good friend who's a senior officer with the Met. I know he's had a bit to do with Isha's case. If you like, I could pass this on, unofficially, and then, you know, it'll be out there. He might want to talk to you himself, but it could be quite low key – and I'm sure you wouldn't be charged with anything.'

The woman groped in her bag and produced a small white card. 'That would be brilliant,' she said. 'This is me – *Beth Hart-Carpenter, Interesting Interiors*. What a relief bumping into you!'

As her grandmother tucked the card away in her bag, Freda thought that there might be more than one way of being a witch.

# Chapter Sixteen

## PRO BONO

*Monday 1st August 2016*

The morning starts with Freda coming into my room to pinch-punch me the first of the month, and I realise that, for the first time in weeks, I have slept late. She is all of a bustle to be up and off to collect Nico. I warn her that getting discharged from a hospital takes forever, with forms to be signed and medication to be collected and explained, but I get up nevertheless. I find Ellie and Ben already at the breakfast table, and while I am still reviving myself with my first sips of coffee, they are gathering their bags and packing them into Ben's car, which has stood undriven in my resident's parking space for the past week.

There is a plan: Ellie, Ben and Freda will walk round to the hospital and wait there until Nico is about to be released. Then Ben will come back for the car, and I will go with him to the hospital so that I can wave them all off as they depart for Kent. This is an excellent plan, as far as it goes, but it does not take account of my need to complete my task of the day, which is to talk to Cressida Long and find out more about Isha Anand's life. So I am relieved to get a call from Ellie to tell me that Nico won't be discharged until mid-afternoon at the earliest – results of final blood tests have to be awaited. This is bad news for them, but it enables me to get on with my day.

I am tempted to strip the sheets from my bed and reclaim my bedroom, but I restrain myself, feeling that Fate is lurking about and waiting to be tempted by any precipitous move. Instead, I ring Annie. I heard once more from her yesterday. She texted to say that Asmil Anand had responded to her text message, saying that he could, of course, be counted as a friend of Bimal's, since he was his cousin, but that was the only further response she had had. Thin pickings, but I passed his name on to David, together with Harry Yeoman's. While David does the official stuff, I want to talk not just to Tom Yeoman and Asmil Anand, but also to the other people in the *Measure for Measure* cast, in case I can find out more about Isha's life from them.

I am breezy and casual with Annie.

'I just wondered,' I say, 'if you're having a run-through in the next couple of days, and if you'd like me to come along.'

'Really?' she says.

'Yes. Unless you don't want – '

'No, no. Tomorrow evening. Do come. You haven't seen the final scene.'

'Which is a nightmare, I imagine.'

'Pretty much. Any suggestions would be gratefully received, I think.'

'I don't want Tom to feel I'm interfering.'

'Tom can get stuffed.'

'OK, then. See you tomorrow.'

Fine. Now I have to address the question of what pretext I find for approaching Cressida Long. Even I, the queen of *chutzpah*, haven't the nerve to pretend that I was a friend of Isha's or that I am on the police team – both claims that would crumble under the most superficial examination, let alone one carried out by a competent lawyer. And even I can see that using Annie's name to gain access would be embarrassing for all concerned. So, what to do?

I make some more coffee and sit with it in the garden, and it is possibly the influence of my surroundings, as natural as central London allows – birdsong and a gentle breeze – that draws me to the unusual idea that telling the truth might be the answer. Or a version of the truth. I shall ring Cressida Long's chambers and explain to her – or to her clerk, if necessary – that, in my capacity as a linguistics expert, I have been consulted by the police team investigating Isha Anand's death, with regard to a document that may provide significant evidence. It might help me in my analysis of the document to know more about Isha's professional life, and I am wondering if Ms Long, among others, could find time to talk to me briefly. Well, it is almost true, isn't it?

I go to my computer, google the chambers, find the phone number, and ring. I am disconcerted when the clerk who answers turns out to be female – not the crusty cynic of television legal dramas, but a pleasant, youngish-sounding woman. I give her my rigmarole, and she says that she will relay my message and that Ms Long will, she is sure, be in touch in due course. This is all very well, but I am not patient; in due course won't do.

'It is quite urgent,' I say, mildly. 'I understand that the police are concerned for the safety of another person, so time is of the essence.'

I can picture David's fury if he ever finds out that I have said this, but needs must, I think, and I get the desired effect.

'I'll just see…' the clerk says, and suddenly I am speaking to Cressida Long herself, and she is saying, 'How soon can you get here?'

'Fifteen minutes,' I say, and I gather my bag and my wits and run out to find a taxi.

I have no trouble locating the chambers, since they are next door to Annie's, but for the same reason I skulk a bit, anxious not to be seen by her. A shiny brass plaque bears eight or nine names, including *Ms Cressida Long*. The clerk inside turns out not to be as young as her voice suggested, but she is cordial and shows me the winding way to Cressida Long's room, which is decorated in Georgian green with white trimmings; it is fresher, and contains less polished oak than I expected.

I had no clear expectation of what Cressida Long herself would be like, but I suppose the harassment case predisposed me to expect someone slightly fragile. If so, I was wrong. She turns out to be a tallish, wiry woman, with neat, crisply curling, iron grey hair and a lean, rather leathery face that speaks to me of weekends spent sailing. She shakes hands, ushers me to a chair and, without preamble, asks, 'So, what can I do for you?'

I am flustered. I haven't, I realise, prepared myself for this. Once again, I am bounced into telling the truth.

'I teach in the Linguistics department at SOAS,' I say, 'and I was approached by the police to look at a letter – an anonymous letter concerning Isha Anand, sent shortly before her death. It is unsigned, and they wanted my view on the likely author – age, gender, education and so on.'

I pause. She says nothing.

'So…' I say, groping for where to go from here.

She leans forward across her desk. 'Why you?' she asks.

'I'm sorry?'

'Why were you asked? The Met has its own experts for this kind of thing, doesn't it?'

Now I feel snappy. 'Well, I don't know,' I say. 'I was asked, so I took it on. On the principle that saying no to the police is rarely a good idea.'

'Are they paying you?' she asks.

'No,' I say. 'It's an act of citizenship.'

She smiles. 'I take it you have a personal connection with someone at the Met?' she says.

Damn the woman. Has she rumbled the whole thing?

'One of the officers on the case is an acquaintance of mine,' I say.

'Yes,' she says.

'Anyway,' I plough on, 'there are indications in the letter to give me a likely profile, but the main thing is that the writer is clearly someone who knew Isha Anand quite well, so I am trying to get a sense of the people who were close to her, and that includes work colleagues.'

She leans back. 'Well, I wasn't close to her,' she says. 'I'm a senior barrister and she was doing her pupillage.'

'Oh, I understand that, of course,' I say. 'But your name was given to me because she worked on the Jake Steel case with you.'

Her face tightens. 'Is there any indication that Isha's death is connected with that case?' she asks. 'Because, if so – your phone message said that the police were concerned about the safety of someone else. Is that someone me? Is this by way of a warning that I may be in danger?'

*Oh God, what have I got into here?*

'No, no!' I protest. 'No, nothing like that. I'm afraid I was trying to get your attention. I mean, someone else might be at risk but it's not … I'm so sorry, I didn't mean to alarm you. It's just –'

She picks up her phone, and I am convinced that she is about to call the Met.

'Would you like a cup of coffee?' she asks.

'Do you have decaff?' I ask, weakly. I am jittery enough. I should probably ask if they have any camomile.

'Emma,' she says into her phone, 'could we have a couple of coffees here, do you think – one decaff?'

'I was surprised by your clerk,' I say, by way of chit-chat to lighten the tone. 'I thought all clerks were crusty middle-aged men.'

'Emma's not our clerk,' she says.' She's our receptionist. Martin is our clerk. He's a crusty middle-aged man.'

She doesn't smile, so I don't either.

When the coffee comes, we sip in silence. Then she says, 'Now, would you like to start again?'

'Thank you,' I say. I am meek now. 'The thing is, this letter that I've been asked to look at was clearly written by someone close to Isha, and it has a distinctive idiolect, so – '

'*Idiolect?*' she enquires.

'Individuality of linguistic style.'

'Right.'

'So, it would help me, of course, if I could talk to the people who were close to her and see if I can spot similarities – speech patterns and so on.'

This sounds thin, even to me, and she is on to it. 'But speech patterns and written style are different, aren't they?' she says.

'They are, of course,' I concede, 'but we do find overlap.' I am pleased with *we find*, and hope it manages to suggest that I am right there in on-the-ground research.

'This letter – was it a threat?' she asks.

'No. A warning.'

'But a warning can be a disguised threat, can't it?' she says, and I remember that she has probably been the recipient of some of those recently.

'This reads like a genuine warning.'

'All right.' She leans back and waits for me to carry on.

I try a new tack. 'Was Isha popular here in chambers?' I ask.

'Popular? She was pleasant and competent. I really can't say more than that.'

'Did you think of keeping her on here at the end of her pupillage?'

'I don't remember it being discussed.'

'Why not?'

'We're not looking to take on anyone new at the moment.'

'But she was offered a place elsewhere?'

'Yes. At St Albans Court, I believe.'

'Are they good – well thought of?'

She smiles for the first time, revealing rather stained teeth.

'Excellent,' she says. 'Would you expect me to say anything else about neighbouring chambers?'

'They're next door?'

'Two doors down. She did apply to the chambers next door, but nothing came of it, I think.'

'She was turned down?'

'I really don't know. I did ask her about it, as she was working on a case of mine at the time, but she just said she had decided to go to St Albans Court instead.'

'Could there have been prejudice against her?'

'Prejudice?'

'As an Asian woman.'

'I think you need to adjust your own prejudices,' she says. 'The bar isn't any longer the domain of white men.'

'Although I did pass a lot of those on my way in here,' I say.

'It takes time,' she says. 'Talking of which,' – here she looks at her watch – 'I really need to be getting on.'

And with that I am shown the door.

I have very little to report to David from this encounter, except that Cressida Long's answers were so bland that they have made me suspicious. She was like a witness primed by a good counsel to answer the questions put to her in court without actually giving anything away. Isha was pleasant and competent at work; the only reason she was not offered a place in their chambers was that they weren't recruiting; there is no racial or gender bias at the bar any more; the St Albans Court chambers are excellent. *Why is she lying to me?*

Annoyed at having nothing more than suspicion to report to David, I go on the attack.

'Are you alone?' I ask, when he answers his phone.

'I am. And you are out in the street. Where are you?'

'On my way back from seeing Cressida Long.'

'Anything from her?'

'Never mind that now. Have you found Bimal?'

'No.'

'Well, why not? What are the bloody police for if they let a vulnerable seventeen-year-old get snatched from under their noses and then can't find him?'

'We are following up several leads.'

'Which is code for *we're running around like headless chickens*. Did you get anything useful from Tom Yeoman or Asmil Anand?'

'Possibly. Now, have you rung up to tell me anything or just to shout at me, because – '

'Does Bimal's uncle know he's missing?'

'Yes.'

'And?'

'His staff are checking whether Bimal made any calls to the UK from his home there, and he is coming over.'

'If he kicks up a real fuss, you could lose your job, couldn't you?'

'Thank you for pointing that out.'

'Well, why are you being so feeble? You sound so – laid back about it all. Is there something you're not telling me?'

'What possible reason could I have for not telling you absolutely everything that is going on in this very sensitive case?'

'One reason for telling me everything might be that I am busting a gut trying to help you. What are your lot doing? Why hasn't anyone tracked down the computer or phone those sexting messages originally came from? I appreciate that it's been the weekend, and all your techies have probably been sitting at home in the dark, watching back-to-back episodes of *Star Trek,* but it's Monday now, and unless there's a special techy holiday I don't know about, I would have thought that this was urgent enough to – '

'Gina,' he says. 'How is Nico?'

'What? Nico's fine. Why do you … Nico's fine. He's going home today. They're all at the hospital waiting for him to be discharged.'

'Well, that's good news, isn't it?'

'Of course it is.'

'But now you're going back to an empty flat, and the drama is over, and you are going to obsess about the case.'

'David, you asked me to do this! And anyway, why aren't you obsessing about it, when your job's on the line?'

'I obsess differently from you. And, yes, I did ask you to get involved, but now I'm standing you down.'

'You're what?' I manage to say this right into the face of a man who is passing me, and he looks as though he might punch me.

'I'm standing you down. We're handling it now. I don't need you.'

I am so outraged that I have to stand still to shout at him.

'How bloody dare you?' I yell. '*Standing me down?* You don't get to tell me what I can and can't do.'

'Well, I do, actually, because this is my case.'

'Which you've been at pains to tell me wasn't your case. As a justification for doing bugger all and getting me to do unpaid work for you.'

'Yes. But now it's my case and we're dealing with it, and you can go off and do something else.'

'And supposing I don't want to?'

He doesn't answer, and I think I've lost him. Then he says, 'It's not safe, Gina. There are things we know now that we didn't know before, and you're not safe getting any more involved.'

'What things? What do you know?'

'I can't tell you. Not yet. But this isn't a game. The guy is dangerous. Take a step back.'

'I suppose it's all right to go to Annie's rehearsal tomorrow? Will your suspect be there?'

'Probably.'

'I was going to do a bit of probing.'

'Don't. Go to the rehearsal, if you must, but concentrate on dramatic criticism. Nothing more.'

'If you know who the killer is, why haven't you arrested him?'

'We're gathering evidence.'

'And if I talk to people, I might get you your evidence.'

'No! I'm serious, Gina. For once, listen to me. If you go blundering in there you could wreck everything, as well as putting yourself in danger. All right?'

'All right,' I mutter. 'All sodding right.'

# Chapter Seventeen

## ARTICLES OF ASSOCIATION

*Tuesday 2nd August 2016*

I won't bother you with a tedious account of the domestic trivia with which I have distracted myself since my conversation with David – the stripping of beds, the washing of sheets, the planned restoration of the kitchen to its *status quo ante*, the discarding of outdated food and, when all else has failed, the half-hearted attempt to impose order on my rampant garden. They have distracted, but not enough. Whatever I may have said to David, I know that he doesn't scaremonger without a reason. If he thinks I am in danger, then I probably am, and I am jumpy and bad-tempered in consequence, working myself up into a rage against him. Wouldn't knowledge make me safer? If I knew where the danger was coming from, wouldn't I – possibly – find it easier not to bump into it? If going to the rehearsal tonight is dangerous, then is Annie in danger, too? Why can't he tell me what's going on? Once, just once, I let slip a piece of information in one of his cases. How long ago? Freda was a baby, so ten years ago, nearly. Is he never going to trust me again?

Well, you will have noticed that I haven't told him about Isha's neighbour, Beth Hart-Carpenter, and the story she told me about finding Isha in tears. I know I told her I would pass it on, and if David hadn't used the phrase *blundering in*, I would have done, but as it is he can just do it his way, and let's see how far that gets him.

By the time I am dressing to go off to the rehearsal, I am jittery and sick – partly, I realise, because I haven't felt like eating anything. The sky, as I start walking towards Gray's Inn, has a mustardy tinge to it that threatens thunder, and my head has started to ache with a nagging throb over my right eye. I feel vulnerable, weary and pissed off in more or less equal measure. Even the people who pass me on the pavement seem bent on harassing me, but then I should probably stop scowling at them.

We gather, as ever, under the tree in the green and pleasant courtyard, but everyone seems odd. Maybe it is the effect of the lurid sky, which is casting a sickly, greenish light onto people's faces through the tree's spreading leaves, but I am reminded suddenly of the effect you see in some TV whodunnits of the Agatha Christie variety: the colour goes monochrome, and ordinary faces are caught in expressions of exaggerated suspicion, anger and fear. I should have eaten some supper; hypoglycaemia is playing tricks with me.

Or is it? Tom Yeoman has definitely cut me. He saw me and looked straight through me. Does he resent my being here? Did Annie not square it with him? Or have the police questioned him about Bimal? In which case, does he hold Annie and me responsible? *Tom can get stuffed,* Annie said. Maybe she told him so to his face and I am just collateral damage from that encounter. I could believe this, except that he is not alone in his unfriendliness. Piers Upton, our pretty Claudio, greets me rudely, with 'What are you doing here again?' and I have twice caught Lyle Fenton, slimy Angelo, watching me with a narrow-eyed, unfathomable expression on his face. Only Asmil Anand appears normal, talking about Bimal and asking if I know whether the police have made any progress. Annie is nervous and snappy, but at least I am used to that.

I watch out hopefully for Roderick; if he is also odd, then I will know I'm in trouble. But he arrives at the last minute and is on stage immediately, so all I can do is watch and wait. And as I watch, I can see that there is something wrong not just with the people but with their performances, as well, and that – surely – can't be anything to do with me.

Roderick starts off all right, with his usual crispness and control, but Lyle Fenton is completely off his game, losing lines and hardly putting in a performance at all. The chap playing Escalus, the Duke's old advisor, has always been a bit weak, so the scene feels lopsided. The Duke is supposed to be handing power over to Angelo – with some help from Escalus – because he has failed to get a grip on the city's morals and thinks it's time for a new broom, but Roderick's energy and polish would make any audience wonder what on earth this super-competent ruler is doing by throwing everything up and leaving Vienna to be run by a pair of incompetents. He isn't really giving off the air of a man who fears, deep down, that he has failed in his office, and Lyle certainly doesn't have the aura of the zealot who believes that he alone can cleanse the city of corruption. True, Angelo protests that he is too inexperienced for the job, but you need to see that he doesn't really mean it. Lyle, who is unappealing (to me, at least) in everyday life precisely because of his air of invincible superiority, can't manage to fake it this evening at all.

Roderick does at least drive that scene on. It is when we get to the next one that I really start to worry. It is a comic scene, set among the city low-lifes, involving Asmil as the rake, Lucio, a couple of unnamed gentlemen and Mistress Overdone, the brothel-keeper, with her pimp, Pompey. It depends for its humour almost entirely on an unending supply of jokes about the hilarious subject of venereal disease, so you can see that it might take a bit of work to make it actually funny. It is not remotely funny today. The thing that is needed, to get away with a scene like this, is rapid-fire banter together with the speed and energy of a confidence trickster. Then you just might be able to make the audience believe that they should be laughing. We have none of that today. In fact, we have the reverse. The moves, the cues, the very words are so sluggish that the actors seem to be performing in slow-mo action replay – or possibly under water, or in outer space. Even Asmil is devoid of his usual Lucio swagger. I sneak a look at Tom Yeoman. He has his eyes closed.

I move to sit next to Annie, who is watching from some distance away.

'What's happened to them?' I hiss.

She turns to look at me and I can see a struggle in her face. She is worried, so I know she would like either to argue with me and say there is nothing the matter, or to agree that things are wrong and find a way to blame me for it. Eventually, she says, 'The police have been in chambers most of the day – questioning people and searching offices. They've taken some of the computers away.'

*So, I was right. David does have a lead that he's not telling me about. Damn him.*

'Have they only been to your chambers?' I ask.

'Yup.'

'And how many of the cast are in your chambers?'

'Lyle, Asmil, Piers. And Emma and Simon.'

'Emma and Simon?'

'Those two – doing Mistress Overdone and Pompey.'

'Not Tom?'

'No. He's at the chambers where Isha was. I don't understand why the police aren't swarming all over them rather than us.'

'Mm,' I say. And I think, *Asmil, Lyle, Piers – and what about this Simon, who is a completely unknown quantity?*

At this point, Piers enters – Claudio being led to prison for the crime of getting his girlfriend pregnant. Is it my imagination or is there a personal edge to his railing against *the demigod Authority?* Personal or not, his tone is whiny and petulant in a way that makes me quite happy to see him banged up, and I'm not sure any of the audience will be rooting for his release in a hurry. They really are an unlikeable bunch, the men in this production. I thought Tom Yeoman was all right, but Annie told me he is a predator. The best word for Lyle Fenton is supercilious. Do you know the original meaning of supercilious? It means eyebrowish – from the Latin for eyebrow – *supercilium* – so it means going around with your eyebrows raised in haughty disdain. Well, that's Lyle Fenton for you. And then there's Pretty Piers, so self-regarding, so entitled. Couldn't any one of them have turned killer if their vanity was punctured by rejection?

Annie goes backstage now, to wait for her first scene, and Roderick is back on, picking things up a bit, and then we move on, via another drearily unfunny comic scene, to the first encounter between Angelo and Isabella. I have low expectations. The two scenes between them were terrific last time I saw them, but I can't believe that they can be so again, in this soggy atmosphere. I am right, and the scene doesn't hit the heights, but it is good enough. Annie is clear, passionate and poised, and she seems to steady Lyle, who is more secure on his lines and properly focused. This is all right. And it gets better. They manoeuvre through their second encounter admirably, with Lyle's Angelo negotiating his way towards his sleazy bargain – Claudio's life in exchange for sex with Isabella – and Annie, clever but innocent, taking Isabella to outraged realisation and passionate denunciation:

*Seeming, seeming!*
*I will proclaim thee, Angelo; look for't.*
*Sign me a present pardon for my brother,*
*Or with an outstretch'd throat I'll tell the world aloud*
*What man thou art.*

And then I see it. I understand. As Lyle starts his reply – *Who will believe thee, Isabel?* – I turn it over and I am sure I am right. I don't know everything, but I know why, at least. I look from Lyle to Annie and I realise that she is looking at me. She has seen the look on my face and she is frozen by it. I wave a hand in front of me as if dispelling a cloud of flies, but she has seen me, and she knows I know. When Lyle finishes his speech with the abuser's mantra, *My false outweighs your true,* and exits, leaving Annie with her final soliloquy, she stumbles for the first time this evening. *O perilous tongues,* she says, instead of *perilous mouths,* and then comes to *self-same tongue,* at the end of the line, and hesitates, registering her mistake and losing her rhythm, so that she is in no fit state to manage the wretchedly difficult couplet,

*Then Isabel, live chaste, and, brother, die*
*More than our brother is our chastity.*

The lines emerge clunky and unconvincing. Others have noticed her sudden lapse. One or two are looking at me. Did anyone else see my face when she did? What did they read there, if so? Is it obvious that Annie knows that I know? Is she safe? Am I safe?

She exits unhappily, and I sit waiting to see if she will come and talk to me. She does not. Even when we take a break at the end of the next scene, she avoids me. I would like to go home. I want to think, and I want to talk to David, but I also don't want to arouse suspicion, and I did tell Annie I would watch the last scene, so I do. I take in very little, however, as my busy brain pursues the ramifications of what I have understood. The final scene is predictably a shambles, but I have no suggestions to make. The storm that has been threatening has not yet broken, but it will at any moment; the air is so thick you can taste it. No-one feels the rehearsal has gone well. They pack up almost in silence, and though they are clearly heading for the wine bar, no-one – not even

Roderick – invites me to join them. How could I, anyway, knowing what I know? I can't extricate Annie from the group; I have to trust that she is not in danger. With a vague wave, which is mostly ignored, I go to hail the safety of a taxi and get home before the rain.

At home, though, I can't relax. I shouldn't have left Annie. There is a killer in that group, and I am afraid I have put him on the alert. For want of anything more constructive to do, I ring David with a view to shouting at him.

'Scott,' he barks on the first ring. He was obviously waiting for a call, but not from me.

'Good evening,' I say.

'Gina. I can't talk now. I need the line clear.'

'Because you're nearing a dénouement?' I ask. 'Am I allowed to ask what you found on the computers from Annie's chambers, and if you've made an arrest yet?'

'I'm dealing with a bunch of lawyers here, Gina. I have to go strictly by the book. They put up quite a fight about the search warrant this morning. So I'm not making an arrest until I've got hard evidence.'

'But meanwhile I'm in danger?'

'Where are you?'

'At home. Back safely from the dangerous rehearsal. Where, by the way, I think I realised what – '

'Stay at home. Don't open your door. I'll talk to you in the morning.'

And he rings off.

# Chapter Eighteen

## FREDA

*Wednesday 3rd August 2016*

'Couldn't I just write her a letter,' Freda asked. 'I could write a really, really nice one on that paper I had for my birthday.'

'You wrote her a letter before, remember?' her mother said, as she stacked breakfast plates in the dishwasher. 'That's what you're apologising for.'

'I wish I could tell her it was me who worked out where Jasper was. That would even things up. Then I wouldn't even have to apologise for running away – she would have to thank me instead.'

Her mother turned away from the dishwasher and looked at her. 'We talked about that,' she said. 'We agreed that we couldn't tell her that without telling her that Grandpa got Ted to steal Jasper. And that would cause too much upset – for Auntie Lavender and for the boys.'

'It was Granny who did a deal with Grandpa,' Freda objected. 'She said she wouldn't tell Lavender about it if he got Jasper back home. I never promised. I don't see why he should get away with it. It's not fair.'

*It's not fair.* Even as she said it she could hear how whiny and babyish that sounded. But it wasn't fair, all the same.

'And would it be fair to Auntie Lavender to tell her?' her mother asked, sitting down at the table to start writing a shopping list. 'Does she deserve to be hurt and disappointed?'

'Well, she was silly to marry him. That was her mistake.'

'Well, Granny made the same mistake, didn't she? But he's not all bad, you know. He helps people in his work. One day, when you know a bit more, you'll be proud of him.'

'I won't ever be proud of a dog-kidnapper.'

'We'll see.'

Freda watched her mother as she wrote her list.

'You're sure Grandpa won't be there, aren't you?'

'Positive. He's in Turkey.'

'Well, all right.' Freda got up from the table. 'Cos I'm not apologising to him under any circumstances. He ought to apologise to me.'

Her mother laughed. 'Well, that's not going to happen. I shouldn't think he's ever apologised to anyone in his life.'

She added a couple of items to her list and then said, 'Mind you, Granny's not a big apologiser, either.'

'Which is probably why they couldn't be married to each other,' Freda said.

'Out of the mouths of babes,' said her mother, which Freda didn't understand because Mum must have meant Nico, but he wasn't even there.

'Well, if I'm not a good apologiser,' she said, 'it's obviously not my fault. It's in my genes.'

She looked at her mother, still bent over her list, and said with as much semblance of casualness as she could manage, 'Was my dad any good at saying he was sorry, I wonder?'

Her mother looked up, and Freda saw a blush spread up into her face. 'I don't know, Freda,' she said. 'I didn't get a chance to find out.'

She went back to her list, but then pushed it away and looked at Freda. 'We're not just our genes, you know, There's such a thing as nurture as well as nature.'

'What's *nurture*?'

'How you're brought up. What you're taught. Look at Ben. He doesn't have any trouble apologising, does he?'

Freda considered this, and it struck her that Ben's greeting, when he came to pick her up from somewhere, was more likely to be *Sorry* than *Hello*, because he was so often late, always rushing to try to fit in one extra thing. The thought made her smile.

'I wish Monika was still at Aren't-We-Grand Hall,' she said. 'I'd like to see her.'

'Isn't she there any more?'

'No. She texted me. After they blamed her for me running away she was really fed up, and her friend in London told her about a job in a family near her, so she's gone there. She says it's much better. She texted, *So I ran away to London too.*'

'Maybe you could see her next time you go to stay with Granny.'

Freda felt suddenly more cheerful. 'All right,' she said. 'I'm going to put my new dress on to make me strong for coping with Auntie Lavender, and then let's go.'

Crunching up the drive of Aren't-We-Grand Hall, however, her courage started to seep away. 'I wish you'd told Auntie Lavender I was coming,' she said. 'Then she'd have been prepared.'

'I thought that would make it awkward, if she was here waiting for the apology. So, I just said I'd be popping in to pick up your things, and then she'll be surprised and pleased to get you, and the apology, and the chocolates.'

Freda looked at the box of Belgian chocolates in her lap and resented them. Mum had insisted that she paid for them out of her birthday money, and the deep unfairness of this rankled alongside all the other unfairness. But then, here was Auntie Lavender, dressed in a floaty skirt and pink sandals, running out to the car, with Jasper leaping around her, and saying what a lovely surprise it was to see her, and those were her very favourite chocolates, and how did she know? And then they were ushered through into the flower garden, while Nico went off to play with Arthur and Hubert.

Mum looked a bit anxious as the boys approached, and said, 'You know he's only just out of hospital, Lavender. I mean, he's all right, but he's not up to rough games.'

Lavender smiled. She did seem very cheerful, Freda thought, and younger somehow – less worried.

'You need to meet Emily,' Lavender said, as a cheerful-looking young woman with a mop of curly hair appeared behind the boys. 'Emily, meet my stepdaughter, Eleanor, and her daughter, Freda. And this rascal is Nico. He has just had a serious heart operation, so can you make sure the boys don't rough him up?'

Emily smiled. 'A game of statues, I think,' she said. 'And then we'll go in and work on our Lego creation.'

Lavender watched them go through to the play garden. 'When Monika left,' she said, 'I decided to bite the bullet and do things properly, so I rang a Norland agency.'

'Norland?'

'Don't tell me you've never heard of Norland nannies, Ellie? You and your mother are so alike – you're impossible to impress. Norland nannies are the cream – employed by royalty and superstars. Terribly expensive, of course, but I told Andrew this is our children's future we're talking about. At the moment they look as if they're growing up to be little savages and, after all, it won't be long before we'll be paying prep school fees for them, and then the Abbey School, so we might as well get used to it.'

'Do the boys like her?' Freda asked.

'They do, darling. They really do. She is very firm, and Arthur resisted at first, but within forty-eight hours he was a different child. And, of course, if he doesn't play up, then

Hubert doesn't either. And she's fun. If they follow her rules, they have a lovely time.' Lavender beamed at them. 'Coffee, Ellie? Apple juice with ice, Freda? And I think we might open those chocolates.'

She went into the house and Freda whispered, 'She hasn't given me a chance to say sorry. Will the chocolates do?'

Ellie looked at her. 'I'll try to make a moment,' she said. 'Take it when it comes.'

Lavender returned with a tray, talking as she came.

'The other great thing about Norland nannies,' she said, 'is that they're combat trained.'

Freda had an alarming picture of Emily in a helmet and army uniform, and from the startled way her mum asked, 'Really, Lavender?' she thought she probably had the same.

Lavender set down the tray. 'Well, maybe not combat,' she said, 'but self-defence and anti-kidnap techniques. I feel the children are much safer now – it was so scary when Jasper went missing. I was sure they'd be coming after the children next.'

'But nobody kidnapped Jasper, really, did they Aun –' Freda started to say, but her mum stopped her with a frown.

'Freda has something she wants to say to you, Lavender. Haven't you, Freda?' she prompted.

Freda took in a breath. 'I'm very sorry that I went off without telling you, Auntie Lavender, and caused you worry. It was very rude,' she said, and then looked at her feet.

Lavender put an arm around her. 'I do understand,' she said. 'I didn't realise how worried you were about Nico. And I'm only used to little children, you know – I thought if we didn't talk about Nico then you wouldn't think about him and worry, but I should have seen how anxious you were. Only the boys were being such little beasts, you know, and then there was Jasper disappearing, and Andrew – well, you know…'

She tailed off, and Freda thought for a moment that she was going to cry.

'Really, it was my fault,' she said. 'And I'm sorry I got Monika into trouble.'

'Oh, poor Monika,' Lavender said. 'I can see now that she was out of her depth. I wonder if she's happier in London.'

'Oh yes,' Freda said. 'She's got friends, and a car of her own to drive, and lots of things to do.'

'Well then,' Lavender said. 'That's all right. No harm done. Who wants a chocolate?'

Soon afterwards, Emily and the three boys came through from the play garden to go into the house, and Freda was astonished to see Arthur walking between Nico and Hubert, holding their hands and, apparently, not planning to fight with either of them. As they went into the house, Freda turned to Lavender. 'How does she get them to do that?' she asked.

'I have no idea, darling,' Lavender said, and took another chocolate.

When they were leaving, and Lavender was seeing them to the car, she said, 'Your grandpa will be so sorry to have missed you.'

Freda said nothing. She had done the apology – she wasn't going to be nice about Grandpa, too. Then, in a flash of devilment, she said, 'I expect he's pleased to have Jasper back, isn't he?'

She watched a frown crease Lavender's sweet, smooth face. 'I'm sure he is, really,' Lavender said. 'But I wish I knew what happened. It's all very odd – the keys to the gates and so on – it doesn't add up. And it's an odd coincidence that it was Ted who found him. I can't help wondering, you know…' Then she smiled. 'Still, never mind. Least said, soonest mended, and all that.'

She kissed them all and stood waving as they drove off down the drive.

'Did you think it sounded a bit as though she suspected Grandpa?' Freda asked.

Ellie glanced at her. 'People often know only what they want to know,' she said. 'I think she suspects but doesn't want to think about it.'

Freda thought about that. 'I'd want to know,' she said. 'I couldn't leave it like that.'

'No,' her mum said, 'I don't suppose you could.'

# Chapter Nineteen

## COSTS

I don't sleep, of course, after my Damascene moment at rehearsal. I churn over what I think I saw and I start to doubt my certainty, but I am sure, at least, that Isha Anand's murderer is involved with *Measure for Measure* – Asmil Anand? Lyle Fenton? Piers Upton? Tom Yeoman? Who knows? One word seals it. Beth Hart-Carpenter, when she described the night she found Isha in tears, told me that Isha said she needed to declare something. But the word wasn't *declare*, was it? And it wasn't *something* but *somebody*. And my theory makes better sense of Bimal's disappearance, too. I don't know who the killer is, you understand, but I know what sort of person he has to be. I think I will ring David and tell him this, and then I think I won't, because he may know already, and has left me to find my way there by myself. In my groggy state, I haul myself up and try to get my thoughts straight. David thinks Isha's death is linked to Annie's chambers – that's why he has searched them – and to the play – that's why he told me that going to rehearsal last night could be dangerous. So, what do I think I know that he doesn't? What, exactly, was my brilliant realisation at last night's rehearsal? It eludes me, and yet it must be something. It's to do with the play, and David doesn't know the play like I do, so how can he have got ahead of me? And he is not telling me anything, is he? He said he would call me in the morning. If he does, and if he shares anything substantive with me, then I might try giving him the benefit of my insights, but I can feel them melting away as I imagine putting them into words. It is possible that there is nothing there.

It is 02:58, according to my phone, when I come to these conclusions. *02:58.* Can there be a more discouraging hour to find oneself awake? It is neither late at night nor early in the morning. Our cortisol levels are their lowest, and we are in no fit state either for fight or flight. It is the hour when people die. With this thought, I decide to get up. It is summer, after all, and even though I can't expect the outrageously early dawn of midsummer, I don't really have long to wait. So, I make coffee and I warm croissants and I read the bits of yesterday's paper that I thought weren't worth bothering with yesterday, but that now seem to demand my attention, and I try to pretend that I am not a crazy woman eating breakfast in the middle of the night.

I eat a lot. I somehow failed to eat yesterday, and I seem to be making up for it now. Without really thinking I load my two croissants with butter and jam and then, for contrast, I eat two slices of toast and marmite, followed by a banana and a mango yoghurt. I am actually considering a mug of hot chocolate as the dawn comes up, when I pull myself together, hide the evidence of my surfeit in the dishwasher and go off for a shower.

David does call. He is on an early schedule, too, it seems, or he hasn't been to bed. I think the latter. David isn't usually at his best in the early morning, but today he sounds wired and – anagrammatically – weird.

'Are you going to the dress rehearsal tonight?' is his opening gambit.

'Dress rehearsal? *Measure for Measure,* you mean?'

'What else would I mean?'

'Who knows, David? I'm not exactly privy to – '

'Are you going to be there?'

'I hadn't thought. I wasn't particularly welcome yesterday. Are you warning me off? Do dangers lurk again?'

'You should be there.'

'Why?'

'Because I say so.'

'And that's a reason that usually works well with me, isn't it? Let's try again. Why should I be there?'

'Because you'll be sorry if you're not,' he says, and hangs up.

When I stop being furious, I think about this. There was some talk about the dress rehearsal last night, but I was preoccupied and not paying attention. There was mention of running the dress and technical rehearsals together, on the grounds that there is very little tech. The lighting is rudimentary, and the music provided by a live fiddle player, so tech cues are minimal. There was also talk of inviting a few people to come and make an audience. No-one invited me, though, and I am not sure if I will be welcome. On the other hand, David seems to have stopped regarding rehearsals as perilous, so perhaps I will go, even though I resent his gnomic instruction to turn up.

I am tired of finding ways to pass the time and domesticity has lost its charms, so I decide to go into my office and do boring things that I can manage even in my sleep-deprived state. In practice, this means a lot of chatting. I drop in at Reception and listen to Maria's tale of woe about managing the children during the school holidays – a sports course cancelled, an unhelpful husband, a grandmother with a broken ankle – and then I intend to go into my office, but as I am passing the common room I hear voices. I put my head in just to see who is there, hoping I might find a group in idle, mid-vacation mood, up for inconsequential chat, but instead find an intense discussion of the consequences of the Brexit vote for universities. I am not strong enough for this today, so I wave vaguely and back out. There is no help for it but to tackle whatever is waiting for me in my office.

I open the window, although last night's rain has brought a change in the weather and the sultry heaviness of the past week has been washed away. An insistent breeze shuffles the papers on my desk as soon as I let it in. I open my emails with a slight internal flutter, as I wonder if Roderick might have sent me something. I had no more than a wave and a smile from him yesterday at rehearsal, but he was busy, of course. Maybe, I think, he has sent me something charming down the wires.

Well, he hasn't, and I do suspect that I may have made too much of David the other night, in what now seems a rather adolescent attempt to get Roderick feeling competitive in pursuit of my desirable self. As so often, I may have overplayed my hand. I am surprised at how disappointed I feel. I have called my stratagem with David and Roderick adolescent, and so is this feeling of deflation – the sense that something full of exciting possibilities was offered and then snatched away. If I were actually a teenager, I could yell and weep and slam doors; as it is, I allow myself to shout, 'Bollocks!' once, and then get on with answering the emails I do have.

This constitutes more chatting, really, but then I get serious. I get down to some filing. This is, in fact, a deeply satisfying activity. Piles of stuff that have accumulated randomly over the busy term get taken in hand, subjugated, disciplined and ordered smartly into labelled files. Documents that I had a niggling fear I might have lost are rediscovered; work plans and lecture notes appear freshly satisfactory; my sense of competence rises anew. As a process, I think, there is nothing like it in the ratio of effort to sense of achievement. It is like taking all the chaos out of the world. It is the defeat of entropy. I realise that caffeine and sleeplessness are driving me to hyperbole, but I do recommend filing therapy. If you haven't an office, then clearing out drawers at home is a pretty good substitute. Expensive Life Gurus will tell you that attainable goals are among the chief keys to happiness. Start with filing.

And so it is that, some hours later, I am glowing with self-congratulation as I make my way to the canteen, where I do find a few people in idle vacation mode, and I pass a pleasant hour, lingering over an underdressed salad and an overfilled sandwich, discussing the horrors of air travel versus the discomfort of London in August, the horrors of Paris in August versus the discomfort of London in general, and – at my instigation – the discomforts of the English seaside versus the delights of London. I do a *tour de force* on my sojourn on the Kent coast. I omit desperate asylum seekers, of course, and bodies on the beach. I know when to keep things light.

Finally, I go home and think about the evening ahead. It probably won't rain tonight, but it will be cold, and I know, from years of experience, just how cold one can get on an English summer evening, sitting watching a three-hour play. I put on trousers and a sweater, and I find a padded anorak with a hood to carry with me. I put on socks but then take them off again, feeling frumpy, and put them in my bag for emergency use. I look longingly at a tartan blanket, which I use occasionally as a picnic rug. It would be cosy, over the knees, but I haven't entirely abandoned hope of Roderick and I don't want him to look out into the audience and glimpse me looking like a granny at the seaside.

I eat some pasta with a quick pesto sauce made of whizzed-up, out-of-date salad leaves and the end of a lump of parmesan, and then I set off. I am surprised to find that my legs feel heavy and that the prospect of the walk seems unusually daunting. I wonder if I'm sickening for something, and then remember my sleepless night, and the fact that I have already been up for fifteen hours. This entitles me to a cab, so I hail one and arrive early at Gray's Inn. The courtyard is deserted – the actors are all in the dressing rooms, presumably. I wonder where they are dressing – in one of the sets of chambers, I suppose. A couple of rows of chairs have been put out, and I settle myself in the second row. I send a good luck text to Annie, and then sit back and close my eyes.

When a voice says, 'Back again?' I jerk awake. It is Roderick, resplendent in a very fine suit and tie which are, I assume, his costume. I knew they were going for modern dress, and thought it was a shame, given the antiquity of the setting, but gathered that hiring costumes for three performances to small audiences was beyond their budget. He sits down beside me. 'I'm sorry we didn't get a chance to talk yesterday,' he says. 'You sped off. I don't blame you. It was pretty dire, wasn't it?'

'You were fine,' I say, sitting up straight and doing my best to dispel the dozy old woman picture that I must present. 'You carried it, in fact,' I add.

'You're very kind. Age, you know – we get better at riding the bumps. It was a bumpy day in chambers, as you may have heard from your friend the DCI.'

'He doesn't talk to me about work,' I say – truthfully, at this moment, as it happens – 'but Annie told me.'

'She did well last night. Kept her cool.'

'Yes. Just one bad moment.'

'Was there? Well, we're all entitled to one. Listen, do stay around afterwards and have a drink. If it's disastrous and you don't want to face the cast, we could slip off somewhere.'

Then he is up and off, and I call, rather feebly, 'Break a leg!' and watch him striding away. *Well, there!* Who needs a blanket when they have the nice, warm inner glow of a woman who is fancied by a good-looking man? *Slip off somewhere.* How attractive that sounds.

A few other people are drifting into the audience – a couple of groups of young people – friends or colleagues of the cast, I suppose – and some older ones, who might be parents. They are mostly inexperienced outdoor theatre-goers, I see. They don't have enough clothes on.

Eventually, only ten minutes behind schedule, lights come up on the stage area, the fiddle player starts with a commanding flourish and Roderick steps onto the stage. At the same time, the seat next to mine is occupied. This is an entirely familiar feeling, and I know who is there without looking. During the years when we were actually going out on dates, I became quite used to David's last-minute arrivals in theatres, cinemas and restaurants. I deliberately don't turn my head until the end of the scene, and then I whisper, 'What's going on?'

'Oh, you know…' he says, swatting the question away.

Well, I don't know, and I am annoyed. If Roderick looks out into the audience and sees David sitting all snugly beside me, he may well rescind his invitation; I see the *slipping away* – well – slipping away. David has no right to commandeer me like this, and I am about to tell him so and send him away when I realise that he is simmering with suppressed excitement. It is palpable, coming off him like heat.

– 'Tell!' I hiss, but David puts a finger to his lips and turns to look at the stage.

Lucio and the gentlemen enter for the next scene. They are taking too long between scenes, I note. Professionals would have this lot entering while the others were leaving. Dare I tell Tom? The performances are not bad. Their costumes mostly help them, and the presence of an audience seems to give them a lift rather than intimidating them. Annie is secure as ever, and she looks quite good in her postulant's uniform. We have had a lot of discussion about her costume. I remember seeing Kate Nelligan's Isabella in a BBC production in the 1980s. She wore a complete habit and wimple in snowy white, which did make Angelo's propositioning particularly outrageous, but equally outrageous was the Duke's not-to-be-refused proposal of marriage at the end of the play. The point is, as I explained when Annie was talking about habits and wimples, that Isabella is a postulant. Although she gets referred to as a 'sister', she has only just gone into the convent. She is still being told about the rules when Lucio comes to take her to Angelo; she has only one foot in the convent, as yet. Annie has, eventually, compromised with a white shirt and a calf-length black skirt, worn with thick black tights and flat shoes. Novices, apparently, often wear black headscarves, but that gave her a bit of a Greek peasant look, so she has pulled her hair back into a severe bun. The effect, actually, is to make her look not like a nun, but like a schoolgirl at a particularly traditional school. And that, too, makes Angelo's propositioning even more outrageous, if we need extra outrage.

I wait for the moment of my lost revelation yesterday, hoping for enlightenment but afraid it may derail Annie again. She is unaffected, though; it was my face, yesterday, and not the lines, that made her stumble. I, on the other hand, know what I saw, and more. I hear again Isabella's cry, *I will proclaim thee, Angelo,* and I look again at Lyle Fenton's face, the sneer as he says, *Who will believe thee, Isabel?* Now, I really know. Does David know, too? I plan to wait until the interval to ask him, but he disappears as soon as the lights go down on stage, muttering something about going to the loo, and comes back only as the lights come up again.

He is more keyed up than ever now, and so am I. We sit there with an electric charge of excitement crackling between us. No, not sexual – more exciting, actually. Am I aware that

David is glancing from time to time into the shadows at the side of the stage? Yes, I am. Am I outraged when, as I start to squirm with impatience at the intolerable length of the rambling final scene, I am quelled by a very firm restraining gesture from David? No, I am not. Am I puzzled when, before the very last lines are spoken, David gets up and slips away? Not at all. Something is about to happen, and when it comes it is quite unsurprising. I am not surprised when the lights go down on stage and Tom Yeoman calls, 'We'll do the curtain call, people.' I am not surprised when I see the actors lining up in the gloom on either side of the stage, ready to come on. I am not surprised when the line on the prompt side moves smoothly onto the stage but on the other side there seems to be a disturbance, a scuffle, some actors backing away. I am not surprised when I make out a couple of police uniforms in the little crowd, and I am suddenly not surprised, not at all surprised, when I see a man in handcuffs being led away, and the man is Roderick Gillard.

# Chapter Twenty

## AFTER THE FACT

*Thursday 4th August 2016*

Do you know the Paul Temple mysteries? They were very early radio dramas by Francis Durbridge, hugely popular in the 1940s and 50s. My father had loved them and, when I was a child, spoke of them as being vastly superior to the TV mysteries of the 1970s, so when new recordings were made for radio a few years ago, I was very excited – and then dreadfully disappointed. They were impeccably acted, with wonderful 1940s accents, but they turned out to be quite ludicrously formulaic. In any episode, certain tropes were guaranteed. Paul Temple would be sent a message by someone with information to offer about a murder, but when he got to the appointed (and strangely isolated) meeting place, his informant would invariably be dead; if Temple left his elegant London flat and drove his expensive car out of town, he would, without fail, be run off the road by villains wearing hats and motoring goggles; if Temple's plucky and glamorous wife, Steve, tried any sleuthing of her own, she would undoubtedly be kidnapped and need rescuing; at the end of any case, the murderer would be revealed at a smart party in a glamorous venue, and, finally – and this is the point of my diversion – the following morning, Sir Graham Forbes, the head of Scotland Yard, would inevitably drop in on the Temples while they were having breakfast, and all would be explained in response to Steve saying, 'But what I don't understand is ...'

This is a roundabout way of telling you that I don't get the whole picture (and nor does David,) until breakfast the next day. Well, it is only technically the next day, actually. What happens is this: after Roderick is arrested, David disappears – of course – and we all catch the sweep of the headlights of the two police cars as they drive away. Then, Annie emerges from the crowd and comes at me, blazing. 'What the hell does David think he's doing?' she demands, grabbing hold of me and taking me away from the throng of disoriented actors. 'This can't be about Isha, can it? They're going to say they've found porn stuff on Roderick's computer, aren't they? They're so stupid. If you're doing a case, sometimes you have to look stuff up – it's professional. They can't – '

I stop her. 'I'm pretty sure it's about Isha,' I say.

She laughs. 'It can't be. That's crazy. Why?'

'Why have they arrested him or why did he kill her?'

'Both.'

'Well, David hasn't actually told me anything, but I assume they've arrested him because they've got evidence against him, and the reason he killed her will have been sexual, basically. But then we always knew that would turn out to be the reason, didn't we? Why else do young women ever get killed?'

'But you don't believe it, do you? I thought you liked Roderick.'

'I did. Mainly because I thought he liked me. Now I'm beginning to see that he just wanted to find out what I knew. Tom didn't do me any favours introducing me to the cast as an amateur sleuth. Roderick just saw me as a potential danger that needed to be neutralised. I suppose I should count myself lucky that he decided to charm me rather than bump me off too – or kidnap me. I wonder if they've found Bimal.'

'Stop it, Ma,' she hisses at me. 'Come on. You don't really believe he did it, do you?'

'I'm sure he did it,' I say.

She still has hold of my sleeve, where she has pulled me away from the others. I shake myself free. 'I can't tell you anything, and I'm tired,' I say. 'I didn't sleep last night.'

Actually, I'm not just tired. The adrenaline build-up of the past two or three hours is draining away fast, and I am feeling wobbly and light-headed. 'I need to get a taxi home,' I say, 'before I fall over. I'll talk to you when – if – I know more. But it's true, Annie. He did it. Just think about Angelo and Isabella and you'll get it.'

'Really?' she asks.

'Really.'

I totter off to find a cab, and I sit in a daze as we snake through the traffic to my door. Once inside, I want nothing but to sleep and to stop thinking. If I had a bathroom cabinet full of pharmaceuticals, I would take whatever I could find to knock myself out, but I know I have nothing but a tube of Germolene, a box of plasters and a packet of paracetamol in my bathroom. It was, after all, less than two weeks ago that I moved in here and stashed my meagre supplies away. I don't even have any grappa left. I consider making tea but can't see the point. I pace around the flat for a bit, twitching at things. I think about the business of going to bed, and I picture myself, staring, wide awake, into the semi-darkness. In the end, I simply switch out the light, kick off my shoes, lie down on the sofa, cover myself with the tartan picnic blanket discarded there earlier, and close my eyes.

When, some time later, I jump awake, it is because I am summoned by bells. Sirens? A fire alarm? I struggle up and identify the ringing as my still unfamiliar front doorbell. I peer at my watch. It is just before two. If someone is leaning on my doorbell at two o'clock in the morning, this can only be bad news. Or danger. But the danger is past, isn't it? Roderick Gillard is in custody. He surely doesn't have criminal cronies who are out to get me? All the same, I don't turn the light on, but grope my way to the front door, where I see through the door's glass pane, backlit by the street lamp, two heads with a male look to them. Surprisingly, I hear myself call out not a feeble *Who is it?* but a pretty aggressive, 'What do you want?'

'Just let us in, Gina,' comes the reply.

'David? Who have you got with you?'

'Someone you'll be glad to see. Now, open the bloody door.'

I do, and I find that David's companion is a gangly young man, almost as tall as David, with tousled black hair, troubled dark eyes and bruising round his mouth.

'Bimal?' I ask.

'How do you do?' he says. 'This is very kind of you.'

He stretches out a hand and I shake it automatically, while shooting a look at David.

'Bimal has had a hard time,' David says, 'and he needs a bed for the night. We could have found him a hotel room, but after what he's been through, I thought he could do with some motherly comfort.'

Suddenly, embarrassingly, I find my eyes filling with tears. This boy, this motherless boy, who has flown alone to London to help find his sister's murderer, who has been ill-treated in who knows what ways, has been brought to me to be mothered because David believes I'm the person to do it. Inexplicably, I am deeply touched.

To mask the tears, I snap into action. 'Come, come!' I cry. 'Food, drink, a clean bed – I have them all. Follow me.'

I lead my guests back into the sitting room, where I switch on lamps and settle them down before I go through to the kitchen to consider what I can offer them to eat. Knowing David's tastes, I feel bacon and eggs would be the best option, but I think Bimal probably won't eat bacon, so I decide on cheesy scrambled eggs with lots of butter. I sense that Bimal will probably be too polite to refuse anything, but I ask anyway.

'Scrambled eggs all right?' I say. 'And tea? Coffee's probably not a great idea – unless you want some, David? I assume you're not going to bed yet? There's orange juice, Bimal, if you'd prefer that to tea?'

He smiles, and I can see that he's really a very good-looking boy. 'Perhaps both?' he says, 'if that's not greedy?'

'He's got a bit of catching up to do,' David says. 'And I could do with as much caffeine as you can muster.'

So, I go to make a pot of tea and some double strength coffee. I scramble six eggs with grated cheese and ladle them onto thick slices of buttered toast. We sit round the kitchen table as they eat and I sip tea and think how much I would like a cigarette. I hope you have noticed that I haven't yet asked a single question – not about Roderick Gillard, not about where Bimal has been. Motherly comfort was asked for and is being supplied. But I have no intention, of letting David leave this flat without telling me something.

After the eggs are eaten, I make more toast and offer it with jam and marmalade. Then, when the loaf is finished, I usher Bimal into my study-cum-spare room, load him with clean towels, then show him into the bathroom, where I demonstrate the workings of the shower and find him a temporary toothbrush, appropriated from a hotel room at some time. I can't offer pyjamas, but I don't expect he'll mind. I realise, looking at him properly, that his clothes are filthy, and quite smelly. Cooking smells masked this in the kitchen, but in here it is noticeable.

'If you would like to leave your clothes outside the bathroom,' I say, 'I'll wash them for you and have them dry for the morning.'

'You are very kind,' he says.

I look up at him – he is much taller than me. 'I'm so sorry about your sister,' I say. 'It was a terrible thing.'

He drops his head, and I see the tears in his eyes. I would like to stand on tiptoe and smooth his tousled hair and kiss his cheek, but I think this goes beyond the acceptable, so I pat his arm instead and tell him to sleep well.

Back in the kitchen, I'm ready to tackle David. 'So, where has he been?' I ask. 'Was Roderick holding him? How did you decide it was Roderick? Have you got evidence? Will he get away with it?'

David pours more coffee. 'I thought you might try and tell me I'd got it wrong and your charming admirer couldn't possibly be a killer.'

'Oh no,' I say with what I think is convincing insouciance. 'I've known for some time.'

'But you resisted telling me?'

'You weren't telling me anything.'

'I think I have explained this to you before – the public are supposed to give the police information, but we are not obliged to give information back.'

'Which is hardly fair. Anyway, before you threaten me with obstructing a police inquiry, I should say that I have actually only known properly since about nine o'clock last evening.'

'Why then?'

'*I will proclaim thee, Angelo.* It says it all.'

'But you'd heard that line before.'

'I had. But I didn't get it. I don't know why. Stupid of me.'

'Well, we don't know what we don't want to know, do we?'

'Oh, for heaven's sake,' I snap. 'Listen to yourself – *full of wise saws and modern instances.*'

'And where's that from?'

227

'*As You Like It.* The seven ages of man. The fifth age – the pompous old justice, *with eyes severe and beard of formal cut.* You want to watch out – *the lean and slippered pantaloon* comes next.'

'Well, I'm sorry if I was pompous.'

'Oh, you weren't. I'm just … it's so bloody, bloody awful. Of course I didn't want to know. But not just because of my bruised ego. Because it's vile and tawdry and tragic, and it says things about human nature that we none of us want to confront.'

'Some of us have to.'

'I know, but most of your villains have some excuse, don't they? Rotten childhoods, neglect, abuse, a life without opportunities or rewards.'

'You are sounding very bleeding-heart-Guardian-reader.'

'OK. But Roderick Gillard didn't have a deprived childhood, did he? He is clever, successful, cultivated, charming, but he thought it was his God-given right to demand sex from a young woman just because he thought he could get away with it – because, presumably, he had always got away with it in the past. And then, when she threatened to blow the whistle, he killed her – just disposed of her as an inconvenience – and then tried to blacken her name and frame her teenage brother. And I know it ought not to feel worse that Isha was clever and beautiful, but it does.'

'You sound very sure about what you think happened. You didn't get all that from one line in a play, did you?'

'This is awkward. There's something I didn't tell you.'

'Then do you think you could make some more coffee and tell me now?'

'Are you sure you should have more? I made it double strength.'

'I had a work medical last week. I think my heart can take it.'

I go to refill the cafetière and say, 'Oh, what the hell, I'll join you. I'm not going to be sleeping tonight anyway, am I?'

Fortified by coffee, I make my confession. I tell David the story Beth Hart-Carpenter told me about finding Isha in distress, and Isha's saying she needed to *declare* something. 'But I bet the word was actually *proclaim*,' I say, 'only that was such an odd word to use that Beth normalised it to something more familiar. Isabella's line must have rung in Isha's head.'

'All right. But even if you intuited that Isha's 'proclamation' was going to be about some sort of sexual assault, how did that take you to Gillard?'

'Well, it didn't at first – not till tonight – but it ought to have done. There's the power thing, you see. Angelo thinks he can demand sex from Isabella because he has all the power, so I did begin to think that whoever had propositioned, or – more likely – assaulted Isha was someone older, with influence, and that made sense of the odd business about her not getting a place in Annie's chambers. Both Annie and Cressida Long told me that it had looked as though she was going there and then she got a place somewhere else instead, and neither of them gave a reason. If she was offered a place but there was then some suggestion of a *quid pro quo*, that would explain why she didn't take it – and that ruled out the young men, because they don't have that sort of influence. I thought you ought to investigate the senior barristers there, but I didn't think of Roderick because he, of course, had taken care to make sure that I wouldn't.'

'It's too crude, isn't it? *Yes, you can have a place in these desirable chambers, but the price is sex on demand.*'

'Well, of course it wasn't like that at all. I'd guess that she got offered the place – you need to check whether he was the person who interviewed her, by the way – and then he dropped in at her flat, all very charming – delighted that they were going to be working together, and would she like to come out for dinner to celebrate? Then, when she turned him down, he was affronted, got pushy, maybe made a lunge at her, or possibly just kept it verbal – suggested that if she couldn't be a real part of the team, the offer of a place could be withdrawn. As her neighbour Beth described it, Isha was really distressed, almost in a state of collapse, so whatever he said or did must have been pretty vile.'

'You've not actually got evidence for any of this, have you? It's a good story, but it's just a story.'

'Well, of course it is. You wouldn't give me anything, would you? I had no evidence to go on. One thing I do know, though, is that Roderick is an ace at computer and phone technology. He positively dazzled Freda, and he boasted to me about it. So, he will have known how to do the sexting stuff, and also how to bury the evidence.'

'Not all that effectively, as it turns out. He's not quite such a whizz as he thinks he is. It didn't take our people long to find the pictures on his office computer.'

'So, there you are: your plodding old police work, my amateur intuition – a marriage made in heaven.'

'I think we ruled out marriage some time ago, didn't we?'

'You know what I mean.'

'Anyway, it's not as good as you think. I'm afraid he's claiming not to know anything about the photos – says anyone could have used his work computer. He'll know where to get the very best defence team, of course, so we're not home yet. The CPS might even decide it's not worth prosecuting.'

'For murder? And the victim's uncle a senior Indian politician? And, anyway, what about Bimal? I assume it was Roderick who was holding him – and knocking him about, it looks like? Bimal will give evidence against him, won't he?'

'Again, it's not straightforward. We found him in Gillard's garden shed – one of those smart sheds designed to be used as an office – but Bimal says he never saw his kidnapper's face. A man wearing a peaked, police-style hat, pulled well down, met him at the airport and said he had instructions to take him to the police station. When they got out of the car he was knocked out, and he woke up in the shed, tied up, blindfolded and gagged. Someone came and brought him a sandwich and some water a couple of times, but he didn't speak and Bimal couldn't see. Gillard is claiming he's being framed – with the photos on his computer and with the use of his shed. He says everyone at work knows he uses the shed as an office, and he has occasionally asked juniors to go and pick up files from there. The clerk keeps a key in his desk drawer, apparently, so anyone could have taken it and copied it. At the moment, we've got a Swiss cheese of a case, but I'm buzzing now, and Gillard has had time to stew – and don't tell me I'm mixing metaphors because I know I am – so I shall go back and give myself the pleasure of trying to break him.'

'You need to talk to other people in his chambers,' I tell him, as he starts to look for his jacket. 'See if he was known for propositioning the younger women. My guess is he was, and everyone turned a blind eye. I think he's probably got away with it for years because no woman would risk her career by speaking out, but Isha was different – she was outraged – and the times are changing. I bet Cressida Long suspected the reason why Isha didn't take up the place in his chambers – that's why she was evasive with me – but she's old school, assuming that women put up and shut up and everyone looks the other way. But workplace harassment is becoming a concern. Employers are less ready to look the other way. Soon they'll all be huffing and puffing, wanting to put themselves among the righteous. *Completely unacceptable*, they'll say *a policy of zero tolerance*. Roderick realised that he couldn't be certain of his colleagues' support. If Isha had 'proclaimed' him, they might have been ready to hang him out to dry, and he knew it.'

'What he may have done in the past still isn't evidence. We won't get away with that in court.'

'A good prosecutor could use it, surely? And another thing – we couldn't work out how anyone knew that Bimal was arriving at Heathrow that morning, but Roderick knew because he overheard us talking in the sitting room when he went to the loo. In fact, I think he went to the loo precisely because he thought we might talk and he might learn something useful. The bathroom walls in this flat are like cardboard. I realised how much you can hear just now, when I could hear Bimal running the shower, even from out here in the kitchen.'

'Circumstantial, Ms Sidwell. Still not good enough.'

'So, you're just going to try and batter a confession out of him, are you?'

'I think that will be unnecessary,' a voice says, and we both swing round to see Bimal standing in the doorway, wrapped in a towel.

'Thank you for the shower,' he says. 'And it gave me the chance to clean up this.'

He walks over to David and hands him a memory stick. 'Roderick Gillard phoned Isha on her house phone while I was staying with her and I could see that his calls upset her – scared her – so I recorded three of them – just picked up the extension and recorded the call on my phone. It's not great quality, but you can hear what he's saying, and he's threatening her. It's always the same thing – she's 'overreacting' and he's not going to let her wreck his career. I recorded them because I thought they could be protection for her, if he knew I'd got them, but then it was too late.'

David looks at the memory stick. 'And the calls are on here now?' he asks. 'Why?'

'I transferred them from my phone before I came over here. I thought the police might take my phone, and I – well …'

'You didn't trust us not to 'lose' the evidence.'

'Yes.'

'With some reason, I have to say.'

I stare at the memory stick. 'But how have his phone conversations got on there?' I ask, bewildered. 'How does that work? Phone calls and memory sticks – they're two different things.'

Bimal has been mainly addressing David, but he turns to me now and says, kindly, 'There's an app you can use. It's quite easy.'

'Right. Of course,' I say.

David cuts in. 'More to the point, didn't Gillard search you while he was keeping you in his shed ? He'll have wanted to take your phone, and I assume he went through your bag to see if you had a tablet or laptop with you.'

'He took my phone. That was all I brought, apart from this – which I hid quite effectively.' He glances uncomfortably at me and then looks back at David. 'I know where the boys at school hide things when there's a drugs search.'

We all of us look at the memory stick in David's hand.

'I did clean it up,' Bimal says.

'The benefits of an English public school education are endless, aren't they?' I say. 'It equips you for being a pillar of the establishment, but if it's a life of crime you're after, it offers all the skills for that, too. Parents can certainly be assured that their money is well spent.'

Bimal smiles. 'And if you do end up in prison, seven years of boarding school will have given you all the survival skills you need,' he says.

'Let's hope that stands Roderick Gillard in good stead, then,' I say, and Bimal's smile fades.

'You will get a conviction, won't you?' he asks David.

'You bet,' David replies.

Bimal goes off to bed and I look at David, who has picked up his jacket.

'With Bimal's evidence, it's not quite so urgent to get back to questioning your suspect, is it?' I say. 'Wouldn't it be a good idea to have a couple of hours in bed first?'

'It's not worth going home.'

'I was going to offer you a bed here.'

'Bimal's sleeping in your spare room.'

'I have another bed. A very large bed. Plenty of room for two.'

He looks at me, hard. 'What is this, Gina?' he asks.

'Well, we're neither of us going to sleep, are we? We're both too wired. But we could try to relax.'

He puts his jacket down, 'You realise,' he says, 'that we shall probably regret this in the morning.'

'I do,' I say, 'but the world is infinitely disappointing, and sometimes the only thing to do is to live dangerously.'

# Chapter Twenty-One

## PATERNITY SUIT

*Thursday 11th August 2016*

This play will not let me go. You might have assumed, as I did, that the arrest of one of the leading actors at the dress rehearsal would scupper the leaky vessel conclusively, but it is refusing to sink. Determined to keep it afloat, Lyle Fenton has found a university buddy of his, now a professional actor, who has played the Duke before and is willing to plug the hole, so here we are, a week and a day after the dress rehearsal drama, sitting in the damp gloom of an unfriendly summer night, applauding a respectable, if uninspired, delayed first night with rather more enthusiasm than it deserves and a good deal of relief. When I say we, I mean the entire gang. Ellie and Ben are here, as is Freda, who has insisted on coming and has invited Monika to join us. Annie did invite Andrew – this is, after all, his old stamping ground – but he is in Belarus, which must be some kind of punishment, surely. Jon, her boyfriend, is here, though, looking mildly stunned by his surroundings – surely one of the odder manifestations of English life for someone who has just spent six months in a developing country. And David is here – having actually arrived before curtain-up and sat waiting with me, which is a new experience. Whether this means anything significant about the current state of our relationship I really can't say, and I don't suppose he can, either. Professionally, he is not sure where he is. His superiors seem to have accepted his pursuit of Isha Anand's murderer, and the subsequent arrest of a prominent barrister, with reasonably good grace, and the CPS will prosecute, but David suspects that his card has been marked. Does he mind? I'm not sure about that, either.

We make the rounds, offering congratulations and lavish praise, and then we leave Annie and Jon to party with the cast – poor Jon – and the rest of us cram into a cab to go back to my flat, where we had supper before the show, and where we plan to have pudding now. It is only when I have dished out ice cream, meringues and berries in varying proportions, and we are all eating, that I realise that Ellie has been unusually quiet and is not eating. She has pulled her chair back from the table and is looking at the *Measure for Measure* programme. It is a rather lavish affair for a shoestring production, but someone has desktop publishing software, and so it has run to cast photos and mini-biographies. Ellie studied drama at university and teaches it in what we nowadays call a *challenging* school. I wonder if seeing Annie on stage has made her yearn to act again herself. Now the drama of Nico is over, does life threaten to become humdrum and dull? On the pretext of getting more ice cream from the fridge, I go around behind her and ask, quietly, 'Are you all right?'

She looks up, startled. 'I need to make a phone call,' she says, and leaves the room.

I assume she has gone to ring Lavender, to check on Nico, who is spending the night at Aren't-We-Grand Hall under Norland Nanny Emma's reassuring care, but it is a while before she comes back, and when I ask if he is all right, she says, 'Yes, I expect so,' in a vague way, and then explains, 'I was ringing Annie.' She sits down at the table and eats some of her melting ice cream, but then she puts her spoon down and says, 'Ma, can I talk to you for a moment? And Ben, can you come too?'

236

I feel a bit bad about leaving David to Freda's and Monika's girl talk (Monika's phone is in action, and she is showing something to Freda), but Ellie sounds urgent and panicky, and I am scared.

The open-plan layout of the flat offers little in the way of privacy – not even in the bathroom, as it turns out – but my bedroom at least has a door, and it is at the other end from the kitchen, so we go in there and close the door, and then Ben and I perch awkwardly on the bed, while Ellie paces around the small area of floor space available to her.

'The thing is,' she says, 'Lyle Fenton is Freda's father.'

'Jesus!'

'Oh, for heaven's sake!'

Ben and I both speak at once. Ellie says, 'I knew I recognised him, as soon as he walked on stage, even before I'd looked in the programme. I don't know what to do. I've just talked to Annie. I wanted to know if he's in a relationship – if he has children – other children.'

'I'm in the dark here,' I say. 'You've never told me anything about Freda's origins. I assume he was at Manchester with you?'

'No. He wasn't. Ben knows about it. I was in a debating team, when I first started at Manchester, and we went down to Cambridge to debate against his college, and he was in their team – a second year and very smooth. Anyway, I drank too much afterwards, we ended up back in his room, I was too drunk to be careful, and a few weeks later I realised I was pregnant. I thought about an abortion – of course I did – but I couldn't do it. I'd made a mistake, but now there was this little life, and I couldn't just wipe out the mistake. So, then there was Freda, and of course I've never regretted her.'

'You told me Freda's father didn't know about her,' I say. 'It would have been easy enough to contact him. You knew his name and his college. He needed to take some responsibility.'

'No, Ma. He didn't. I was the one who got pregnant, and that was my responsibility. What would have been the point of telling him? I wasn't going to marry him, was I?'

'He could have helped to support her. He should – '

'He would have wanted me to get rid of her. And I had no right to say *I'm going to keep this baby and you have to support it.* It was much simpler to leave him out of it and do it on my own.'

'With a quite bit of help from me,' I mutter.

'Yes, with help from you. And with help from Ben. But neither of you has ever wished she wasn't here, have you?'

'But now,' I say, 'she wants to know where she came from. She doesn't have a first beginnings story, and everybody needs one of those.'

'That's the problem.' Ellie jumps up and starts pacing again. 'I've always known I would have to tell her some time, but it's not a romantic story and I didn't know how to make it sound anything except grubby. Now there's this actual father, and he's respectable, at least – quite good-looking, successful and so on – so should I tell her? Should she meet him? Will he want to meet her?'

'I don't like him,' I say, helpfully. 'I think he's slimy.'

'I think,' Ben says, 'that you have to tell Freda – she has a right – and then she can decide whether she wants to meet him.'

'But is she old enough to make a decision like that?' Ellie demands. 'It's too much to ask of a ten-year-old, isn't it?'

'Freda has been through a lot recently,' I say. 'Nico being ill, escaping from Aren't-We-Grand Hall, finding out that her grandfather is – untrustworthy. She is pretty grown-up.'

Ellie looks from Ben to me, and then back again. 'Would you mind,' she asks Ben, 'if Freda wanted to have contact with her biological father?'

'All I'll mind is if she gets hurt,' he says. 'And then he'll have me to answer to.'

'OK, then,' Ellie says. 'Let's do it.'

I assume that this means that I am to be involved, and perhaps Ben assumes the same, but when we get back to the kitchen, Ellie says, 'Freda, my love, can you come and have a talk with me?' and off they go without a backward look.

It's a bit awkward now, because Ben and I are in possession of a momentous piece of information, and David and Monika are not. If it were David alone, I would tell him, because he has known Freda since she was a baby and at one time aspired to be her step-grandfather, but it's really not something that should be discussed with an outsider like Monika, so I offer more wine and, when David says he really ought to be going, I beg him to stay, and we carry on a stilted conversation in which we both interrogate Monika about her experience of living in London – all ten days of it.

Eventually, Ellie and Freda return, and Freda, looking very pink and bright-eyed, says, 'Monika, can you come and talk now?' and off they go.

I realise that I am telling this tale vilely – too many important conversations are happening offstage, while I am telling you what is going on in the kitchen, where nothing is happening. The problem is that I can only tell you what I hear and see. If this were a play, it would be different. The significant dialogue would all happen in one place, and characters not required would be given reasons – not always convincing ones – for leaving the stage. They would go off to answer phone calls, pop out for more wine, make cups of tea and so on. In fact, you wouldn't set the scene in a kitchen at all, because kitchens are useful offstage places for people to exit to. And you would set it earlier in the day, so that people could go out into the garden, preferably visible through open French doors. So, this is all inside out, and I apologise for that and for the fact that I really have nothing to entertain you with until Freda and Monika return. I do use the time to fill David in on things, but his reaction is disappointingly downbeat, and hardly worth telling you about at all.

When the girls do come back, Freda is even pinker than she was before, but she sits down opposite Ben and says, 'Ben, I don't want you to think that anything I've decided has to do with you promising to buy me a smartphone. That would be very shallow, and I don't want to be shallow.'

'I won't think that, Freda,' Ben says, and there is not the merest twitch of a smile as he looks back, solemnly, at her.

'But,' Freda says, 'what Monika and I think is that being a dad isn't what you are but what you do, and you actually do all the dad things – like you taught me to swim and to ride a bike. And you calm Mum down when she gets stressed and shouty. So, really, you are my dad and I don't think I need another one who hasn't had any practice at it. So, I'm glad Mum told me about him, but I don't think I want to meet him at the moment – maybe later.'

She pauses, and I see Ellie and Ben give each other a long look which has so much love in it that tears threaten me. But Freda isn't finished. 'So, you are my dad, Ben,' she says, 'but I won't call you Dad, if you don't mind, because I've always called you Ben, and it would feel weird to change. And I don't want to be Biaggi, because Freda Gray feels like who I am, and I don't want to change that either. But you can teach me Italian if you like, because Nonna and Nonno would like it.'

She leans back in her chair. 'I think that's all,' she says.

Ellie reaches across to give her a hug, and Ben raises his glass and says, 'Salute, Signorina Gray!'

In the ensuing laughter, I feel an unworthy pang. Something rather momentous is happening. I am used to being Freda's only effective grandparent, and now I feel unreasonably threatened by Nonna and Nonno and their Italian farmhouse with guaranteed sunshine. I look up to see David looking at me. 'To mine?' he mouths.

I nod. I get up and move round the table, kissing everyone in turn. 'It's late,' I say, 'and you all need beds. I'm going to stay at David's tonight. There's plenty of food for breakfast, and the beds are made up. Give my love to Nico, and I'll see you soon.'

And with that I put my toothbrush into my handbag, and David and I go out into the night in search of a cab.

# APPENDIX

From *The Caretaker* by Harold Pinter, Act 1

DAVIES: *I'll tell you what, mate, you haven't got a spare pair of shoes?*

ASTON: *Shoes?*

DAVIES: *Them bastards at the monastery let me down again.*

ASTON: *Where?*

DAVIES: *Down in Luton. Monastery down at Luton... I got a mate at Shepherd's Bush, you see...*

ASTON: *I might have a pair.*

DAVIES: *I got this mate at Shepherd's Bush. In the convenience. Well, he was in the convenience. Run about the best convenience they had. Run about the best one. Always slipped me a bit of soap, any time I went in there. Very good soap. They have to have the best soap. I was never without a piece of soap, whenever I happened to be knocking about the Shepherd's Bush area.*

ASTON: *Pair of brown.*

DAVIES: *He's gone now. Went. He was the one who put me onto this monastery. Just the other side of Luton. He'd heard they give away shoes.*

ASTON: *You've got to have a good pair of shoes.*

DAVIES: *Shoes? It's life and death to me. I had to go all the way to Luton in these.*

ASTON: *What happened when you got there, then?*

242

DAVIES: *I used to know a bootmaker in Acton. He was a good mate to me.*

*You know what that bastard monk said to me? (pause)*

*How many more Blacks you got around here, then?*

ASTON: *What?*

DAVIES: *You got any more Blacks around here?*

ASTON: *See if these are any good.*

DAVIES: *You know what that bastard monk said to me? (pause)*

*I think those'd be a bit small.*

From *Entertaining Mr Sloane* by Joe Orton, Act 1

KATH: *We always planned to marry. But there were difficulties. I was very young, and he was even younger. I don't believe we would have been allowed.*

SLOANE: *What happened to the baby?*

KATH: *Adopted.*

SLOANE: *By whom?*

KATH: *That I could not say. My brother arranged it.*

SLOANE: *What about the kid's father?*

KATH: *He couldn't do anything.*

SLOANE: *Why not?*

KATH: *His family objected. They were very nice, but he had a duty, you see. As I say, if it'd been left to him, I'd be a widow today. I had a last letter. I'll show you some time. D'you like flock or foam rubber in your pillow?*

SLOANE: *Foam rubber.*

KATH: *You need a bit of luxury, don't you? I bought Dadda one but he can't stand them.*

SLOANE: *I can.*

KATH: *You'll live with us then as one of the family?*

SLOANE: *I never had no family of my own.*

KATH: *Didn't you?*

SLOANE: *No. I was brought up in an orphanage.*

KATH: *You have the air of lost wealth.*

SLOANE: *That's remarkable. My parents, I believe, were extremely wealthy people.*

KATH: *Did Dr Barnardo give you a bad time?*

SLOANE: *No. It was the lack of privacy I found most trying. And the lack of real love.*

KATH: *Did you never know your mamma?*

SLOANE: *Yes.*

KATH: *When did they die?*

SLOANE: *I was eight. They passed away together.*

KATH: *How shocking.*

SLOANE: *I've an idea that they had a suicide pact. Couldn't prove it, of course.*

KATH: *Of course not. With a nice lad like you to take care of, you think they'd have postponed it. Criminals, were they?*

SLOANE: *From what I remember, they were respected. HP debts. Bridge. A little light gardening. The usual activities of a cultured community. I respect their memory.*

KATH: *Do you? How nice.*

SLOANE: *Every year I pay a visit to their grave. Take sandwiches. Make a day of it. The graveyard is situated in pleasant surroundings, so it's not a hardship. Tomb an' all.*

KATH: *Marble? Is there an inscription?*

From *Top Girls* by Caryl Churchill, Act Two Scene One

NELL: *So just describe your present job to me.*

SHONA: *My present job at present. I have a car. I have a Porsche. I go up the M1 a lot. Burn up the M1 a lot. Straight up the M1 in the fast lane to where the clients are, Staffordshire, Yorkshire. I do a lot in Yorkshire. I'm selling electric things. Like dishwashers, washing machines. Stainless steel tubs are a feature and the reliability of the programme. After-sales service, we offer a very good after-sales service, spare parts, plenty of*

244

*spare parts. And fridges, I sell a lot of fridges specially in the summer. People want to buy fridges in the summer because of the heat melting the butter and you get fed up standing the milk in a basin of cold water with a cloth over, stands to reason people don't want to do that in this day and age. So I sell a lot of them, big ones with big freezers, Big freezers. And I stay in hotels at night when I'm away from home. On my expense account. Stay in various hotels, they know me the ones I go to. I check in, have a bath, have a shower. Then I go down to the bar, have a gin and tonic, have a chat. Then I go into the dining room and have dinner. I usually have fillet steak and mushrooms. I like mushrooms. I like smoked salmon very much. I like having a salad on the side. Green salad. I don't like tomatoes.*

All three extracts given here are taken from Methuen Modern Play editions.